STOLEN KISSES AT THE LOCH VIEW HOTEL

MARGARET AMATT

LEANNAN
PRESS
INDEPENDENT PUBLISHER

LEANNAN PRESS

CHAPTER ONE

Briony

August

G eorge, the financial adviser, leaned back in his chair, clicking a pen and shaking his head at the screen. Briony knew that look, the one the builders gave her right before they told her it would cost several thousand pounds to fix that crack in the brickwork. But surely it couldn't be that bad.

'With these projected figures, it doesn't look too good,' George said.

Ok. So it was *that* bad. Briony clasped her hands on her knees, rubbing the ridge of gems in her eternity ring and peering around at the spreadsheet. Accounts weren't exactly her favourite thing; all those figures were enough to bring on a migraine and those red numbers never meant anything good.

'The saving grace is that you're not paying a mortgage on it,' he said.

That was something, at least. Inheriting the Loch View Hotel in the small town of Glenbriar was proving to be a curse, not the dream she'd imagined. But Briony was a great believer in 'if it's for you, it won't go past you', so there must be something she could do.

Through the crack in the blinds of George's office, the main street was visible: pretty shops in old Victorian buildings, cafés bustling with tourists, and hikers marching past, heading for the hills surrounding the village. But where was the starry-eyed girl who'd told her family she could run the hotel, no bother? The one desperate for a challenge just like this? And here. Back in Glenbriar, where she'd spent many fun times as a child. That girl was sitting right here, only how could she make those dreams come true? They'd fizzled out in a few short months, leaving a much more frazzled girl, who wasn't sure what to do next.

Leaking roofs, loose floorboards, damp in the bedrooms and an unfit-for-purpose kitchen had swallowed her budget and spat out even more problems in return. It was like trying to patch holes in a sinking ship. Every time one was fixed another sprang open. In the evenings, she crept into the poorly lit staff quarters, curled up in the dingy bedroom and slept – alone. But she wasn't going to throw in the towel yet. A solution would present itself; it just needed to be sooner rather than later.

'So,' she said. 'What are my options?'

'Well.' George leaned even further back, shaking his head with a grave expression. 'With the current debts, I don't think another loan is the answer.'

Why say it then? Maybe to rub in how crazy she'd been to take on the hotel in the first place? She'd only discovered how bad things were after. This was adulting at its finest; she was failing on every level and she didn't like it.

'With a very robust business plan and a substantial increase in profits, you may be able to break even within the next five years, but it would rely heavily on being able to fill the hotel throughout the year and keeping the bar and restaurant open to non-residents.'

Briony pulled a confused pout. How could she guarantee any of that? Who wanted to visit a run-down old hotel that hadn't been redecorated for over forty years?

'And how will I pay for the renovations? I can't afford to staff the bar and restaurant even for residents a lot of the time.'

'If you choose to go down that road, that'll be the purpose of the business plan.' George tapped his pen. 'Unfortunately, even doing all that might not work. The hotel has been left to get into such a state that it's almost unviable.'

How could he say that? Briony's heart slipped out of her chest, off the padded seat and onto the grey carpeted floor. She'd dreamed of owning the hotel since she was tiny. Who wouldn't be inspired by a pink hotel next to a glassy loch? As a child, it had seemed the most perfect place in the world. She'd played at the lochside or in the woods with her sister, renaming herself Missy Peck and inventing her very own stories about adventures and romances that took place at the Pink Hotel. Only she wasn't really Missy Peck, she was Briony Dalgleish, and the pink hotel wasn't a cute backdrop for exciting adventures or even a cosy place to have afternoon tea by the fire after having solved a local mystery. No. It was a draughty old pile of bricks with a heap of debt. Without the necessary repairs, the building would be condemned and there wouldn't be a Loch View Hotel in Glenbriar anymore, just a sad old ruin of what might have been.

'Sadly,' George went on, 'your best option is to sell it as a going concern or look for an investor who's willing to take it on and retain you in a managerial role with a salary to be negotiated.'

'Sell up?' Briony's jaw fell open. This could be the shortest ownership in the hotel's history. She'd barely had it six months. The big break had turned into a big hole and she'd fallen in. This was the only way out? Admit defeat and walk away? What would her parents make of it?

'Yes, unless you want to run into further debt trying to save the building. It's almost unfit for purpose.'

'No other options?' She kept her tone light and playful. Maybe she could tease a better answer out of him if she smiled enough.

He cocked his head and shook it slightly. 'Not unless you have another source of income or savings that can fund the renovations.' He floated his pen above the screen indicating the long list of repair work needing done.

Briony considered the small income she made from the children's book she'd published under a pen name. It was her pride and joy and told the story of Missy Peck, taking Briony back to the dream world she wished she could inhabit. It was better than the stress and debts of real life. She wanted to write more, but the time that took plus the marketing and publicity that followed were too much; the royalty it brought in was pocket money and nowhere near enough to save a business. With the hotel in the state it was, she couldn't devote time to anything else. Her pencils and sketchbook were gathering dust in a box by her bed and the files on her computer with her story ideas hadn't been opened for over three months. A great weight pressed on her brain, crushing the creativity she was desperate to let spill out. If she could just push it off and see the way forward.

She pressed her lips together, swallowing back a lump in her throat. Bad emotions didn't get the better of her – not in public anyway. Putting on a face was part of her life front of house, and she was good at it, even if she said so herself. And she had to, because at the end of the day, who else would? She'd taken this on alone, with faith and high hopes. Her parents had been sceptical, but she'd been determined. Her dad had signed the title deeds over to her and she'd never looked back... Until now. What on earth was she going to do?

George tilted his head, a sympathetic expression etched on his brow. Briony sighed and smiled as though everything in the world was perfect, but inside her heart ached for someone to share this with – not just a friend she could talk to about it; her bestie, Felicity, was a saviour when she needed a shoulder to cry on, but she craved more. Someone to share the burden and shoulder the weight of responsibility. Not her parents. She needed to show them she could do this. Only she wasn't sure how she'd pull it off.

Maybe she should think about dating again and looking for that special someone. The one she knew was out there somewhere; she just hadn't found him yet. The one she'd believed was her ex-husband until she'd woken up and smelled the coffee, realising she'd wasted years on the wrong person.

She let out a half laugh, half snort, making George frown. Eek. That wasn't an appropriate response to this predicament.

'Sorry.' She cleared her throat. 'It's just that lovely table. So pretty.'

'Er… Thank you.' George frowned at the upcycled coffee table. 'My fiancée made it.'

'Gorgeous.'

But Briony's mind had wandered off. Marrying Darren Dalgleish hadn't brought her someone to help and share problems with – no. It had just added more grief and caused more headaches. *Can't afford to go down that road again.*

Not that she had the time. She'd met Darren when they worked together at The Gladstone, a high-class hotel in Edinburgh, but never again would she date someone she worked with… Or a guest. Not that she had ever dated a guest, technically, though she'd committed a minor indiscretion with one – a very attractive American one. She swallowed and stared at the line of red figures on the spreadsheet, trying to pull her focus back to the here and now. That American had been proper gorgeous and irresistible, until she discovered his real motives. At least they'd only kissed – not *that* bad but enough to lose her job at The Gladstone. And she would have done if Darren hadn't stepped in to save her. Wearing her Missy Peck tinted glasses, she'd thought it was a sign and decided he was The One. Only Missy Peck had been wrong.

'It's your choice, Mrs Dalgleish,' said George. 'But selling up looks by far the best option in this case.'

'Right.'

Ok. If that was how it was meant to be, then fine. If getting out of this mess and saving the hotel meant selling, then sell she would. But as a believer of everything from unicorns to pots of gold at the end of rainbows, she was convinced that exactly the right person would turn up to save the bright-pink liability. She just didn't know exactly where to look or who they might be.

CHAPTER TWO

Zach

October

Rain. Rain and more rain. The wipers slashed across the windscreen, skating over the surface and leaving nothing but streaks. Zach squinted forward. Tall pines on either side of the road closed in like high walls, barring the light. The clock on the dash said fifteen twenty-six but greying skies and gloom made it feel closer to midnight. That and the jetlag.

Everyone had warned him about it, but had he listened? What was the point wasting time sleeping in a drab airport hotel when he could be on his way north? Compared to the road trips he took back home in the States, driving from Edinburgh to the Highlands was nothing. A different kind of nothing if this weather and these roads were to be believed. But starting the job straight away meant he could get it done quicker. It'd be wound up by Friday. Easy. He'd be back in Kentucky by Saturday, ready to start his vacation. And it couldn't come soon enough.

First he had to find the hotel. The GPS, which had dipped in and out since passing a town called Perth, was now jammed on a giant question mark, flashing like a warning. *For real?* He jabbed the off switch.

'I don't appreciate you telling me what to do anyway,' he muttered. Much as he loved *Star Trek*, he didn't need AI bossing him around in reality. Not unless Alexa had learned how to beam him from his Louisville apartment to this crazy-sounding pink hotel in the Scottish Highlands and back in the blink of an eye. A pink hotel. Yup. His latest mission took the cake – locate Barbie's Highland home or, as his employer, bourbon billionaire Daniel Beyer, more accurately said, 'Find out everything you can about the hotel's historical value and determine if it's worth my money.' And if it was, Mr Beyer was ready to throw his bucks at the place known officially as the Loch View Hotel. Mrs Dalgleish was the contact name he had and Zach imagined a somewhat stout lady in her mid-sixties ready to sell up and blow the money on a round-the-world retirement cruise. Lucky woman.

'Where is it?' Zach slowed, screwing up his eyes and leaning forward. Nothing was there. Well, technically, there were trees – lots of them. Clouds. Grey ones. Even more of them. Rain, gallons of that. But nothing else. Nothing he could see anyway. Maybe beyond that impenetrable mass of cloud something lingered but he was damned if he knew where to go next.

He'd visited Scotland once before, years ago, when he'd been a green newbie at work. Not much had changed. He still didn't know what he was doing most of the time. That trip had been an out-and-out disaster. He barely remembered seeing anything Scottish. Most of the time was spent banged up in a fancy hotel in Edinburgh. And to cap it off, he'd fallen foul to his colleagues goading. *No way can a nerd like you pull someone as hot as that waitress.* They even placed a bet on it. Alcohol-filled Zach had proved them wrong. Easy. Unbelievably easy. Because she'd not only been hot, but a kindness superhero. Her smiles made everything feel natural and she seemed to genuinely like him. Until some idiot told her about the bet, and he never saw her again. Story of his life.

A barman from the hotel confronted him before he left the next day and told him the waitress would lose her job unless Zach paid him to make up a story. Zach had handed over the five hundred dollars he'd made from winning the bet and left with no knowledge of who she was or what happened to her. Not exactly a visit he cared to remember, funnily enough. Though without meaning to, he often wondered about her.

At least Mr Beyer had never found out about any of it. He was too obsessed with counting his dollars and trawling the world for the rarest whiskies he could find to add to a collection that now took up a whole building at his Louisville mansion. He employed twenty-four-hour security and rumour had it the collection was worth more than a billion dollars. Zach had never understood the fascination, not something he dared admit in the office. You didn't work for a bourbon billionaire and confess to having zero interest in the industry.

Crawling along, he came to a small opening and a gravelly road shot off up a steep slope to the side. A green sign displayed Dalarvin Wood Forest Trail Car Park. Spinning the wheel abruptly, he pulled into the opening. The tyres shrieked in protest, whirling in the mud, but he hammered the pedal, motoring forward. Why were rental cars so ridiculously unsuitable for the countryside? This kind of saloon would be fine for Daniel Beyer if he wanted to coast around town, attending his latest meetings. But off-roading in the Highlands? No.

Zach slammed into a space. Technically not so much as a space but a muddy puddle next to one other vehicle – an ancient-looking Jeep. Ancient maybe but better suited for these roads than the fashion wagon he had.

Would the rental company have provided a paper map? Did people still use them? He opened the glove box and peered inside. *That'll be no then*. Resting his head back, he let out a sigh. What now? If GPS didn't work, his phone wouldn't either. He was stuck in the middle of nowhere.

He closed his eyes and a yawn escaped him. Rain battered the car from all directions. A firm clinical bed in the airport Travel Inn looked quite luxurious now. 'What am I gonna do?' he muttered, not opening his eyes. He wouldn't even mind if the

GPS answered him this time – any sign of it coming back online would be beyond awesome.

A voice outside made his eyelids spring open. The view from every window was completely obscured by thick raindrops. He opened the door and peered out. Beside him, the Jeep's trunk door slammed shut.

'Hey!' he called, jumping out of the car.

An old man with a sopping wet coat, huge thick boots and a long, bushy white beard peered around at him.

'Can you tell me the way to the Loch View Hotel, please? It's close to Loch Briar, but I don't know where that is either.'

The man nodded. 'Aye, I know the place. Who doesn't? That pink eyesore.'

'Yeah, the pink place.' Zach's heart lightened. This had to be good. Someone who knew where it was.

'You're not far now, but if it's a room you're after, you'd better go elsewhere. It's a dive, that place. Gone to the dogs since old Hilda died.'

Rain started to penetrate Zach's clothing. His thick curls grew lank, sticking horribly to his forehead and the back of his neck. 'Sure, I hear you, but I need to find it.'

'Keep on the road until you reach Glenbriar. Just through the village, you'll see a sign for Heather Glen Campsite. If you head down there, you can't miss the hotel. It'll be on your right.'

'Great, thanks.'

'Oh, and mind the monster.' The man chuckled.

'Pardon?'

'Aye, you Yanks have all heard of the Loch Ness Monster, but the Loch Briar one is a lesser-known beast. Much more potent though.'

'Yeah, funny.' Did people think Yanks was an acceptable term in this day and age? And technically he wasn't, being a Kentucky guy born and bred.

'If you dinny believe me, ask anyone. And you should ask about the legend of the stolen kisses.'

'What does that mean?'

The man tapped his nose. 'Ask the owner for a stolen kiss and see what happens.'

Zach barely held onto his eye roll.

'Travelling alone, are you?' the man asked.

'Yup.' When was he not alone? Not that he minded. Being alone was safe.

'Have your friends abandoned you in the woods?'

Friends? Zach almost laughed. Though being abandoned was fairly common in the life of Zach Somerton. 'No. I'm here for work.'

'Work? Dear, dear. Well, you get back to work then and remember to look out for the monster.' With an almost manic laugh the man got into the Jeep and Zach jumped back into the car. Was everyone here this crazy? Or was it his bad luck to run into the one escaped looney?

He fired up the engine and revved out of the car park before the ancient Jeep. He didn't want to follow that along a country road, especially one where he couldn't see around the bends and when he was used to driving on the other side. The blowers were on the top heat setting and hummed full blast. Hopefully that would dry him off. He separated strands of hair with his fingertips, one hand clamped on the wheel.

All he needed was for a zombie to limp across the road and all his fantasies would collide. He'd been sent on a crackpot mission to an Endor-like world, met the local Gandalf who introduced him to the legend of the loch and now he must fight off the walking dead in the zombie apocalypse. Trip finally looking up?

He slowed at signs of habitation and let out a low whistle. *Phew*. He passed a few houses and a sign announcing Glenbriar. 'So far, so good.' Slowly, he edged through the village, checking out cute cottages and a mismatch of old and new buildings. Gorgeous colours flooded the grey vista as he passed a park full of deciduous trees. These were better than the grim pines he'd been lost in moments before. Red, amber and gold leaves covered the grass while some clung on to the almost bare branches.

As the old wizard had said, the sign for Heather Glen Campsite appeared after the last house in the village. Zach turned onto the road. It curved around. Swathes of misty cloud hovered like steam from a giant cauldron close to the surface of what must be the loch. Perhaps the monster would rise before him.

'Get real, man.' Sometimes his overactive imagination took him too far. Make that most of the time. At twenty-eight – according to his mom – he was too old for *Star Wars*, comic books, *Harry Potter* fanfic, making *Lord of the Rings* genealogy charts and watching reruns of *Voyager*, wishing every time the ending would be more satisfying. But when were endings ever satisfying? Not in real life anyway. Happy endings were fantasies for dreamy-eyed kids or reserved for people who could afford them.

Through the mist and across the steaming loch, an unmistakeably pink building materialised. Almost unremarkable. If it wasn't for its unusual colouring it would be nothing but an average coaching inn. And yet, Daniel Beyer had decided this was a place he wanted to invest in. Who knew why? But when Mr Beyer snapped his fingers, Zach jumped. And this was where he'd landed. Now to complete the business and get the hell back home.

CHAPTER THREE

Briony

'No, no, just no, get off there.' Briony lifted the duvet and yanked it, trying to shake it, but Becker was too heavy. 'Come on, Becker, get off, please. Oh god, look at the mess. Who let you in?'

Becker stared at her, his big brown eyes droopy and content, like he had no intention of moving for at least an hour. What had been a pristine white cover adorning the four-poster bed in the best guestroom was now covered in mud and stinking of wet dog.

'Becker, move.' Briony leaned into the middle of the bed and pushed his big brown hairy backside. He turned his good-natured gaze to her hands and watched with interest. His expression said, *Is this the best you could do in the petting department? Tut, tut.*

'Move, you great lump.' She gave him a huge shove and with a grumbly moan he heaved himself onto the carpet.

Briony pressed her fingers into her forehead. Seriously? This wasn't good. Becker slouched onto the tartan carpet with a humph and started nibbling his back leg. Exactly what type of dog he was, Briony had no clue, some kind of schnauzer-labradoodle cross type thing, but one thing was certain, he was definitely the troublesome type. Why Granny Hilda had permitted him into the bedrooms was anyone's guess. Even now she was gone, Becker thought it was his right to go anywhere, especially if it was warm, clean and strictly off-limits for dogs. Briony had learned the hard way that year, you really couldn't teach an old dog new tricks. If Becker wanted to lie on the bed, then lie on the bed he would. She tried her best to keep him away from the bedrooms, but he just made those big eyes at passing guests and they granted his every wish. But today? Ugh. Why today?

She'd actually got someone interested in investing in the old pile of bricks and she had to make a good impression. It wasn't every day American billionaires called. If that wasn't a sign, she didn't know what was. Not only was he interested in buying her out, but he was happy to let her keep working for him. Maybe not the most ideal solution but it would be a way to save the hotel and allow her to keep her job. How he'd found out about the hotel when she hadn't started the selling process was a mystery, but didn't that reinforce the serendipity? She needed a buyer and the universe had provided. Or maybe he'd seen the interview she'd done with Highland Home magazine on Scotland's most colourful hotels. It hadn't done anything for business but if it had attracted a rich investor then perfect. His representative was arriving today. The would-be investor was interested in the hotel's history, so where better to put his representative than in the newly named Bonnie Prince Charlie suite? Bonnie Prince Charlie rooms graced hotels the length and breadth of the country and who could prove he'd really been to them? Briony vaguely remembered he was an Italian-born prince with a taste for the luxuries in life, exactly the type to have loved a pink hotel. Voila! She smiled inwardly at her own brilliance before gritting her teeth. What the prince wouldn't have loved was a duvet covered in muddy dog, a carpet with a pawprint trail and a host who had no idea how to get it clean before he showed up. Most likely Mr Beyer's representative would feel the same. The vision of a very slick man, dressed like a *GQ* model with a shiny leather briefcase and a penchant for everything neat, tidy and perfectly aligned flickered through her conscience.

This room wasn't exactly straight at the best of times. The cornicing didn't meet correctly in one corner. The floorboards creaked and she was pretty sure if she put a ball on one side it would roll down to the other. Maybe tartan wasn't a good choice for the carpet. It made the room feel even wonkier as none of the edges lined up. Maybe she was the one with the obsession about things lining up. Whatever, it didn't matter right now. Wet dog was definitely worse than squinty carpets.

'Come on, Becker.' She tugged him by the scruff of the neck. 'Time to go downstairs.'

After giving her a woeful look for a few seconds, he got to his feet and trotted into the hall, leaving more muddy footprints everywhere. Not unusual. If she found the guest who'd let him in here, well, she'd like to throw them out, though it wouldn't exactly help her make money. Shari, the cleaner, had just left. How horribly inconvenient with such an important guest due. And this American wasn't the only person arriving. Most of the rooms were full as the Amber Gold Music Festival was on in the village that week.

Briony still wanted to drag the hotel out of the mess herself, no matter how impossible it seemed. George's advice had suggested keeping the bar and restaurant open to non-residents. While she couldn't afford to staff that all the time, she could open for special events and try to restore links with the community. Links that had been lost over years of neglect when her grandmother was in charge. Briony's BFF Felicity worked for a local distillery that was sponsoring the Amber Gold Music Festival. Briony had loved working with Felicity, forging a link between the businesses and ensuring the Loch View Hotel had plenty of gigs over the weekend. In her heart she wished this could be Plan A, but since the American investor's interest, it had become Plan B, and she'd had to shove it on the backburner while she concentrated on preparing for his rep's arrival.

Soft chatter sounded from the foyer as Briony reached the bottom of the stairs. Becker had gone on ahead and a couple who'd checked in earlier were fussing over him. Water dripped from the hems of their jackets, pooling on the carpet at their feet – feet encased in thick-soled boots caked in mud. Briony drew in a silent breath. These carpets may have been industrial strength when they were fitted in the seventies but now they were verging on threadbare. Hoovering this latest mudfest might open a chasm in the floor, hopefully one that revealed hidden treasure under the hotel.

'That rain hasn't gone off then?' She rubbed her hands together and summoned her best smile.

'It has now,' said the woman. 'It's still grey but what a downpour we got caught in. Coming down like stair rods it was.'

'Go into the lounge if you like,' Briony said. 'The fire's on.' She needed them off the carpet. Then she had to get Becker into her private rooms, through the passageway next to the kitchen. The hotel might be shabby but it was six steps up from the kitsch staff quarters. Who could blame Becker for wanting to escape to a bit more luxury?

The couple took off their wet coats.

'That's a lovely coat you have,' said Briony. 'If you hang it over the back of the chair near the fire it should dry nice and quick.' She opened the panelled door off the foyer that led into the lounge bar and dining room. Paintings of fish, hares and Victorian men with rifles standing over dead stags hung around the walls. No matter how often she cleaned them, the dust reappeared within minutes, and maybe it was better to leave them like that; it obscured the ugly subjects. One day she'd change them for something less morbid and dull. If she got the chance.

'Take a seat.' She indicated the brown tweed chairs next to the fireplace. The long wooden bar on the far side was highly polished but empty – always empty. She couldn't afford staff so hardly anyone came to sample the local craft beers and whisky she had in stock. If only the olde worlde-ness was quaint and not just old-fashioned.

The guest house her parents ran in Ayrshire was full every night and had a minibar in the lounge that was busier than this. But they'd worked hard to get where they were and sacrificed loads. *Like my childhood.* Little Missy Peck tugged at Briony's chest, reminding her not to think like that. It hadn't done her any harm, just shown her the value of hard work.

A car door banged outside. Becker's ears pricked and before Briony could grab him, he'd weaved his way through the half-open front door and out.

'Oh, sorry, we didn't shut that properly,' said the woman.

'It's not a problem. You just get warm.' Briony legged it after Becker. This was another of his 'tricks'. Enthusiastically greeting guests – not all of whom wanted to be greeted by a great big hairy dog.

Briony swung open the glass-panelled front door in time to catch Becker flinging himself onto his hind legs, splaying his filthy great front paws onto the white t-shirt of a man who had been tying the laces on black Converse boots. 'Oh no, Becker.' Briony flung up her hands.

Almost wholly on the ground, the man staggered to get to his feet; Becker pawed him playfully.

'Becker!' Briony yelled.

The man straightened up and gaped at his t-shirt and formerly black, now mud-coloured, jeans. He was kind of scruffy looking with a denim jacket slung over his arm. Probably one of the festival goers. Not the representative of Mr Beyer then. If that had been a slick white shirt Becker had pawed all over... Briony held her breath – *relax, it isn't*. Just as well, because she still hadn't fixed his room.

The man's thick dark hair flopped around his face with some wet strands stuck to his forehead and his expression was thunderous.

'Becker. Leave him alone.' Briony tugged his collar, dragging him away from the man's leg, and looked up at him. Her heart started to pound. A memory stirred. The hair was longer, a bit more stubble, and he was older, obviously. But he was an absolute ringer for the American she'd almost lost her job over some years back. Couldn't be him though, could it? That would be ridiculous.

He stepped back, holding out his arms and glowering at his t-shirt and jeans with deep liquid brown eyes. His skin was tanned, his nose very straight and his stiff jaw covered in a dusting of stubble. So handsome. Briony swallowed. It *was* him. She'd thought him attractive before, spotted him watching her across the room and been ok with it; they'd seemed on the same wavelength. Only they hadn't been. He turned out to be a prat who was doing it for a bet. Days later she fell in with Darren. Would she ever learn? One day her soulmate would turn up, she was sure of it, but she needed to stop being so impulsive and make damn sure this time.

She cleared her throat, wondering if the man would recognise her. He was still too obsessed with his t-shirt to have looked her way. 'Sorry about that. He gets a bit overexcited.'

The man glared at the paw prints ranging from his shoulder, down his front and all over his right thigh.

'Er... Yes. So, are you here for the festival?' Briony gabbled on, ignoring his locked jaw and flaring nostrils. 'By the weekend everyone will look like that if the rain keeps up. The field will be a mudfest.' She was blabbering, but nerves tingled up her arms. What the hell had brought him here to her hotel? After all these years. She believed in coincidences. Of course, they happened. How often had she thought about someone she hadn't seen for a while, then gone into town and bumped into them? Or spied someone on the other side of the road, thinking it was someone else, only to see the actual person later? But this. This was mad.

He raised his eyes to her, his brow furrowing so his thick eyebrows joined in the middle. He blinked, looked away again and swiped at the muddy marks.

'You can put it in the hotel laundry if you like. I'm sure it'll come off. It's lovely quality fabric, cotton, I think, and that usually washes well.' Briony reached over and ran her fingertips over it to check if it was ingrained or purely on the surface.

The man staggered back. 'Hey. Watch where you're putting your hands. How would you like it if I did that to you?'

'I... er... Sorry.' Heat flared in her cheeks.

'Wait a sec.' He squinted up again and frowned.

His accent. He was American. It had to be him. Just had to be.

'Yes.' She gulped too much air and almost coughed it straight back out again. Did he recognise her?

'I'm not here for a festival. I'm Zacharias Somerton, representative of Daniel Beyer.'

Her eyes widened and she temporarily forgot he might be the man she'd once kissed in a posh hotel room in Edinburgh. This news was worse. 'Oh.'

'I'm booked into this hotel for the week, so I can investigate its potential for investment.'

Briony closed her mouth and swallowed. So much for the uptight businessman. Daniel Beyer had sent *him*. What were the chances and what did it mean? Heat burned on her face. Bang went the cool, calm and collected hostess.

'Come in then.' She turned away from him. *Help.* How to get out of this? She'd never known the man's name, but she was convinced it was him – or else he had an identical twin. Should she ask him? Or keep quiet and act like she didn't remember? That, apparently, was his tack.

She stole a glance at him. It felt like he'd been watching her, but his gaze roamed over the hotel front and his thick dark brows closed together. Briony clung to Becker, painfully aware how many patches of paintwork had fallen off the hotel, leaving unsightly dark blotches. The front door didn't close properly and had to be jammed shut every night. Untidy bushes clambered around the windows and so many slates were missing from the roof it was no wonder the attic was a swimming pool and most of the rooms in there were permanently closed for damp. This was the place she was trying to sell. She'd had it eight months and accomplished so little. Practically nothing. If anything, it looked worse now than it had done over the years when Granny Hilda ran it.

Zacharias Somerton shook his head. 'This place... It's... Well, not exactly what I expected.'

'Why don't you come inside, Mr Somerton?' Briony floated her hand in the direction of the door. 'It looks like the rain is about to come on again.' Getting him soaked through as well as muddy was asking for more trouble.

He glanced at the sky, blinking his long dark lashes. 'Nobody calls me Mr Somerton.'

'Ok. Zacharias then?'

'Nobody calls me that either.'

Briony held her plastered-on smile. *Do not let it budge.* She was well-practised at this. Awkward guests were a common hazard in this job. But if this was the same guy she'd met before, he'd soured a lot in the past five years. 'What would you like to be called then?'

'Zach is what people call me.'

'Great. Well then, Zach. Would you like to come in?'

His half pout half sneer said *not particularly* but with a quick flick of his luscious locks, he moved towards the front door.

'Don't you have luggage?' Briony squinted around, checking it wasn't dumped in the middle of the car park.

'I'll get it later. I'd like to go to my room first. I'm exhausted and jet-lagged. I just want to lie down and sleep.'

'Of course.' Briony stared at Becker as Zach opened the door and trudged inside. 'Oh my god, Becker,' she said as soon as Zach was out of hearing. 'You naughty dog. What am I going to do now? His bed is covered in your mess.'

CHAPTER FOUR

Zach

Zach wiped his feet on the mat, noting the faded words Loch View Hotel in an old script font. Judging from the threadbare and mud-stained carpet with some highly suspect dark patches, he was one of the first people to bother this week. He blinked and his eyes adjusted to the orangey-gold light in the lobby coming from... er, wall sconces? Maybe in a dungeon but in a Highland hotel? No. It was like falling into a faded seventies photograph. Daniel Beyer wanted history and this place had it, heaps of it, but not the right kind. This was hardly an investment opportunity, more like a cash drain.

'Excuse me, two minutes, Mr... um, Zach. Let me get this daft dog safely into his bed and I'll be right with you.'

Zach's pulse quickened and he watched the woman retreat through a door just past the reception area, dragging the wet dog by the collar. Zach roughed up his cheeks and shook himself. She was the double of the woman he'd fooled around with on his last visit to Scotland. But what the actual...? No way could it be her. Jet lag had made him crazy. He associated her with Scotland and his brain was tricking him into believing it was her.

He raised an eyebrow at his reflection in the large, gilded mirror between two flickering sconces. What a mess. He raked his hair. Not much of an improvement. His vision blurred and a scene played in his mind. That same woman flashing a smile across a crowded dining room. Him returning it, even though he wasn't a great smiler. All through the meal their gazes had connected. They shared glances. She'd even flicked him a little wink. Wordlessly they'd fallen into an understanding.

Back then, she'd had longer hair. Now it was super tidy and so well-styled it was like a Lego wig that came in one piece and she just clicked it into place. She was the kind of woman his colleagues married – several times over, including Mr Beyer: four different versions, four separate occasions. Zach was the odd man out at company functions, missing the perfectly coiffured wife and the well-manicured life. On the surface anyhow. Dig a little and cracks were there. Everyone knew the squeaky-clean image of the Beyer company was a good front, but who married four times without a little scandal or two? And yet Mr Beyer was considered an upstanding man and expected the same moral standards from his employees – the type he preached even if he didn't practise.

Where was the receptionist? Zach shoved his hands in his back pockets and bored himself reading the fire safety certificate.

He'd had his own scandal. Oh yes. Not The Gladstone one, which Mr Beyer was happily oblivious to. Last year, he'd almost brought down the Beyer empire by handing over confidential papers to his business rival. A mistake – a bona fide one. He hadn't realised who he was dealing with. *Which just goes to show I'm in the wrong business.* Something he suspected more and more every day.

But Mr Beyer had headhunted him straight out of college, which was the reason he remained loyal. Though why Mr Beyer had picked him in the first place was a question he asked himself every day. His qualifications were good, yeah... He was lucky. A relative of his mom's had died and left him money to fund his college education. Zach had stopped asking who the relative was. His mom could be so closed about things, especially her family. And after Grandma died, it got worse. Zach had found solace in a big screen, earphones, and a console in his hand rather than in his mom's arms. But whoever the philanthropic relative was, Zach was grateful. It was just a shame his qualifications were rarely compatible with the type of jobs Mr Beyer threw at him. But who knew how the mind of a billionaire worked? A mystery of life. *And I'm not knocking it.* He pulled in way more money than he could hope to make elsewhere, even though he was on his last warning. Miracle he still had a job. The lowest of jobs. Because Daniel Beyer held his destiny and could send him to the furthest outposts of the world whenever he wanted. One word from him and Zach could be cut loose. He couldn't afford to let that happen; his mother's healthcare didn't come cheap. She may not be the most demonstrative of moms, but she was all he had left, his only living relative.

Zach let out a long sigh that turned into a groan. This job should be a cinch but this woman complicated things. Could he survive the week pretending he didn't remember her if in fact it was her? Well, he spent his life pretending he knew how to do his job, so why should this be any different? Ever since his grandma died when he was thirteen, he'd had a weird sense of being an imposter in his own skin.

He rubbed his hands together, skimming over the reception desk. The almost red mahogany construction was an eighties classic with two levels, a higher one for guests to lean on when standing to write and a lower section, playing host to a laptop, a phone and an in-tray.

As far as the hotel went – his nose twitched at the musty smell and the peeling wallpaper in the corners – he could report back to Mr Beyer this minute and tell him it wasn't suitable, but he had strict orders. *Fully investigate every historical aspect of the hotel. Leave no stone unturned.* No stone or piece of mouldy carpet?

'Right.' The woman reappeared through the door. Smile still in place, white teeth shining, lips sparkling. Zach's gaze travelled over her and his stomach gave an unwelcome little swoop. It was her. Without a doubt. He'd kissed those lips and he wasn't about to forget it. Flesh memories of her petite form pressed against him slammed him in the groin. Christ, this was going to be hard.

But what was she doing here? He didn't dare ask. Not when she either didn't recognise him or didn't want to. Had she lost her job because of him? He'd never discovered the outcome. Maybe she'd taken a job here to hide and never wanted to see him again. How could he blame her?

She sat behind the low part of the desk and woke the laptop. A plum-coloured sheath dress encased her neat curves. Not that he should be looking but he couldn't stop himself. She tapped at the keys. Her nails matched the colour of her dress perfectly. No surprise. He'd bet his last dollar her underwear matched too. Not that it was any of his business. This did not bode well. *Do not go there this time.*

'Now. Would you like to have a drink in the lounge before going to your room?' She flashed that million-dollar smile once more and he clenched his jaw. 'The fire's on and I can get you a drink.'

'I just wanna lie down now. That drive was...' So much longer than he'd expected, and the roads... Jeez. They were something else. 'Well... I can't think straight until I get some rest.'

The woman sank her teeth into her plump lower lip. Seductive. *Please stop.* She probably didn't mean to be. There he went again, off down that crazy path. A definite sign of a jet-lagged brain. 'Thing is...' Her smile morphed into an apologetic cringe. 'Your room... is not quite ready yet.'

'How can it not be ready? It's like' – he checked his watch – 'four in the afternoon. How long does it take?'

'We're short-staffed,' she said. 'And it's busy with the festival being on.'

'Ok. I get that but...' His shoulders sagged. He needed sleep. 'Where's the manager? I have to talk to her anyway, it might as well be now. Mrs Dalgleish is her name.'

'You're looking at her.' She locked eyes with him and an unspoken current of understanding flowed between them – exactly what had happened before.

Zach's jaw fell slack. Ok. That was unexpected. Not only was she married but Mrs Dalgleish was not a woman of a certain age who'd owned the place for decades and wanted rid of it to fund her pension.

'Ok, you're Mrs Dalgleish?' Finally, he could put some kind of name to the face that had unconsciously invaded his dreams for five years.

'I am. But nobody calls me that.' Her smile was still in place but something flickered in her bright-blue irises as she slapped his own words back at him. The current between them filled with her unsaid thoughts. *And I haven't forgiven you, maybe I never will.* He read her mind though her expression didn't change.

'Right. So what do they call you?'

'Briony. And I'm not technically a Mrs anymore.'

She wasn't, right. 'Well, Briony.' Briony. Her name was Briony. A beautiful name. His eyes locked on hers and he couldn't move them. Did she have a built-in tractor beam? It lured him closer, messing with his head. Exactly what she'd done five years ago. 'So... My room. Yes, my room. Why isn't it ready?'

'I told you.' She leaned forward as if to emphasis her point. 'We're short-staffed. But if you would take a seat in the lounge for half an hour, I'll see to it personally.'

He stifled a yawn. 'I don't seem to have much choice.'

'The other option is a room in the attic. It's small but it's made up and you can sleep in there until your room is ready.'

'Yeah. I'll do that.' Why had she made up an attic room no one was using and not the main suite? Mental. But no time to consider it, closing his eyes was top priority. And getting away from her.

Briony led him up the stairs to a wide corridor, then opened a door to reveal a winding staircase. Kinda creepy. The peeling paintwork on the walls looked like scratch marks.

'Has anyone been up here in the last forty years?' He couldn't help voicing his concerns.

'Of course. Though this is the only room in use. The others are... um, out of action.'

'Oh-kay.' What did that mean? Like dangerous? Was she shoving him in an attic where the roof might cave?

The sweet smell of her perfume was like a drug, wafting over him, inviting him to do all sorts of wicked things. His focus lingered on her dress and the way it hugged her curves, tapering neatly at her waist then rounding over her hips. The long zipper snaked up her back, perfectly centred.

At the top of the winding stairs was a small landing with three further doors. 'This one.' She opened a door and gestured for him to go inside.

He peered in. It had a dormer window and a bed covered in pure white linen, which was about all he could say for it. He sidled past her, heavily aware of her proximity and the hyper tick of his pulse. He inched forward. *Crack.* His head collided with the ceiling. 'Fuck's sake.' He slapped his hand to his forehead.

'Oh gosh. Sorry. It's quite low,' said Briony.

'Yeah. So I see.' He rubbed his head, then sat on the end of the bed with a groan.

'Are you ok? Would you like me to get anything to put on it?' She trailed a fingertip along her lower lip, watching him.

'No. Just go,' he said, not meaning it to sound so abrasive. 'And please don't wake me. I'll come down when I'm ready.'

'Sure.' Her broad smile pinged back in a flash. 'There's a bathroom at the bottom of the stairs if you need it.'

'Thanks.' He threw himself onto the bed as the door clicked shut. Jesus Christ. What was going on? How the hell had this happened? Fate? He'd never believed in that. Not in real life. It was great in his favourite fantasy books, but he was Zach Somerton, not Luke Skywalker. He didn't have any crazy destinies – unless Mr Beyer decreed it.

The rain tapped on the windowpane. What kind of insane place had he landed in? *Just one week.* He could do it. His eyes closed. This was where a fancy-shmancy degree in history got you. Twenty-eight and clueless about what he really wanted to do. Still faking his way through life, waiting for that letter from Hogwarts, the chance to hop on the Millennium Falcon or to discover he had the power to balance a car with one finger. He was the company liability and he had a week to prove otherwise. Only he wasn't sure what the parameters for failure were. How would he know when he'd fully investigated? What did Mr Beyer want him to find? Good things? Bad things? Now Zach was thousands of miles away from everything familiar, this felt more like a test than a job.

A test made a hundred times harder by the fact that the hotel owner happened to be someone who hated his guts. Her cooperation was necessary, but he couldn't hide from the fact he'd been responsible for her losing her job once before. He'd paid off the sleazy barman in the hope he'd stay true to his word, but the guy had probably taken the money and run. Zach let out a growl. He'd landed in his own worst nightmare.

CHAPTER FIVE

Briony

The door had barely shut on the attic room when Briony legged it down the stairs. She quickly attended to the couple in the bar, then hightailed it into the Bonnie Prince Charlie suite.

'This is unreal. I can't believe he's here. How is it possible?' she muttered, grabbing the duvet and hauling it off the four-poster bed. The top layer peeled off and she screwed up her face. 'Nooo.' Becker's muck had soaked into the duvet itself. 'That dog.' Coming straight from her city life to this place, she'd never had a pet. Keeping one in her flat wasn't fair and she couldn't deny life had been a lot easier *sans* Mr Messy Paws. When Granny Hilda died, Becker was left to the family with everything else. Briony's parents didn't want to take on a Highland hotel – they already managed their own upmarket guest house in Ayrshire. Her younger sister had taken one look at the place and laughed. She'd forged a successful career singing on cruise ships and taking on something like this was not for her. To Briony, with her degree in hospitality, it presented an unmissable opportunity, and her parents were delighted she wanted it after spending so long at The Gladstone. The fancy Edinburgh hotel had lost its appeal. And she'd always been edgy, never putting herself forward for promotion in case the scandal came back to bite. She'd only escaped getting the sack because Darren had told her boss he'd overheard the Americans 'forcing' Briony into their room. Going along with the story had saved her skin, though how her boss ever found out in the first place was a mystery.

When Darren did the dirty on her, she called it a day. Mr done-dusted-and-divorced Dalgleish was no more. Marrying him in the first place was one of her biggest mistakes, but she'd been so grateful and convinced he'd been thrown in her path for a reason. Now, it was like she'd wasted years of her life on him. She would change her name back to her maiden name were it not for the fact it was hideous. McClurg. Such a yucky word. Like dirty water draining down a plughole – exactly where she hoped Mr Dalgleish had found himself.

She dragged the messy duvet onto the landing and unlocked the large walk-in linen cupboard. The overheads and upkeep of this place were thousands more than the profits. How could she make any improvements when she could barely afford to keep it open? She lifted another duvet from the shelf and scuttled back into the Bonnie Prince Charlie suite. It wouldn't be sensible to put all her faith in this investor, but the other options were paper thin. The innocent voice of Missy Peck chirped up, reminding her good things happened when you least expected them.

1001 Stain Remover was usually good at getting out anything. She scrubbed the worse stains on the carpet with it, then knelt for who knew how long, blasting them with the hairdryer. This room was her one nod to improving the accommodation. She'd given this room a facelift and renamed it in the hope of drawing in more tourists, or at least being able to charge more for it. Neither had worked so far.

Now, how best to sell the hotel to Zach Somerton? Maybe bet him he couldn't get it so he would prove her wrong? 'Ugh.' She groaned. *Why does it have to be him?* She knew his style, turn on the charm for cash. But he hadn't seemed very charming so far.

Briony stood back, glaring at the carpet, and sighed. Selling the hotel wasn't what she wanted but this deal presented a solution that would allow her to be heavily involved in the hotel's future minus the financial responsibility. Surely that was perfect. She'd have more free time to indulge Missy Peck. They could go adventuring together again. Only a handful of people knew she'd written and illustrated a book. She used the pen name Bee Mack – best not to let on. No one liked a boaster. But before she got carried away with wishful thinking, she had to convince Zach she was the best person for the job. One of the only people in the world who knew her record wasn't exactly clean. Would he hold that against her? Maybe he wouldn't want to draw attention to what happened. Or maybe he was proud of his part in it.

On her hands and knees with a bucket ten minutes later, she scrubbed the muddy paw prints from the carpet on the landing. This was what her life had become and it couldn't go on. She wasn't afraid of work, but this? Nope. Time to pull out the razzle dazzle and flash it in the smouldering dark eyes of Mr Somerton.

Oh god. Easier said than done. Had he been a perfect stranger, it would have been simpler. But a sickening sensation formed in her tummy at the thought of even seeing him again. He appeared brooding and gruff these days, but he'd been persuasive and deceptive in the past. Maybe she should play up the hotel's attributes just a little? Like she'd done with his room. Harmless exaggeration. She pummelled the scrubbing brush along the carpet.

First, she had to get him in here. The attic wasn't suitable, and he'd had to crack his head, hadn't he? *Nightmare.* She facepalmed. He said not to wake him, so she left him, but how long would he sleep? At least she had time to fancy up his room and the least time spent with him the better. Surely a moment would come when they'd have to admit they recognised each other. It was awkward enough already, but a confession? She winced and shuddered. The longer she could hold off that moment, the better.

She dashed downstairs and into her private quarters. Becker was sprawled out, taking up the whole sofa, and barely raised a bristly brow. Pulling open the one of the retro – and peeling – upper cabinets in her kitchen, she grabbed a packet of shortbread. Somewhere in one of these cupboards was a decanter. The fryer came out, the mixer, liquidiser, an ornate cake stand, an oddly shaped vase. *Aha!* Briony's grip closed around the neck of a decanter. The cut crystal ridges pressed into her fingertips as she pulled it out. All she had to do was shine up this beauty, polish a matching glass and stick it on a tray beside the bed. *Don't forget the shortbread!* She veered across the room and put the packet next to the tray so she would remember to take it up.

Granny Hilda had a cabinet full of whisky and other select liqueurs. Briony hadn't been close to her – no one had, except maybe Becker. Granny Hilda kept everyone at arm's length and was private to the point of being shut off. No small wonder the hotel had gone downhill under her management. She hadn't exactly presented a friendly face to weary travellers. But she must have had a love of alcohol, judging by the well-stocked cabinet. Briony pushed bottles aside, scanning the labels. A half-full whisky bottle from Glenbriar Distillery with a quirky old-fashioned label stood out. May as well stay local. Felicity worked there and, as her friend had helped her bring in lots of guests for the festival, Briony could repay the company a little with this.

'That'll do.' She pulled it out and popped out the cork. The deep peaty aroma hit her immediately and she held the bottle away from her nose. It wasn't a taste she'd acquired. As she poured it carefully into the decanter, she smirked at the name.

Whisky Kisses. That sounded ridiculously twee. Whisky didn't normally have a name like that, did it? It felt like ladling out a love potion. Perhaps if Zach drank it, she'd get a whisky kiss in the morning. A little tingle crept down her spine and she shook her head to get rid of it. Nope, she'd travelled that road before. Her fingertips brushed over her lips. Weird, really, how well she remembered that kiss and the promise of where it might lead. She normally wouldn't have dreamed of behaving like that with a guest, but there had been something about him. Something she now knew had been fake. Good but fake. And she'd do well to remember that.

When Briony got downstairs after leaving the complimentary tray in Zach's room, Meg swished in the back door in time to cook the evening meals. She was the only other member of staff, along with Shari, and she was completely indispensable. Cooking for one, even two was doable but hotel guests with dietary requirements and everything else was too much and way beyond Briony's skillset – not to mention her human capabilities. She couldn't be in the kitchen, behind the bar, serving the food and watching the front desk.

The door to the kitchen swung back and forward as Briony brought out steaming plates laden with Meg's good old-fashioned home cooking. It wasn't comparable to the gourmet meals in The Gladstone, but this was an old Scottish coaching inn, and people had different expectations. Good pub grub was allowed and should be celebrated. Hopefully anyway. What Mr Zacharias Somerton would make of it was another issue. Maybe it didn't matter anyway. If his boss bought out the hotel, who was to say what would happen? Daniel Beyer could sack Meg and change the menus as he pleased. A sickening pang twisted in Briony's chest. Poor Meg. Would it be possible to make it a condition of the sale that she should be kept on too? But how? Briony didn't exactly have much leverage. Make that none. The reality of the situation started to press heavily on her shoulders.

With so many guests, dinners ran on past nine o'clock. Briony's feet were throbbing in her not-so-sensible heels. *Must wear flats tomorrow.* She gave herself a mental check as she took the last plates into the kitchen and leaned on the worktop. Meg was shoving crockery into the washer and scrubbing like mad, her neatly bobbed hair covered by her cook's hairnet and her face red.

'What a night,' Meg said. 'Hasn't been this busy for ages.'

Too true. Even in the summer months, they hadn't been full.

'Is that everyone done?'

'Everyone except Mr Somerton,' said Briony. 'But I think he must be asleep for the night.'

'Is he this investor man?'

'He's representing him, yes.' Briony nodded. She'd been upfront with Meg, but Mr Beyer had never indicated whether he would keep on all the staff or just Briony. Maybe Meg was ten steps ahead and already looking for other jobs, or did she think she'd automatically be kept on? Briony was too tired for that conversation tonight, especially when she didn't have the answers. They could discuss it properly tomorrow or when she knew more. 'He went to bed when he arrived. Jet lag. I haven't seen him since.'

'Do you think he'll want this place?' Meg's tone had a pleading note in it. 'It's in such bad nick. You were brave to take it on. I don't know how Hilda kept it going in her last few months.'

No one had grasped just how bad she was until she was overcome by heart failure. Such was Hilda's way. Never let anyone close. It explained why the hotel – not to mention the accounts – were in such a terrifying state.

'When she died,' Meg went on. 'I thought I'd be out then.'

'Of course not, you're a great cook. I honestly couldn't survive without you.'

'But with all the cutbacks these days. How do we know if this American will keep us on? It's not easy working with that in the back of your mind.'

'I understand,' said Briony. 'But he'll need staff and who better than the people who know what they're doing?' She ignored the wishful thinking-ness of that statement. Rarely had she worked for a boss who didn't want to change the regime as soon as they took over. 'I'll try my best to get you a fair deal.' What else could she do?

They cleared up and shut the kitchen. Briony served the last few drinks, then closed the bar. As the last guests drank up, she nipped into the private quarters and let Becker out. Grudgingly he got off the sofa and stood beside her at the door, hanging his head as rain battered the ground.

'Go on,' Briony said. 'I'd rather not be up at three in the morning when you decide you need to go. Now's your time.' She gave him a light slap on the rear and he grumbled off into the darkness. She waited for him with a giant towel spread in her arms. As soon as he reappeared, she wrestled him dry before he returned to the sofa.

A yawn escaped her and she massaged her face to stay awake. Bed wasn't an option until the last guests were done. More reasons she couldn't keep this up. Exhaustion wasn't a good look.

Sitting at reception, she flicked through some emails. Ooh, she had some responses from local businesses interested in Christmas party nights. That was good. And a cancellation for next month. Seriously? That knocked the wind from her sails. She sighed and opened the booking system to cross it off.

People were still chattering in the lounge. A creak on the stairs made her peek up. She barely suppressed a giggle. A bleary-eyed Zach shuffled in, ruffling up what was already a fairly impressive bed head of thick dark curls. His t-shirt still bore the mucky footprints but now it was untucked and creased too.

'Is my room ready yet?' he asked, through a half yawn. He looked like he could do with a big cuddly teddy bear and someone to tuck him in for the night. Not that she'd be volunteering.

'It is indeed.' Briony pulled out her biggest smile. 'Would you like me to show you to it?'

'I need my luggage first. And food.'

'Food? At ten o'clock? I'm afraid the kitchen's closed.'

'Well, what do you expect me to do? Starve? I haven't eaten since about two.'

'Of course.' And he couldn't have thought about this before he decided to sleep for six hours – more than she'd get. 'I can fix you a cold plate to eat in your room if that would suit?'

'Yeah, sure. Just no pork or bacon. Pig stuff. You know the deal.'

'Er... Sure.'

He turned and strolled out the front door, audibly muttering about the rain and the cold.

Seriously? Food now? But here was a chance to give him the full Scottish experience. She yawned and flapped her hand at her mouth. *Come on, let's do this. Did haggis have pork in it? It was sheep, right? Can't put that in a sandwich though.* Cheese then. She sliced some local cheese and a selection of salad vegetables, some grapes and bread. That would have to do. Grabbing the cling film, she covered the plate and returned to the foyer.

Zach stood waiting, his eyebrows knitted together, his thick hair, slick and wet, dripping down his face. His mucky and soaked t-shirt clung to a very shapely torso. The feel of that was embossed in her memories. In room 414 at The Gladstone, she'd enjoyed a too short skim of it beneath his shirt. But she'd been sober. He hadn't. She'd stopped before they'd gone too far, though he probably told his chums they'd gone all the way.

Briony ran her eyes over the ridges of muscle under his t-shirt. He was even more well defined these days. She sucked the inside of her lip. Couldn't blame a girl for looking. Actually scratch that. It always led to trouble and she'd had enough problems with this one already.

'Here you go, Mr... er... Zach. Your cold plate.'

'Thanks.' He peered at it.

'Let me bring it up for you. Or would you prefer me to carry your bags?'

'No. I'll take the bags.'

'I'll show you to your room then. Follow me.' She lifted the plate and led him upstairs, taking calming breaths as she reached the landing. He was close behind and the fresh rain-washed scent from his hair and skin permeated into her consciousness. With a little cough, she halted outside a wood-panelled door. 'Here it is. The Bonnie Prince Charlie suite.'

He stopped close and raised an eyebrow. 'I suppose it still has the original bed he slept in?'

Was he being serious? Was that what he thought? Wanted? 'I, um, don't think so. But he travelled all around the Highlands after...' She snapped her fingers. What battle was it? She always got mixed up. Culloden or Bannockburn?

'Culloden?' he said. It sounded like a question, but that sarky-smug expression said *I know I'm right.*

'The very one.' She beamed as though he was a very clever child and his answer was wonderful, not just irritatingly precocious. 'So, it's possible he stayed at this hotel during that time.'

'Right. Even though that battle was in 1745 and this hotel looks like it was built about a hundred years after that.'

Oh crap! 'Well, not necessarily this very building.' Were her cheeks as red as they felt? 'There's always been a hotel of some sort here.'

'Has there? Right.' His flat tone said he didn't believe one word of it.

She wrenched her eyes from him, opened the door, switched on the light and laid his plate on the small table by the window, painfully aware of what had happened the last time they were alone in a hotel room. Rain splattered against the panes. 'I've left you some complimentary local delicacies. That's Glenbriar whisky in the decanter, a rare and potent variety, I believe.'

'Sounds dangerous.' His eyes met hers and the wire of understanding between them crackled into life again.

'All whisky is dangerous in the wrong hands or if drunk too much,' she said with a slight quirk of her eyebrow.

'True.' He huffed a half laugh, opened the decanter and sniffed it. 'As we know to our cost,' he muttered so low she barely caught what he said.

She cleared her throat, unsure if he'd meant her to hear or not. 'Right. I'll leave you to it. And hopefully we can talk in the morning... about business.'

'Sure. But I leave the business to Mr Beyer.'

'Isn't that why you're here?' She swallowed. He couldn't have any other motivation, could he? Had he deliberately tracked her down?

'I'm here to see if this place has the kind of historical clout Mr Beyer wants. And I need to investigate it from top to bottom to find out.'

Briony's heartrate picked up. Historical clout? And she couldn't even remember the difference between Culloden and Bannockburn. Oh great.

'Wonderful,' she said. 'See you in the morning then.' She snapped the door closed, threw back her head and let out a silent scream. When she'd asked the universe to send her the perfect person to save the hotel, she hadn't meant a person with perfect cheekbones and a fit body. Help! What was she going to do? This was not going to plan.

CHAPTER SIX

Zach

Sleeping for six hours in the evening when his brain was still on Eastern Standard Time was messing with Zach's head, and that was before thoughts of Briony, and what she was doing here, crept in. His cell phone told him it was now three in the morning, but he felt wide awake. Travelling wasn't his thing; sticking with the status quo was infinitely safer. The hassle of planning and executing a trip was never worth the payoff. This trip was proof of that and he'd barely been here twenty-four hours. How was he going to last the week?

He cast a glance over the bedroom, dimly lit by a bedside lamp fashioned out of antlers. Were they real? Zach frowned. Was this seriously the kind of place Mr Beyer wanted to invest in? No real history existed here. Decorating it in tartan, leaving some whisky and calling the room after a barely Scottish, supposed heroic, but actually deeply narcissistic, historical figure was hardly the right way to create mystique. The Gandalf man's mention of a monster in the loch was more plausible than the idea of Bonnie Prince Charlie ever having been here – and more fun.

Zach leaned over to the bedside cabinet and pulled the stopper from the whisky decanter. Warm smoky undertones tickled his nostrils. Mr Beyer was the fanatical connoisseur and would have been able to give a proper evaluation, though he probably wouldn't even lower his nose to this. To Zach's untrained palate, it smelled nice but could easily be cheap muck turfed into a fancy decanter. Or poison. Zach's undiscerning palate was another reason working for a bourbon billionaire was a joke. One he lived daily, though it wasn't particularly funny; it cemented his lifelong status of misfit.

His grandma had always told him to be himself and not be ashamed of who he was – though he wasn't sure he knew who that was. He returned the stopper and lay back on the pillow. The paw print t-shirt and mucky jeans were off, and he was in his black and red TIE Fighter boxer briefs, lying atop the covers on the massive, ornately carved bed. A pleasant warmth had filled the room when he first came up but now it was freezing. He pulled a hefty blanket from the end of the bed and draped it over himself. His grandma would have loved this place. She always wanted to travel but never had. One day, Zach had gone off to school and Grandma to work. She never came home. She'd collapsed at work and couldn't be resuscitated. The gap her death had left in Zach's soul was unfixable. Grandma was the glue that held him and his mom together. Without her they drifted into an odd, lonely and repetitive existence. Zach hadn't noticed how sick his mom was until Grandma died. Staying in bed seemed to be what she needed, so he'd left her there, neglecting her, and concentrating on getting himself sorted for school. In the evenings, he'd play computer games until his eyes went square or he fell asleep. Warm hugs became a thing of the past and online gamers took more interest in him than his only living relative did. Now he could afford to pay for proper care for Mom, make up for when he'd been too young to know what to do. She would be ok. He'd make sure of that. He owed to her and his grandma.

He shoved on his glasses and looked heavenward, hoping she was watching and not disappointed in his life choices. *Goodnight, Grandma.* He resumed reading his latest sci-fi thriller download on his iPad. Half an hour later, it slapped him on the face and he jumped. His glasses were askew, his head nodding. Damned jet lag.

He was awake again by six. That was a respectable time to get up, right? He stretched and yawned, not feeling rested at all, kind of teetering in limbo between not being tired enough to sleep but not awake enough to do anything constructive. His dreams had been full of aliens – most resembled Briony – giving him bizarre instructions or trying to get his clothes off so they could perform extremely kinky alien moves on him.

The en-suite bathroom was the room's high point. Genuinely old-fashioned and dazzlingly clean. Navy and white geometric tiles trimmed the walls around the bath and sink while the rest had mock William Morris wallpaper. He ran his finger over a chunky faucet on the sink and shivered. Jeez. Frigging cold though.

Were there no heaters? He dragged a fluffy white towel around his shoulders. Grin and bear it time. If the water was this cold, it would soon wipe out any lingering memories of those dreams. The glass screen creaked open and he turned three levers on the shower without a clue as to what they did. Why were they so different from the showers back home? When he finally got the water running hot, he waited until steam filled the room, then flipped open a bottle of body wash and sniffed it, blinking at the potent tea tree fragrance. When he couldn't procrastinate anymore, he took off his boxers, dropped the towel and jumped in. The hot water blasted heat through his system. He soaped himself up, taking his time because he didn't want step out onto the stone-cold tiles. Parts of him might shrivel and fall off – parts he was pretty attached to.

When he was in danger of drowning, he bit the bullet, leapt out and grabbed his towel, barely drying himself before he jumped into the bedroom. Not that it was much warmer there. Perhaps half a degree. At least it had a carpet. Slightly better underfoot. He rummaged through his case, pulling out a black *calm you shall keep and carry on you must* Yoda t-shirt and a charcoal zip-up hoody. Everything he had was what Briony would dub festival-goer. She may even have a point. So what? His idea of a fun vacation was attending a *Star Wars* convention –

and if he was done here by Friday, he'd be winging it home and flying to Anaheim for The Return of the Fans festival. It was the carrot keeping him going.

A neatly bound book containing important information about the hotel and the local area was on the dresser. He flipped through it looking for breakfast times. From seven thirty. Well, seven was close enough. Surely someone would be around to serve him? Or he could wait in the lounge. He ruffled his hair, drying it out as he went downstairs. He never bothered with hairdryers or styling products. A year ago, he could have rivalled Jon Snow from *Game of Thrones* for the thick curls. He'd had it trimmed since, but it was still a big floppy mop, unlike the perfectly cropped hair his colleagues all had and how he'd worn it when he met Briony first time around. He stuck out like a sore thumb in the office. Maybe one day Mr Beyer would order him to have it cut.

He approached the reception area and blinked. Briony again? Had she been sitting there all night? When she'd said they were short-staffed, just how short-staffed did she mean? Was there anyone else working here at all?

'Hi,' he said, and she glanced up.

'Oh. Good morning. Did you sleep well?'

How could she be so cheery and chatty so early? How could anyone? And still nothing to confirm she recognised him. 'Not really.'

'Oh dear. That's not good. Was there a problem with the room?' She tugged at the floaty sleeve edge of her floral top. It was a variation of her plum colour scheme from yesterday. Her nails still matched perfectly. The neckline dipped towards her chest, leaving an exposed V of peachy skin dappled with freckles. A sparkling petal-shaped pendant dripped around her neck; its intricate design worked in harmony with the pattern on her top. The whole ensemble was perfectly pulled together and made her look delicate and feminine; it gave Zach a jolt deep down. A light fragrance in the air matched her outfit and Zach breathed it in, suddenly aware of the strong tea tree scent lingering on his skin. Was finding Briony here a second chance? Maybe a gift? Could they carry on where they'd left off? Her fragrance kicked him where it hurt, reminding him things hadn't exactly ended well. 'No. It's the jet lag.'

'I see. Well, would you like some breakfast? Maybe some strong coffee might help. Or eggs?'

He blinked. 'Do coffee and eggs cure jet lag?'

'I don't know. But they work wonders on a hangover.'

He nodded, then leaned his forearms on the high part of the desk. 'Let's drop the act for a moment.'

'What act?'

'The one where we pretend we've never met.'

Her cheeks coloured and she pressed her lips together. 'Ok. But does it change anything?'

He half raised an eyebrow. 'I don't know. But I don't want to keep up the pretence.' He did that every day at work – in fact, he'd pretty much done it every day since he was thirteen – pretending he was a competent human, not a pantser who flew through every day hoping nothing would go wrong.

'No?' she said. 'I thought you enjoyed that kind of thing.'

Ouch.

'Wasn't that what it was all about last time?' She blinked slowly, tapping a nail on the desk, waiting like a cat preparing to pounce.

He huffed and stepped back, raking his fingers through his hair. *Not for me.* The last time he'd met Briony had been the one time he'd felt real, like he'd finally shrugged off the role of bumbling sidekick and stepped up to be the hero in his own life. *Yeah, and how long did that last?* All of a few hours. 'It was a dumbass thing to do. I'm not denying it.'

She got to her feet and pushed her chair in. 'Indeed, it was. Now, would you like that breakfast?' Her smile leapt back into place and she clapped her hands. 'This way to the breakfast room.' She pointed to the same door she'd tried to get him through yesterday when she'd suggested he went into the lounge. 'That's a fun t-shirt you have.' She smirked as she opened the door and her gaze landed where his hoody hung open.

Zach let out a sigh, toying with the zipper. So much for the big confession. She may as well have lifted a strip of that grotty carpet and swept it under. 'Is the breakfast room different from the lounge?' He thrust his hands into his back pockets and followed her.

'Well, it's one big room as you'll see.' She opened the door, gesturing around like she was a real estate agent doing a tour. And he thought he was the master of faking it – nothing compared to this mistress of fakery. The phoney sweetness was grating, not like the warmth he'd felt the first time around. 'We have the bar here and on this side is what we call the lounge. It's the comfy side and it has the fire.'

'Yeah. I see.'

'Then through the arch here is the dining room, which I call the breakfast room in the morning when it's laid out for breakfast. It has a great view to the loch and...' She peered out of the window into the semi-darkness. 'I think we'll be able to see it today. It's hard to tell before the sun's fully up but it doesn't look as cloudy as yesterday.'

'Right.'

She'd turned on the full sunshine, but every word held a sharp blade, reminding him of what a bastard he'd been. How could he deny it? He *had* chased her for a bet. What had made it easy was how much he liked her. No point telling her that now. How lame did it sound? Even thinking it made him cringe. The oldest excuse in the book. That starring role he'd had back then now felt like a botched audition.

'You can sit here by the window if you like. Watch the sun rise as you eat. The menu is here.' She lifted a faux leather-bound book-style menu with gold swirly writing on it. The spine was peeling away and when she opened it, the plastic-coated pages crackled like they were stuck together. Yet another piece of history – the not good kind.

Zach plonked himself on the seat she'd indicated and she placed the open menu in front of him. He scanned the breakfast choices.

'I'll give you a few minutes to decide.' She bustled off and he lifted his gaze from the blurry text on the menu and followed her path; her pert bottom, encased in a tight grey pencil skirt, swayed as she wound around the tables set with white cloths and little vases containing purple plastic thistles bound with tartan ribbons. Heat rippled through his stomach, scorching his insides, reminding him of the first time. Only she'd been a willing party then. For a fling. She'd known he was leaving the next day. If the bet hadn't been discovered, her pride would still be intact and they could have parted as two people who'd kissed in a hotel room. Maybe she wouldn't have looked twice at him for anything more serious. Women never did. Zach could alienate them five minutes into a date by dropping some stupid line from a film or a crazy reference only he understood. Not cool. Blame nerves or whatever but he couldn't help himself and it sucked. In fact, it wasn't just women. He didn't have the knack for making friends either. Not real ones, just the cyber variety who lurked on the same sci-fi forums as him. And if they got bored with him or lost interest, they could just unfriend him. Somehow that didn't hurt as much as being ditched face to face.

Briony had slipped through a swing door he assumed was the kitchen. She was the most vibrant thing in the building. Everything else looked worn and unkempt. He was still staring at the door, his chin resting on his hand, when it opened again and she strolled out, big smile in place. He dropped his eyes to the menu.

'Have you decided then?' she asked, placing a coffee press on the table with a loud clunk.

Had he said he wanted coffee? He didn't drink it. He never had and he had no idea what to do with that gadget she'd set down.

'Vegetarian breakfast.' That was the safest. He'd left his glasses in his room and was struggling to read the small print.

'Of course.'

'Can you pour that out?' He pointed at the coffee press. 'Please.'

The tiniest flicker of a frown intruded on her smile before she plunged the lever into the jug then poured some into a cup. 'Milk?'

'No, thanks.'

'Sugar.'

'No. I'll take it neat.'

'Neat? Ok. There it is.' Her lips closed. Was she biting back a laugh? What was she thinking? That he was an asshole? Or some kind of idiot who didn't know how to make a coffee? Well, fuck it, she was right. But he was damned if he was going to let on.

'Your breakfast will be ready shortly.' She flicked her hair and made to walk away.

'Are you...' He frowned and she turned back. 'Are you the only person who works here?'

'No. I have Meg who comes in to cook the evening meals and Shari who comes in to help change the rooms and clean.'

'That doesn't seem enough for this size of hotel.'

'It's not. That's why I need an investor.'

'How did you get here in the first place? What happened after—'

'That's not any of your business,' she said, lowering her voice as two more guests arrived, sitting at a table on the other side of the room. 'Which reminds me, I need to talk to you about staff arrangements.'

'To me?'

'I want to know what will happen to the staff if Mr Beyer buys this place. He said I could stay on as manager but what about the others?'

'That's nothing to do with me. I'm just here to investigate the history.' Though what exactly that meant, he still wasn't sure.

'Can we schedule a time to talk about this properly? I can't until breakfast is finished but most people are usually out by ten thirty and Shari will be in, so I could meet with you then.'

Obviously no shifting her on this. 'Right. Ok.' Her business-like tone gave him a niggle in the gut. Talking business was above his paygrade. Briony may not know the first thing about history but when it came to business, she'd wipe the floor with him. *Mustn't let that happen.* Mr Beyer would kill him – though Briony might get there first. She strolled across to the other guests and chatted to them as they looked through the menu. Zach sipped his coffee and screwed up his nose.

Ten thirty seemed a long way off. After breakfast, he put on his denim jacket and walked down the short path to the loch side. A walk might clear his head. The path continued through woods but it was muddy underfoot and his Converse weren't exactly waterproof. The rain had stopped and flashes of blue sky poked their way out. A calm stillness settled, broken by the occasional breath of wind stirring the grass, and the call of a bird. Beyond the loch in the misty haze were the silhouettes of mountains. Surely this was why people came here? The history was insignificant next to this. Zach wasn't often moved by landscapes but vibes pulsed through him. This was like Rivendell, the last homely house before the wild mountains. Visitors were on the edge of danger, an unknown, frightening wilderness beyond; they could choose to step outside and journey into the wilds or stay in the safety and confines of the hotel.

But Zach had his instructions. Investigate the history – not the fantasy appeal. If he owned a place like this and had the money to do it up, he'd dig for the real history and beef that up, but also weave in the magic. Who didn't like a little mystery in their lives? Myths and legends were tourist catnip.

On a low shore further up the loch, a couple picked their way across the pebbles, holding a toddler in a bright-blue rainsuit and yellow rainboots between them. The kid giggled as his parents swung him along. Zach slumped onto a fallen tree trunk and rubbed his thighs, watching the happy scene. What must it be like to grow up in a family like that, with two doting parents as opposed to one clueless one? If only Grandma had lived longer. Maybe with better guidance he'd have made better choices and not found himself trapped in a job he hated. But it paid his way. He checked his watch. Ten o'clock. He should go back.

A crashing in the bushes behind him made him spin around. A giant brown shape came loping through and his mind whirred through hundreds of images in quick succession, including bear, Wookie, deer and werewolf before settling on dog.

'Oh no, not you again.' Too late. The dog leapt on him before he could get off the log, smearing his jacket with mud and licking his face. 'Seriously? I don't even know you. Could you be any more forward?'

'Becker! Oh my god.' Briony came racing along the path – well, running was clearly what she was aiming for, but that tight skirt came with limitations. She'd switched her heels for rainboots and had on a belted pink coat but neither were helping her move fast enough. Zach wrestled Becker's feet back to the ground and stood. Briony marched up and clipped on his leash. A bit late.

'I'm not going to have any clean clothes left at this rate.'

'I am so sorry,' Briony said. 'Becker, I don't know what to do with you.'

'Maybe he needs longer walks.'

'Well, sadly I can't. This is all I can fit in.'

'Then why get a dog?' He shrunk back at the irritated flash in her eyes.

'I didn't. He came with the hotel. He's nine and it seemed cruel to send him away, so I kept him.'

Sounded fair.

'I'll walk him if you like.' Where had that come from?

'You?'

'Why not?' Now he'd said it, he felt the need to defend himself, though he'd never had a pet in his life. He'd never wanted one. One day it would die. He didn't think he could pour all his love into something that would leave him too soon. But this crazy dog had shown him more love and affection in the past twelve hours than most humans did over a lifetime.

'I'm not sure I can trust you.'

He shrugged. 'Suit yourself. I was only trying to be nice and I'd like the company.'

'I'll think about it, but you'd have to keep him on the lead.'

He pouted at his mud-stained jacket. 'Maybe you should take your own advice.'

'He's my dog,' she said. 'I'll decide that. Now, see you in half an hour. Come on, Becker.' She tugged gently on his leash and marched towards the trees. As they reached the edge of the wood, she unclipped him and he ran off.

Zach raked through his hair and let out a sigh before heading back to the hotel. He nipped up to his room, discarded his muddy hoody and grabbed his glasses and his iPad. He wanted to at least look like he knew what he was doing. The reception area was empty and had a card on it with a phone number to call in an emergency. A vision of Becker charging through the woods wearing a red cape to save the day assailed Zach and he smirked. Becker the wonder dog. The lounge was empty, and he slipped in and wandered around, trying to get a feel for the history of the place. The windowsills were wide and painted white. Leaflets and local information books were spread across them. He put on his glasses and read over a few. Local water sports, distilleries, craft centres, a light show in a local woodland, the Amber Gold Music Festival in Glenbriar – presumably this was the thing Briony had thought he was going to. He replaced the leaflets and dropped into a seat by the unlit fireplace.

A small coffee table to the side had other books on it and he spied a kid's book. The front cover had an illustration of a rather naughty-looking little girl in front of a bright-pink building. He picked it up. The scenery in the illustration looked remarkably like the loch view he'd had that morning. *Missy Peck and The Pink Hotel*. He flicked open the book and read. A smile grew and his heart lightened. *Ok*. She was a naughty little kid but kinda cute. Her adventure seemed to take place here. She had a little sister and together they solved a mystery that involved doing lots of things they shouldn't. The pictures were stunning and full of little details. The hotel was like a focal point for the residents of Tartan Town and Zach snickered when he got to a page where they'd come together for a ceilidh and were riotously dancing, while Missy Peck twirled in the middle.

Written and illustrated by Bee Mack. He was on the verge of googling the name when the lounge door opened and a young woman came in. She had on a tunic and her hair was tied in a messy bun atop her head.

'Oh... hi.' She goggled at Zach and he looked sideways. What was she staring at? 'I wondered if Briony was about.'

'She's walking the dog,' he said, toying with the leg of his glasses.

'Ah. Ok.' As she pulled the door shut, Briony's voice chirped out.

'I'm here, Shari, what is it?'

The door clicked, obscuring the rest of the conversation. Zach returned to the book. He'd just got to the end when Briony came in. She glanced at the book and her cheeks reddened. Pressing her lips together, she toyed with her petal pendant; the slow motion of her fingertips circling it resonated deep in Zach's gut. With an effort, he rolled his shoulders and wrenched his eyes away. Briony marched across the room and sat opposite him, clasping her hands on her knees and fixing him with a steely gaze.

Zach tossed the book onto the table and peered back at her. Let business commence.

CHAPTER SEVEN

Briony

*M*issy Peck and The Pink Hotel lay on the coffee table in front of Zach. Briony drew in a slow breath, not looking at the cover with the picture she'd drawn so long ago she wasn't sure she remembered how. Her heartrate spiked as she sat, staring into Zach's deep brown eyes. He looked ridiculously sexy and disarming in glasses. Not something she'd noticed in anyone before. But the blend of brooding looks and shapely spectacles worked magic. And she'd caught him reading her books. Then smiling. Zach smiling! Cue disconcerting hiccup. Zach hadn't shown himself to be much of a smiler this time around, fortunately for her – she knew too well what damage that smile had caused before. But what had made him grin this time? Was the book so bad it was hilarious? Or was he enjoying it? She ran her palm down her thigh and sucked her lip. She didn't have the nerve to ask. Best not to draw attention to the book.

'Right. Business.' She patted her knees.

'Business,' he repeated.

'What exactly is Mr Beyer looking for in the hotel? I don't get what kind of history he's after. This is an old building and all old buildings – old anythings – have some kind of history.' *Like us, though we aren't that old.*

Zach shuffled in his seat and tapped the edge of his iPad. 'I'm not entirely clear what he's looking for either. My brief is to make thorough investigations. I think he's deliberately kept me in the dark so I give him an impartial report.'

'Ok. And don't take this the wrong way, but why you?'

'What do you mean?' His thick brows joined in the middle, making a hard line along the top of his glasses. 'I didn't come here searching for you if that's what you think. I didn't even know your name. That was part of the deal.'

'Like I could forget.' *The deal*, aka his bet. Maybe his boss was a gambler too and wanted to take a punt on this place. 'But that's not what I meant. I don't get why he sent you in particular to investigate. Wouldn't it have been better to send someone who was able to discuss business?'

'My background is in history.' A slight edge crept into his voice.

Briony was an expert at keeping her smile in place, but her insides jumped. 'Is it? Wow.' She hadn't seen that coming. 'Sounds fun. What projects have you worked on before?'

His jaw tensed. 'Well, this is my first assignment in this field. My degree is history but I worked in a different sector before. I was recently, um, reassigned to a new post.'

His words came out stilted like he was considering each one carefully before he spoke.

'Ok, curiosity question.' She couldn't hold it in. 'What age are you?'

'What has that got to do with anything?'

'Nothing. Purely curiosity like I said.'

'Twenty-eight,' he mumbled.

'Seriously?' He'd only been twenty-three when they met before. Heat rose up her neck. She was five years older than him. No wonder he'd looked about five steps out of high school.

'Don't tell me. You thought I was older.'

'Er…' She swallowed. 'I'm not sure what I thought, that's why I asked. Though I remember one of your colleagues calling you baby face at The Gladstone.'

Zach rolled his eyes. 'Yeah. I get that all the time. Even now.'

She cocked her head but refrained from saying 'aw'. He'd tried to disguise it with rough stubble approaching a beard but something youthfully cute remained beneath the scowl – though his body looked all man, distractingly so.

'Well, now that I look properly, you look bang on twenty-eight.'

He pulled a fake smile then let it slide away slowly. 'Thanks. Remind me why we're talking about this.'

'Because I was curious.'

'And what age are you? May as well be on an even footing.'

Briony clenched her teeth. 'Thirty-three.' She waited for his reaction. Was the penny about to drop? He'd pulled her when she was the age he was now and he'd been practically a college boy.

His expression remained inscrutable. 'And you look bang on thirty-three, so there we are. Quits.'

'Good.' *But could he not have said I only look twenty-six?*

'Now can we talk about the hotel?'

'Sure,' she said. 'Where were we? Oh yes, I wanted to know what Mr Beyer was specifically hoping to find. I'm sure this building has history but...' She chewed on her lip. Whatever she said might scupper her chances. She wanted to present the best version of the place but unless she invented a colourful past, as far as she knew, the hotel was nothing but an average inn with nothing much to say for itself. 'The kind of flashy history that goes with Bonnie Prince Charlie and all that is, well, fake. Or it is here. I don't think this hotel has anything to do with anyone famous. I named the room that because it appeals to tourists.'

'No kidding.'

She ignored his sarcasm. 'The history of this area isn't showy or exciting. No battles were fought here, no famous people buried here, I don't think it even has associations with witch burning or anything dramatic like that. There's a cleared village on the hill behind the hotel. You can visit the ruins and there's a plaque in memory of the people who were cleared off the land. I've walked there with Becker. But those houses are lowly and ordinary. No runaway princes ever hid in them. And the hotel is the same. There's nothing extraordinary about it.' She let out a sigh. 'So, if Mr Beyer is after some colourful tales of Scottish history, you're not going to find them here. In fact, you may as well pack your bags and leave.' Her tongue had raced on and now she was giving him an ultimatum. But what was the point in lying? If he was a historian he could work that out for himself. Why prolong the agony? If she didn't fulfil the criteria, it was a wall too high to scale.

'That kind of confirms my feelings. But Mr Beyer was insistent. I might take a walk to that cleared village and check it out, then I'll contact him and see if he wants me to carry on with the building.'

'Good plan.' Smile in place, her heart sagged inside. The opportunity was slipping away like sand in a sieve. But as one door closed another opened. Where would it lead? Her eyes linked with Zach's again and that current of unspoken thoughts reopened. Whatever attraction they'd felt across the dining room in The Gladstone five years ago hadn't died. That smouldering look was dangerous. It could do things to a girl. Had done before. But it was fake. *Must remember that.* The gnawing ache in her chest half-wished it hadn't been. Kisses like that weren't normal. Or maybe it meant fake ones were better. How topsy turvy.

'Can I take Becker with me?'

'Um, ok, I guess. I'm not sure how excited he'll be about a second walk in one day, but he might surprise me. Don't go thinking he's deprived of walks. He's a really lazy dog.'

Zach's lips quirked into a half smile and Briony's heart leapt. Honestly, this was crazy. Why were her insides behaving like a teenager on a trip to meet her pop crush? She didn't need this again.

'I'll come get him in twenty minutes.' He checked his watch. 'Mr Beyer won't be up yet, so there's no point in calling until later.' His eyes fell onto the table. *Shit.* He was looking at the book again. 'That story is cute and it's set here.'

'Um... Yes.'

'The pictures are great and the story is funny. Do you know who wrote it?'

'Um... The author's name is on the book.'

'Yeah, I can see that. But do you know her? Is she someone from around here? I thought you'd left it here because someone local wrote it.'

'I think she, um, lives somewhere nearby.'

'What the kid in these books has, that's what Mr Beyer needs to bottle. The feeling you get when you're down by the loch, the community spirit. All these intangibles.'

If only she could kindle that community spirit for real and not just in the pages of a picture book. Even with all Granny Hilda's failings, she'd had the bar jumping with locals when Briony was a child. Briony remembered ceilidhs and karaoke going on well into the night and feeling the vibrations shaking her camp bed in the spare room in the staff quarters as she lay awake dreaming up more stories. But enticing people back was a tough job when the building looked like the hotel time forgot.

'I wish I understood why he's so stuck on the history,' Zach said.

'Maybe you'll find out when you call.'

'Maybe.' He took off his glasses, shook his curly head, then ran his fingers through his thick locks. His hair had been short before but it suited him like this. His wrists were sturdy and tanned, covered in a smattering of dark hair beneath the cuff of his hoody. She remembered how good those arms had felt around her even for a few too short minutes.

'Right.' She slapped her thighs and got to her feet. Enough ogling Mr wanna-bet luscious-lashes. 'I need to make some sandwiches before the walkers arrive.'

He raised an eyebrow. 'You mean zombies are on their way?'

'Oh, very funny.'

His face split into a grin. Briony pulled back. Wow. A real smile.

'You get what that means, huh?' He eyed her over like he didn't believe she could.

'Zombies from *The Walking Dead*. Walkers.' Or maybe she'd got the wrong end of the stick and he meant something else entirely.

He shoved his fingers under the curls on his forehead and rubbed it. 'Exactly.'

'My ex-husband used to watch it.'

'Oh.' His face fell like she'd slapped it.

'I didn't really like it. But Andrew Lincoln is nice, so's David Morrisey.'

'If you say so.'

'I do.' She opened the door to the hall. 'I'll get Becker when you're ready.'

It took a bit of persuading to get Becker off the couch. 'Come on, you like Zach. You must do, you keep throwing yourself at him.'

Zach was waiting outside, mussing up his hair again. Did he ever leave it alone? Becker strained to get to him.

'See, I told you you'd be happy.'

'Hey,' said Zach, looking at Becker. 'Time for us to bond properly, which I might add is much better manners. You really should get to know a guy before you put your paws all over him and lick his face.'

'Advice for us all.' Briony handed him the lead. 'Now take care of my dog. And treat him better than you did with me. If you let anything happen to him, I'll lock you in the cellar and let you die a long slow painful death.'

Zach smirked. 'Yes, ma'am. I will take good care of him.' His warm hand brushed hers as he took the lead and an electric current zapped across her nerve ends. She suppressed a shiver. 'Though, I would like to add, I never meant to treat you badly. Even if there had been no bet, I... Well, let's just say, I'm sorry.'

'Hmm. Ok.' She nodded and ruffled Becker's head. 'Apology accepted.'

'Great.' Zach tugged Becker and he trotted off.

'Have a nice walk. And keep him on the lead.'

'Yes, ma'am.'

Energy fizzed around Briony's chest as she returned inside. She flexed her fingers, unable to settle. Maybe just nerves at sending Becker off with a near stranger? Or the tingly pleasure of someone liking her books? Or the fact he'd apologised. He'd almost said he would have wanted to do what they did without the bet. Could she believe him? And if she did, where did that leave them?

The kitchen was cool and airy, taking the sting out of her cheeks. She pulled out a pack of baguettes and started prepping them. Anything to keep her busy and stop her head filling with wild thoughts. With so few staff, she'd had to limit the lunch menu and only allow bookings. Hardly ideal. After Zach had called Mr Beyer, she might know her fate. Maybe that was the underlying cause of this restlessness.

She needed to talk this out. Setting her phone on the recipe holder, she pressed Felicity's icon. Time for a chat with the bestie.

Felicity had turned up in the spring looking for accommodation after she'd taken a job at the Glenbriar Distillery and the accommodation they'd promised her wasn't ready. Briony had given her the attic room until she was sorted out. It was friends at first sight. They just clicked. Felicity was younger, still in her twenties, but it was irrelevant; they had other things in common – like their joint love of conversation and their shared vice of overspending when clothes shopping. With all Briony's old friends back in Edinburgh, having Felicity on hand was a godsend.

Messenger connected and a crackly Felicity spoke. 'Hey.'

'Are you able to talk?' Briony asked.

'I'm just heading into work, but I've got five minutes. Is everything ok?'

'You remember that American investor I told you about?'

'Has he arrived?'

'His rep arrived yesterday.'

'And?'

'Well, we didn't get off to the best start. Becker got mud all over his bed, then over the man himself. I had to let him use the attic room while I sorted out the suite and he whacked his head off the low ceiling.'

'Oh, my god, no.'

'Yes.' Briony wasn't sure she wanted to share anything else about Zach. The coincidence was one thing but their shared history another. Too much for now. Best stick to the business side of things.

'So, is he not interested?'

'I'm not sure what's happening. He's calling his boss soon and I'll find out my fate.'

'Aw, I wish I could help. Is he hanging about breathing down your neck?'

'No, he's gone for a walk with Becker.'

'You let him take the dog? On his own?'

'I know. I must be crazy.'

That was the only explanation.

'No, but you are very trusting. I just hope he's not a psychopathic petnapper.'

'Oh, don't. If he is, Becker will probably be delighted. He seems very taken with him.'

'Becker is taken with *him?* That's funny.'

'It was love at first sight.' Briony cringed. Back in The Gladstone, she'd entertained that thought for herself for a fleeting moment. But thankfully she hadn't fallen for Zach. How inconvenient would that have been? 'You know,' she said with a sigh. 'I really wish I didn't have to sell up. I was so sure something would turn up, an eleventh hour reprise, a pot of money in a trust fund we didn't know about, anything. Guess I was wrong.'

'Don't give up hope,' Felicity said. 'I have to go to work, but I have faith.'

'Ok. Have a lovely day and we'll speak soon.'

Briony ended the call. Felicity had faith and Briony needed it too. Her inner Missy Peck gave her a little nudge: *remember, rainbows follow rain.*

CHAPTER EIGHT

Zach

Becker loped ahead, making short work of the steep path towards the cleared village. Pale sunshine had cracked its way through the clouds, illuminating purple and russet hills, sparse golden trees and thick brown bracken dripping with fat raindrops. Every now and then, Zach turned and looked behind at the view to the loch and the hotel. Magnificent, the way it sprawled for miles, creating a panorama of individual snapshots filled with light and colour. Each one was beautiful in itself but put together they became a sight to behold.

He dragged in a lungful of pure fresh air and caught the tang of autumn leaves. Photos couldn't do this justice but he took a few on his cell anyway, then raced after Becker, who tugged on the long leash. Zach's Converse were great for speed but were already covered in mud from this short hike. His socks were starting to feel damp, but to hell with it, he was on a mission. He trudged through the plants that covered the boggy path until he spotted signs of the ruined village. Crumbled walls, most of them barely above hip height, overgrown with bracken and bramble bushes. One of them had a tree poking out where the hearth had once been. Zach stood still for a few seconds, frowning. This was it? All that was left of what was once a thriving community, pushed off the land they'd worked for centuries by a rich landlord who wanted to make money from sheep. Homes wrecked and burned. Lives ruined for the sake of money. These humble homes had crumbled and fallen over the years and were now little more than stony walls forming vague floorplans on the overgrown hillside.

Jumping down from a low verge, Zach tramped through the bracken, tracing his way around the village. Briony was right. This place wouldn't interest Daniel Beyer. He was more likely to side with the landlord who'd thrown these people's lives into turmoil, but Zach was drawn to it.

'Wait up.' He clicked Becker onto a short leash and stopped to read a small plaque nailed to a wooden post. The brief history of the village it presented didn't begin to capture the heavy sense of sadness. A thick shroud of forgotten memories and wrecked dreams covered the place, keeping it in darkness, festering from the bitterness of the lives that had been ruined. 'Life sucks sometimes, doesn't it?'

Becker glanced up with his liquid brown eyes, his tongue lolling from the side of his mouth as he panted.

Zach sat on one of the walls, soaking the butt of his jeans. 'Oh crap.' But he didn't move. The damage was done. Becker nuzzled into his arm. 'You really have no concept of personal space or boundaries, do you?' Zach stroked the dog's wiry hair and smiled. 'But I guess it's ok for dogs. You guys have no pretences, right? You like someone, you just bowl them over or sniff their butt. The only time in my life I've done anything that spontaneous was with your mistress.' Part of that had been Dutch courage.

'I really liked her. I wouldn't have done it otherwise. It was like that song, I can't remember what it's called, but it's in an old film that my grandma liked. It's something about seeing someone across a crowded room and just knowing. I knew from the look in her eyes she wanted me and when those guys bet me I couldn't do it, I knew I had it in the bag. I just wish I hadn't needed the bet to make me do it.' He brushed a papery brown leaf off his jeans. 'What does it matter? It's not like we had a future together anyway. That's why I don't believe in fate and all that crap. If fate was real, it would make this kind of thing happen with someone I had a fighting chance with.'

He gave Becker a pat. 'Listen to me, sitting here, chatting with counsellor dog. Thanks for listening, buddy. And not judging.'

Moments passed and Zach didn't budge. Too often he was trapped behind a desk, doing whatever he was told. His escape was to go home and play computer games, watch sci-fi or read fantasy. Latterly he'd tried working out in the company gym but connecting with nature was something he'd never considered. He could get used it. Becker lay at his feet, clearly not bothered by the wet ground. What would Mr Beyer say about the village? Zach couldn't see him being even the slightest bit interested. How he'd even heard of the hotel was odd. Why had he chosen such an obscure place to invest in? Zach shook his head. The idea that this was a test intensified.

'Which means there's no way Mr Beyer will buy this place. It's my punishment. The same way the Roman emperors used to send their least favourite generals to freeze on Caledonian campaigns. I've been sent to this outpost for my sins and your mistress won't be happy with me.' Again. 'This would have been much easier if she hadn't been here.' But she was and he couldn't shake images of her weaving through his consciousness. 'Must stick to the task. I've got one job to do. Just one.' He got to his feet. Time to go back and face the Daniel Beyer music.

Becker leapt to his feet at once, looking up with wide hopeful eyes. Zach swiped at the back of his jeans in a completely futile attempt at drying them before pulling a hopeless face at Becker and starting the descent. A huge rainbow arced across the sky, ending bang on the hotel. 'Well, would you look at that.' Zach pulled out his cell and snapped a photo.

A crashing in the bushes made him look up and two black dogs bounded towards him, followed by a panting man with a long beard. The dogs sniffed around Becker in a mass of tails.

'Hey,' Zach said, recognising the old Gandalf man.

'Morning,' he said gruffly. His brow furrowed as he looked at Zach like he was trying to work out if he knew him. Zach glanced back at the rainbow and the man turned. 'There's poetry ever I saw it.'

'What do you mean?' asked Zach.

'Well, that's the place to look for the pot of gold around here.'

'Pardon?'

'Come on,' the man barked at the dogs and trudged on up the hill.

Zach let out a sigh. This guy was something else.

At the front door of the hotel, Zach reeled in the leash and held Becker by his side. 'Best not let you in, huh? Those carpets are mucky enough without your prints all over them.' He dragged open the door. 'Hey,' he called in. 'I've got Becker here. He's wet.'

Briony bustled around from behind the reception desk and stopped on the top step, glancing at Zach's feet. 'Not the only one by the look of things.'

'You're not wrong. Wait until you see my butt.'

'Sorry?'

He screwed up his face. 'Yeah, bad phrasing. I sat on a wall and got wet.'

'Well, I'll take Becker into the private quarters and towel him off.' She caught Zach's gaze and raised her eyebrow. 'I'll leave you to do yourself.'

Zach pulled a fake grin. 'Yeah. I'll lock my door and hope you don't have blasters.'

She chuckled and stepped outside. Was she laughing because she found that funny? Did she get the reference? Or did she think he was a sad nerd? Which he'd just proved he was. She took Becker's leash and Zach held his breath as her hand grazed his. A force rose inside him, urging him to seize her and touch her again. Pull her close like he'd done in The Gladstone and restart their kiss five years later. But she'd already gone. With a sigh, he returned to his room, took off his wet jeans and boxer briefs, and hung them over an old-fashioned wooden rail. The room was freezing and his butt was like ice. He leapt under the covers and pulled out his laptop. He wouldn't put his camera on. Mr Beyer would have a fit if he discovered Zach was conducting a conversation from his bed – half naked.

After a few back-and-forth messages, checking Mr Beyer was available, he connected.

'So, what's the big deal?' Mr Beyer said in his low gravely tone. His throaty voice was the only hint of his age – maybe it came with drinking too much whisky. In the flesh, he had impressively few wrinkles, and his hair was as dark as Zach's, even though he must be in his sixties at least. 'You got something for me already?'

'That's kinda the point. There's nothing here to interest you. Not really.'

'You've checked every nook and cranny? Searched high and low? Investigated every square inch of the hotel already?'

Zach rolled his eyes. Thank god the camera was off. 'No. Of course I—'

'Have you even looked?'

'Looked for what? I can see from the outside, from the rooms, the decor, all of it. It's not your kind of place.'

'Zach, if I wanted a verdict based on what the hotel looks like, I'd have asked for photographs. Now, get off your lazy butt and go searching. Find out every damn thing you can about the hotel. Everything. And you better have something good come Friday. No excuses. If you have to lift floorboards or climb into attics, then do it. I mean it, leave no stone unturned. Not a single one.'

Zach glared at the screen. This had to be a joke, right? How the hell could he pull up floorboards and climb into attics? And what exactly was he supposed to find? Mr Beyer ended the call with barely a goodbye and Zach flung back the covers, crossed the room and raked around his bag for dry clothes. What was he meant to say to Briony? 'I've got to rip up the floorboards and search for... history?' he muttered to himself in a mocking voice.

The door clicked open and he jumped out of his skin, turning round as someone shrieked.

'Jesus Christ,' he yelled, shoving a handful of clothes over his bare bottom half. The woman in a tunic he'd seen earlier leapt back out of the room.

'Sorry,' she squealed from the other side.

Heat rising in his cheeks, Zach quickly pulled on his briefs and clean jeans. This hotel was worse than he'd thought. Since when did staff barge in without knocking? He'd never had that before, not that he'd travelled extensively. What immaculate timing to walk in when he was butt naked. Checking the coast was clear before he left his room, he nipped downstairs. The fire in his face rose to burning point when he caught sight of the woman in the tunic leaning over the reception desk whispering to Briony.

Briony glanced up and coughed. 'Thank you, Shari. I'll attend to that directly.'

'But...'

Briony stared pointedly at Shari before shifting her head fractionally towards Zach. Shari spun around, turned a shade of scarlet and scooted past him back up the stairs.

'I, um...' Zach rubbed his neck. What an embarrassment. This was like being back at school and having girls snickering at him for being the nerd who liked comics and carried a *Star Wars* backpack.

'Shari told me she walked in on you.'

'Seriously? Is that something she needs to spread about?'

'She wants me to apologise on her behalf. Obviously it was an embarrassing moment.'

'Yeah. That's one way of putting it.'

'She thought you were out and she was nipping in to fill your coffee tray.'

'I don't even like coffee.'

'Oh. You had it this morning.'

'Yeah, well. I decided to give it a try and it confirmed that I don't like it.'

Briony's smile widened, if that was even possible. 'Please accept our apologies.'

'Yeah, whatever.' This trip couldn't get much worse. Well, it could. If Briony had been the one to get an eyeful. That idea teetered between thrilling and terrifying him. But wait – everything *was* going to get worse any second. 'I spoke to Mr Beyer.'

'And how did that go?' she asked, still smiling.

He gave a half shrug. 'He wants me to turn this place over.'

'How do you mean?'

'That's the point. I don't know. He told me to rip up floorboards and search the attics if I had to. But he didn't tell me what I'm searching for.'

Briony's smile slipped and she folded her arms. Her stern expression didn't sit well on that always cheery face. 'No way. If Mr Beyer wants to rip up floorboards, then he can make me a good offer and I might accept. When the hotel is his, he can do what he wants with it, but not before.'

Zach held up his hands. 'Believe me, ma'am, I won't do any damage. I just... I just don't get it. Is there something I'm missing? Anything? Is there some local legend attached to the place?' Now he was clutching at straws. 'Apart from monsters in the loch.'

'You know about that, do you?'

'I met an old dude on my way here, then again today when I was up the hill. I was lost and he told me the way, then he said

I should look out for monsters in the loch, pots of gold, and...'
Zach covered his mouth.

'And what?'

'Something about the legend of stolen... kisses.' The last word
jammed on the way out. Kisses and Briony fit together perfectly
in his imagination, just not out loud.

'What's that?'

'No idea. I guess he was messing with me. When I asked him
what it was he told me to... ask you for a stolen kiss.' Zach
loosened his neckline. Not the first time he'd asked her for one
of them.

She sucked in her lips and nodded. 'Seems to be something of
a habit of yours, having people put you up to kissing me.'

'Yeah.' He ran his hand down his face.

'Did this man have a long beard and two black Labradors?'

'Yeah, that's him.'

'That's Bruce McArthur. Thinks he knows everything about
everyone, but I reckon he makes most of it up. I meet him up the
hill when I'm walking Becker quite a lot and he's always going on
like he knows stuff about my granny, bla bla bla, bad woman, let
the hotel go to the dogs et cetera.' She stopped and pulled a face.
'Sorry, that sounded unprofessional. I'm sure he's a lovely man.'

Zach leaned his elbows on the reception desk and met Briony's
eyes. 'It's ok. I get it. And I don't think he's a lovely man. More
like an old troublemaker and rumour-monger.'

She tapped the desk, pulling a side pout like she was working something out.

'So... Your grandmother lived here?'

Briony looked away. 'She owned the hotel until she died in January. I took it on a couple of months later.'

'Sorry about that. Well, sorry for your loss. I lost my grandma when I was thirteen and, well, it was never the same afterwards. I know how hard it is.'

Briony tucked a strand of hair behind her ear. 'We weren't close.'

Zach flicked a brief nod.

'Were you?' She raised her eyebrows expectantly.

'Very,' Zach said. 'She raised me. My mom...' He shook his head. 'She's not very maternal, not in that way.' But then he'd neglected her for years when she was sick. How could he blame her? He'd shut her out when she needed him because he didn't know what to do.

'Oh dear.' Briony's hand hovered close like she was considering laying it over his.

'It's fine.' Zach shoved his hands in his pockets. 'And sorry to ask, but your grandmother didn't have any big secrets or anything valuable hidden away, did she?'

Briony laughed and shook her head. 'Are you kidding? Sure, she had secrets. She was the queen of secrets. She played her cards close to her chest and no one got close to her, but nothing that could be noteworthy to Mr Beyer. If we'd found hidden treasure,

I wouldn't be selling, would I? And if it's so well-hidden that none of my family know, then how would Mr Beyer?'

'Good point. I'm scraping the bottom of the barrel because I don't get it.'

Briony's smile was back and it sent an arrow straight to his heart, delivering a message he didn't know how to read. Her long, well-defined lashes fluttered and her blue irises twinkled bright. The arrow pierced a little deeper, sending painfully sweet currents zinging through his veins. He cleared his throat. 'So, did you leave Edinburgh to take on this place?'

'Yes. We used to visit when we were kids. My little sister and me. We got up to all sorts and I dreamed that one day... Well, I was just a silly kid.' She sucked her lip and looked back at her screen.

Zach narrowed his eyes and something made him think back to the kid's book he'd read that morning. *Missy Peck and The Pink Hotel*. 'Like stealing a boat and trying to row to the island in the loch?'

Briony's gaze darted back to him. 'How do you know about that?'

'I don't. Not officially. You wrote that Missy Peck book, didn't you?'

'Zach.' She goggled at him. 'Oh my god. No one has ever worked that out before. I never tell anyone. How... Just how?'

'Ha! I called it. The kid looks like you. Did you draw the pictures too?'

She nodded, her cheeks pinker than usual.

'Why don't you tell anyone?'

'I just don't.'

'Because you think no one will take you seriously? Or because you think it doesn't matter?'

'Maybe a bit of both.'

'Well, you should. It does matter. Don't waste your talent. Around here must be a great place to get inspiration.'

'If only I had the time to write.'

'Yeah. I hear you. I always fancied writing my own sci-fi book but I've never had the nerve to start and work always gets in the way. I'm awed that you've actually done it. You should be proud.'

'Thanks. But don't go shouting about it, ok?'

'If you insist, ma'am, though I'd like to.'

'Don't.'

'I won't say a word. Shame Missy Peck can't help me solve the mystery of what I'm supposed to discover in the bowels of the hotel.'

Briony got to her feet. 'Ok, I have an idea.'

'Does it involve locking me in a cellar?'

'Not quite. But I can offer you a cupboard.' She opened a door behind the reception area.

'What's in there?' He peered in at the rows of shelves, every inch covered with boxes, files, stacks of paper and assorted bric-a-brac.

'Heaps of stuff I haven't had time to sort through. I've done everything on this level. It's the stuff I use every day, but the rest of it...' She held out her hands. 'You're welcome to it. See if you can find anything important in there.'

Zach pushed his hair off his forehead and let out a sigh. 'Oh boy.'

'There's a condition.'

'Which is?'

'If there's evidence of a secret fortune hiding somewhere in the hotel, you let me in on it.' Briony winked.

'I'll do that. But why do I get the feeling you're using me as slave labour to clean out your cupboard?'

'No idea. I'm sure I wouldn't dream of it.'

Zach slipped around behind the high desk. He'd never been on this side of reception before. Briony stood before him. Her perfume tickled him and the warmth from her body was palpable. His heartrate intensified and an invisible hand shoved him forward, forcing him closer. His powers of resistance were low. She'd set the tractor beam in operation again and was pulling him in. Their kiss was begging to be resumed.

'Have fun.' She stepped aside.

Zach swallowed, screwed up his nose and entered the cupboard.

CHAPTER NINE

Briony

Cold fingers of disquiet crept up Briony's spine as she sat at reception, updating the bookings. Zach was in the cupboard behind her. She wasn't used to having her back to people. *Make sure you can see everything and never have your back to the room* had been drilled into her since her training days. Part of the hospitality psyche was to always know what was going on everywhere and be able to pre-empt problems. In fact that had been her life. Being five years older than her sister, she'd often been left to watch and entertain Teagan while her parents worked in the B&B. Problem was, Teagan was a troublesome kid and Briony had never managed to keep her in check; she had a way of leading Briony into trouble then vanishing before she was caught, leaving her older sister to take the flak. And it was usually worse because she was supposed to be the sensible one. Briony had left home as soon as she could so she would no longer be responsible for her and wasn't overly sorry that Teagan had decided to travel for a career.

In fairness to Zach, he wasn't being noisy or interrupting her, so she had no reason to complain. But what was he doing?

Hovering over him wasn't an option. She still owned the place and could do what she wanted, but she couldn't spare the time to dredge through hundreds of old files, seeking an unknown pot of gold – or whatever he was hoping to find. The likelihood of anything but heaps of unnecessary and outdated information on hotel policies being in there was extremely small.

She clicked away at the keys, on hyper-alert for any noise from behind – a whoop of triumph perhaps, or an 'oh my god, check this out' – but the dull shuffle of feet, the scratch of a folder being lifted from a shelf and the flick of pages were the only sounds. Her heightened senses were also making her nerve ends spike and tingle. Thoughts of slipping into the cupboard and falling into Zach's arms kept leaping on her and tugging her into fantasies. *Concentrate for heaven's sake.*

'Christ on a bike,' Shari said and Briony jumped, her hand leaping to her chest. With her focus AWOL, she hadn't noticed Shari approaching the desk. 'That has to rate as one of my worst ever days.'

Why did she have to talk so loudly?

'Oh?' Briony frowned. 'Were some of the rooms in bad shape?'

'No, because of what I told you before. I copped an eyeful of the American's backside and when he turned around—'

Briony's finger shot to her lips and she shook her head, glaring intently at Shari.

'What? You can't deny he's fit and—'

Something slapped onto the cupboard floor and Shari's gaze wandered over Briony's shoulders. Briony stood and beckoned to Shari as she moved around the desk.

Shari's cheeks flared and she mouthed. 'Is he in there?'

With a silent nod, Briony opened the door to the lounge and pointed for her to go in.

'Oh my god.' Shari clutched her face, her blonde curly hair escaping from its updo like a frizzy mophead.

Briony pushed the door shut.

'I had no idea. Do you think he heard me?' Shari said.

'Probably.' Briony resisted gritting her teeth. 'You were being quite loud. Do you realise how unprofessional that was? And what a position that puts me in?'

'Oh my god,' Shari said again like a one-track record. 'What's he doing in the cupboard anyway?'

'Looking through the records.'

'Why?' Shari's eyes widened. 'Is he an inspector or a mystery shopper or something? Shit. We're fucked if he is. I barged in on him starkers.'

'No. He isn't either of them but he's the representative of the potential investor I told you about.'

'Christ.' Shari's forehead creased. 'I forgot. But does he actually want to buy the place?'

'I don't know yet. But we have to be careful.'

'Will I get sacked if someone else takes over?' Shari pulled a face.

'Hopefully not.' Briony fiddled with the edge of her top.

'I need this job,' Shari said. 'It fits in so well with Kaiden's school hours.'

Perhaps she should have considered that before opening her mouth and firing off like a loose cannon. How could Briony recommend her if Zach had heard that? He'd said he wasn't involved with the business side, but there was no saying what he might put in his report.

'I know,' Briony said, aiming for a soothing tone. 'But if I don't consider all the options, the hotel will have to close and then none of us will have jobs.'

'Oh god.' Shari rubbed her head like she had a migraine coming on. Briony's heart withered. She knew only too well the struggles Shari had been through, a single mum at twenty-seven with a sick dad to care for and hardly a penny to her name. If Mr Beyer took over the hotel, no guarantees would be in place to safeguard Shari's job. Briony had nothing to bargain with and no power to stop him doing whatever he wanted.

She patted Shari's arm. 'Listen. I'll do what I can. He wants me to stay on as manager, so hopefully I can get him to promise that he'll keep on the current employees.' But she was fully aware even if he agreed, he could fire them all a few weeks later and that would be that. Far from ideal.

'Do you really think he'll do that for me now that I've been telling people about his guy's nice arse all morning?' Shari half laughed through her grim expression.

'We'll see.' Briony patted her arm, but a heavy weight pressed on her chest. Selling the hotel might improve her personal situation but other people were involved, which complicated things. She'd had to let other staff go when she first took over and that hadn't been easy, but now she'd got to know Shari and Meg, it was like letting down friends. Not a good business mindset, but she couldn't help it.

'What's he looking at the records for anyway?' Shari asked, dusting off her tunic.

'Mr Beyer thinks the hotel has some mysterious past and wants it investigated.'

'Mysterious past? This place?'

Briony threw out her hands. 'I know. Ludicrous, isn't it?'

'If he doesn't find anything, will he go away?'

'I suppose so.' Briony twiddled her pendant between her fingertips. Did she want him to find something? What exactly? She sucked on her lip. If she just had the means to put some investment into the place, she wouldn't have to do any of this.

'Can you apologise to him for me? Again,' Shari said. 'And ask him if he's single and fancies a few hot dates before he leaves.' The corner of her lip quirked up.

'Shari.' Briony gaped at her.

'Why waste a good opportunity? I can arrange a babysitter for Kaiden and show Mr Hotstuff a good time. You never know, he might marry me, then I won't have to worry about keeping a job.'

'Dream on. And ask him yourself.'

'I wouldn't dare.'

'Good. Because if you want to keep your job for the foreseeable future, make sure you don't go shouting about his backside.'

'It was a very nice backside.'

Briony cocked her head. 'Irrelevant.'

They left the room together. Zach stood propped against the doorframe between the cupboard and reception, glasses on, flicking through a folder. He raised his eyes, then recoiled inside the cupboard when he spotted them.

Shari tapped Briony's arm, then fanned her face, mouthing, 'Swoon.'

Briony shooed her away and moved in behind the desk. As soon as Shari was safely up the stairs, she peeked into the cupboard. 'Any luck?'

Zach edged his glasses down his nose and peered over the top of them. His luscious lashes blinked slowly and Briony's heart missed a beat.

'Were the two of you having a nice chat?' he said.

'Sorry about what she said.'

'It's completely inappropriate. Do you think I'm stupid?'

Briony held back a smirk. The askew glasses and Yoda t-shirt weren't exactly helping in his quest to look sensible. 'She was embarrassed. She thinks you're...'

'What? A nerd? A geek? I've heard it all before.'

'Er... No. What she actually said was you're fit and have a nice backside.' There really wasn't any way to say that with a serious face.

'Jesus Christ,' muttered Zach. 'Fit? Does that mean she thinks I'm—'

'Hot. Yes.'

'Oh, god, no.' He covered his face, leaning back on the shelves with a groan. 'And she has the nerve to say *she* was embarrassed?' He scoffed.

'Take it as a compliment and forget it.' Briony folded her arms. 'A few years ago you weren't too bothered about staff thinking you were hot, especially if they were willing to stroke your...'

He almost choked and whacked his fist into his ribs.

'Ego,' Briony finished with a quirk of her eyebrow. 'Tell me...' She toyed with her pendant.

'Tell you what?' Zach eyed her.

'If Mr Beyer takes over here, will he sack her? And Meg?'

'I dunno. But probably, yes. He usually likes to employ his own people.'

'He said in his email that I could stay on.'

'Yeah? Well, don't be surprised if he changes his mind.' Zach tossed a file onto the floor and rested his fists on his hips, opening his broad, shapely chest, only just hidden by Yoda's peering head. 'I honestly don't know what he'll do.'

'Right.'

Briony's eyes met his. His deep brown puppy-dog irises gleamed. Shari wasn't wrong. He was hot stuff and always had been. A nerdy element was there with the sci-fi obsession but that was endearing too. An invisible wire crackled between them. If she looked away it would snap but if she kept on staring it would ignite. Already, sparks had started to fizz in her tummy. Her heartbeat flickered and her fingers tingled. Why didn't he look away either? They were closer than she meant to be. The cupboard was small for two people. Small enough for the air to have filled with his scent. Gone was the musty aroma of old paper, and a fresh, tangy, woody fragrance had taken its place. It tickled her nostrils, filtering deep, adding more tingles of need. Her ears throbbed as her pulse revved. A dangerous kiss was on the verge of restarting.

'So...' Zach coughed, pushed his glasses back into place and swung around so his back was to her. The connection snapped abruptly, leaving her dazed. She blinked and rolled her neck.

'So what?'

'One of those documents mentions the contents of a wine cellar. Where's that?' he glanced over his shoulder.

Briony screwed up her face. 'It's accessible from outside the kitchen. But I don't advise going down there.'

He turned to face her, leaning on the shelf behind him, keeping as much distance from her as he could – or it seemed that way. And, really, she couldn't blame him. If he'd experienced the same pheromone rush as she just had, they needed to keep their distance. This was risky territory and she'd crossed the line before for a cheap thrill. This time it could sink the deal faster than torpedo. His eyes were on her again. She held her breath.

'Why? Am I going to get locked up?' He frowned. 'Is it set to trap annoying Americans?'

'No, it's unsafe. Parts of it are ready to cave in and also there's nothing there. It's an old dark passageway. I had a quick look in it when I first arrived and I'd rather not go back. It's dark and fusty and... Yuck.'

Zach smirked. His gaze shifted briefly like he was sizing her up. 'Afraid of the dark, huh? I wouldn't have thought that about you.'

'I'm not afraid of the dark.' Well, not entirely. The dark hid several things she didn't like. 'I just don't like the cellar and I don't think anyone should be down there until it's been made safe.'

'Ok, ma'am. If you say so.' He raised one of his thick eyebrows. 'But can I take a peek anyway? I don't mind going on my own.'

'What if the ceiling caves in?'

'I'll risk it.' His lip quirked at one side and Briony sighed deeply. No getting out of it.

She opened the key cupboard and took out a heavily rusted key. Her tummy squirmed like a jellyfish had been let loose in it. Call it sixth sense or whatever but she had a bad feeling about this. Or maybe it was his presence behind her. 'I think I'd like you to sign a disclaimer first.' She spun around, dangling the key before him. He drew back into the shelf a little and his jaw stiffened. 'Saying this was all your own idea.'

He watched the key for a moment like she was hypnotising him, then smirked. 'After you.'

'I'll show you the way but I'm not going in.' She led the way along the back corridor beside the kitchen into a small courtyard area that housed the industrial-sized wheelie bins and a log store. Squelchy autumn leaves covered the parking area that provided enough space for staff vehicles and food delivery trucks. Both Briony's and Shari's cars had a slick coating of wet leaves and the trees behind the hotel rocked and swayed.

At the far end of the back wall was the door to the cellar, all peeling paint and rusty hinges. Would the key even still work in that cobweb-covered lock? Briony shuddered. She hated cobwebs, spiders and anything creepy and crawly. Becker might be a lazy so-and-so, but he was a dab hand at catching things that moved or freaked her out. He'd got rid of several spiders and an occasional mouse when she'd screamed. Having the canine superpower of empathy, he'd jump to the rescue.

Who knew what might be in the cellar? Rats? Bats? A shiver ran down her spine. Halloween was approaching but she didn't want to find herself in a real-life horror story.

'Cold out here, isn't it?' said Zach.

'What? Oh...'

He rubbed his hands up and down his tanned arms. No bodybuilder muscles but they were in good shape – like the rest of him. The wind whipped by, ruffling his thick curls and blowing them high.

'It'll be worse down there.' She pointed below the door. Once it opened, all they'd see was steps leading to darkness. There was a light switch somewhere but she didn't fancy fumbling around to find it. The idea of putting her hand into anything she couldn't see gave her the heebie-jeebies and she imagined her arm being sucked into a sticky cobweb mess or being chewed by dozens of spiders. She shook involuntarily, warding off the visions.

Her fingers trembled as she pushed the key into the hole. Could she pass it off as the effort of trying to get it to work?

'Should I try?' Zach said.

Who cared if she was being pathetic and letting a man take over, she leapt aside faster than he could say feminist.

He closed his tanned fingers over the key and gave it a wiggle. It creaked in protest. Taking hold of the door handle, he gripped it while twisting the key again. He let out a grunt. The lock clicked and with a look of triumph, he yanked open the door.

Briony cringed, half expecting a flock of bats to assault her, but when she squinted back only a few wispy cobwebs at the top of the door frame barred the way. Zach peered inside, his nose scrunched up.

'Is there a light?'

'On the wall somewhere.' Briony edged closer. She'd only been in once with her dad soon after Granny Hilda had died and they'd found nothing but a few old wine bottles and empty crates. Cellar safety upgrades were on her list but there were other more pressing tasks to do first.

Zach ducked through the door; his neck craned as he peered downward.

'Watch, that goes straight down,' Briony said.

'Yeah, I can see that, but once I get in further, I won't be able to see anything.'

'I'm sure the light's...' She took a deep breath and flung herself through the doorway. Zach stepped down, making room and giving her a funny look. The walls were damp and an earthy smell lingered in the air. Nothing more sinister. The wind whistled past the entrance making an eerie sound.

'Do you have a flashlight?' he asked.

'Do you mean a torch?'

'No, I mean a flashlight, but if you want to start wielding a flaming branch then go right ahead, it's your hotel after all.'

Briony folded her arms. 'You Americans are—'

A howling gust of wind screeched by, followed by a loud slamming thud, plunging them into darkness. Briony screamed. She couldn't help herself. Her insides quaked and she couldn't breathe. Air. There was no air in here. They'd suffocate and die.

'Hey, calm down,' Zach said.

'Oh my god.' Briony's lungs were full of concrete. 'Find the light or open the door, or something. For god's sake. Help. How are we going to get out?' Her pulse thundered in her ears and she was shaking. She hugged herself. *Must not fall apart.*

'Hey.'

Zach gripped her elbow, sending a steadying vibe up her arm.

'The door's right behind you,' he said. 'Shove it open.'

'I... I can't...'

'Why not?'

'I hate putting my hand anywhere I can't see. In case I touch... I don't know what. I just hate it.'

'Ok.' His voice sounded level, not scornful or sarky. 'I'll come up beside you and open it.'

'Right.'

'Don't panic. I'm stepping up now.'

She let out a little whimper of a laugh through her ragged breathing and clenched jaw. He sounded like he was talking her off a ledge or out of a hostage situation. She appreciated it. The very fact she wasn't in here alone was something. Though it was his fault she was in here at all.

Zach's deep woody scent hit her square on, knocking her mind onto a more pleasing path. He brushed close to her and started shuffling around the door. The prospect of taking up their long-past kiss again seemed even more possible in the dark – perhaps it would black out their memory of it after, and the repercussions.

'Hang on,' Zach said, and the door rattled.

'Do you mean you want me to wait? Or actually hang on to you?'

'If you feel the need to hang on to me, ma'am, you go right ahead.'

At least he couldn't see if she was blushing.

'Why do Americans call women ma'am?' she said, steering the conversation away from dangerous waters. 'It makes me sound like the queen.'

'You can play queen to my dark lord.'

'Er... What?'

'You know? The dark lord on his dark throne.'

'I don't know what you're talking about.'

'No worries. You don't have to. I'm just trying to keep you calm because this door' – she felt the movement as he put his shoulder to it – 'isn't moving.'

'Oh god. Are we stuck here?'

A warm hand landed on her shoulder and gave her a brief pat. 'Hey. Let's hope not. You can write an adventure for little Missy

Peck about the day she got trapped in the cellar with the sci-fi guy from Louisville.'

That story might end up X-rated. Highly unsuitable for a children's book. 'Assuming we get out.'

'We will. I just have to figure out how. There's no door handle on this side. It's maybe fallen off.'

'Oh god. This is awful. What if customers are at the desk? There's no one there to staff it.'

'Well, they'll have to wait. Do have your cell on you?'

'My what?'

'Your cell phone.'

'Oh, no. It's at the desk.'

'I've got mine, but I don't know anyone here to call.'

'Nine, nine, nine,' she said. 'Get the fire brigade to break us out.'

'Let's not be that drastic yet.' He shuffled about, then a light flickered on, casting a glow on the underside of his face. 'It has a flashlight.'

'Torch,' she muttered.

She caught his eye roll in the dim light. He held the beam over the steps, illuminating the dank passage walls. Maybe it was better in the dark. She wasn't sure she wanted to see anything lurking down there. The urge to grab him and cling on burned strong. Cold air nipped at the fragments of her exposed skin and she shivered.

'Look.' He jumped down a couple of steps and stooped over something.

'Oh no, what is it?' Briony clutched her neck. 'A dead rat?'

'I think it's the door handle. I'm not entirely sure how it got there. Maybe someone slammed it and knocked it off. If I can get it back on, I might be able to open the door.' He climbed back up. 'Can you hold this?' He passed her his glowing phone and she held it towards the scabby old door. 'Now, we have to hope no walkers are in the passageway, creeping their way towards us.'

She play-slapped the top of his arm. 'That isn't even funny.'

He smirked and fiddled with the door handle. 'It would be a unique selling feature to pass on to Mr Beyer.'

'If you can't get that on in the next five minutes, I'm calling the fire brigade.'

'Yes, ma'am. Nothing like a deadline.' He rammed at the handle, rattled it some more, then the door sprang open and cool light flooded the entrance. 'There you go.'

Briony didn't wait to be asked, she leapt outside into the fresh, breezy air, threw her head skyward and took a long inhale of the crisp autumn scent. They were out and she was never going back down there again.

CHAPTER TEN

Zach

A steady drip of water beat onto the darkened steps from an unknown source. Zach's hands were cold as he checked the handle on the inside of the door to the cellar. After being stuck in there for a few minutes, his eyes took a moment to adjust to the daylight.

He turned to Briony. She was looking skyward, breathing deeply, his lit cell still in her hand, hanging limp at her side. The wind ruffled her hair, agitating her perfect style. For someone who always seemed so calm, he hadn't expected her to go to pieces like that, but who was he to judge? He had phobias too, like being discovered to be nothing but a phoney. He'd blundered on in this job for five years. One day he'd be uncovered and hung out to dry. It had almost happened last year with his big-time blunder. Only a previously unheard-of charitable streak in Mr Beyer had saved him. Now he was clinging onto it by the flimsiest of threads.

Sometimes he felt his colleagues saw right through him, almost like they were watching him, waiting for his next fail.

'Hey.' He approached Briony, fighting an urge to put his arm around her. He wavered, stopping mid-action. In the dark it had been a lot easier to make physical contact but now... He shouldn't. She frowned at him. Ok, now or never. He either went for it or dropped the idea. Both might make him look like a fool. His hand made up its mind for him and coiled its way around her shoulder. He gently squeezed it. 'You ok?'

'Yes, thank you. I can't believe you got us out.' She beamed at him. 'What a relief.' For a moment they just looked at each other, then Briony seemed to come to. She blinked, gave Zach a quick pat and moved out from under his arm towards the door.

Zach flexed his fingertips as she peered into the stairwell. She couldn't have made it much plainer she didn't want him that close.

'If I'm going back in there, we need to put something in front of that door to make sure it can't blow shut,' he said.

'How about the wheelie bin?'

'I'm not even gonna ask what that is.'

She pulled a side pout, spun around and marched towards the side of the hotel that jutted out in an L shape. Her hips swayed and her heels clicked across the courtyard. Zach tugged at the neck of his Yoda t-shirt.

He'd given up thinking or caring about romance – or dating to be precise. His hook-ups were usually short and awkward. He had a way of making a fool of himself. Destined lovers and happy ever afters were to read about or watch. But a voice was talking in his ear. A bit too loudly. *You've been given a second chance with someone you really like – don't waste it.* If he could stick his fingers in his ears and la-la-la, he would. He could not afford to find Briony attractive. Not this time. No matter how good it had been last time. *Just get through the next few days.* Just. Four. Days. Nothing could happen in four days. Nothing at all. Though the first time it had only taken hours, and four days was longer than most of his previous relationships. Christ, he was a basket case.

'This,' she said, uncoupling his thought train with one of her killer smiles. Her hand gripped the heavy-duty handle of a large curb-side trash can. 'Is a wheelie bin.'

'Right.' He ruffled his hair. 'If you say so.'

'I do. Now let's pull it over.'

'Sure.' He grabbed the other handle and they shoved it up against the door. Zach stepped back and dusted his palms together.

'Now, come back in before you go poking about, and I'll get you a torch.'

'Go right ahead, set a fire burning and light me up.' He swallowed. That came out all wrong but annoyingly accurate.

'Seriously, Zach.' She poked his arm. 'I don't think we want to go down that road again, do we? And you'll never get me calling it a flashlight.'

'I'll make it my destiny to try.'

She stopped inside the corridor that passed the kitchen. 'Listen. I should thank you. I was an idiot when that door shut. I shouldn't have lost it like that.'

'It's ok.' He gave a little shrug. 'But if I don't come back from inside there in the next thirty minutes, send someone to look for me, yeah? I don't deserve that long slow death. I brought Becker back safe like I promised.'

'You did, and I will.' She opened a sliding door onto a cupboard and pulled out a huge flashlight with carry strap and rubber handle.

'That's a big one,' he said.

She considered him, a smile playing at the corner of her sparkly lips. 'It's performance, not size, that matters, and this bad boy has all the features. It has an emergency alarm and a flashing light to attract help.'

'A flashing light, huh? A flashlight then.'

'Oh, aren't you funny?' She passed it to him and he was careful not to touch her hand as he took it. No more fuel necessary.

'Remind me why we didn't take this before?'

'Because I thought there was a light switch. But who knows?' She glanced around and sucked on her lip. 'It's on my ever-growing list of repairs to have the cellar fixed up. I've got Pinterest boards full of ideas. I thought I could have whisky or gin tasting down there. It could have its own bar area. I'm sure people from the town and the surrounding area would come. Do you think Mr Beyer will like that idea?'

Zach gave a little shrug. 'I really don't know. He's not an easy man to get to know. His mindset is very fixed and he demands absolute loyalty. If he likes you, he's more likely to be open to your ideas.'

'Does he like you?'

Zach snorted a laugh. 'Not particularly. I mean, he's guided me occasionally when he's in a good mood, but more often than not, he's annoyed with me.' The most likely reason Zach hadn't been sacked already was because Mr Beyer had chosen him personally. Sacking him would make it look like Mr Beyer made a questionable choice in the first place and he couldn't have that. 'But he might go for your cellar idea. He loves whisky and has a whole building kitted out as a shrine to his collection. A supersized version of what you just described.'

Briony lifted an eyebrow. 'Well, I can hardly compete with that.'

'Don't worry. If he throws his bucks at this place, you won't even recognise it.'

'I'm not sure that's a comforting thought.'

'Yeah.' Zach rubbed his chin. 'It seems a shame.' He'd never in his wildest imaginings considered working at a place like this, but faced with this pink fixer-upper, he felt a weird hook tugging him, leading him onto a path filled with visions of things he could do. It was like opening a blank notebook and starting a brand-new story. 'I like your vision better. There's potential here.'

'That's what I thought. But it can only be realised with money.'

Zach reached out, then faltered, quickly raising his hand to his hair and raking it up.

'Well, I should get back to the desk,' Briony said. 'Please don't have an accident down there.'

'I'll be fine, but come back in thirty minutes, ok? I don't want to be stuck there with a pack of walkers for longer than that.'

'Ok, Zach.'

His gaze lingered on her for a moment longer. Her eyes were as blue as a summer sky and her cheeks fresh and rosy. The ever-present smile sent flaming arrows into his gut, lighting more fires and eating him inside. Nothing could quench the throbbing ache building inside. Nothing legit anyway. Even if he resumed the kiss, he wasn't convinced it would do the trick, not completely.

With a brief wave, he returned outside. The cool air soothed his cheeks and neck. *Focus on the job.* He had to check out this cellar. Fixating on a woman he had less than a hundred hours left with was stupid. If they were destined to meet, it was only for a short, tormenting amount of time. Normally that would have been more than enough, possibly too much. But Briony wasn't just a casual hook-up. Sure, he'd once thought that. Kind of. Even back then, deeper feelings had lingered below the surface, but he hadn't given them airtime. Maybe he should do the same now.

In the full beam of the flashlight, he made his way down the stairs. The eerie stillness reminded him of the computer games he'd played as a teenager when he'd had to solve quests around Hogwarts or find a way to Mordor to destroy The One Ring. Stairs like this always started out benign, but the second you turned a corner, you were attacked by monsters or flying objects. Maybe this led to a secret passageway and the lair of the monster of Loch Briar. He grinned as he reached the bottom step and his feet hit an earthy-floored passageway with doors on either side.

'Jeezo.' He let out a low whistle. 'This is a cryptic test, isn't it?' His gaze travelled between the two doors. Which one to choose? Did one lead to freedom and the other certain death?

First, he pushed the one he surmised led under the hotel. It opened without resistance but was creaky and cobwebby. Briony would have freaked. He shone the flashlight around. The beam flitted over ancient shelves, some of them with wine bottles still on them. Dusty crates were stacked in a corner. Zach wedged the flashlight against the door – just in case – and made his way towards the crates. He shifted the top one easily. Empty. Looked like they'd been abandoned long ago. Using the mini light on his cell, he scanned over the shelves of wine bottles. He wasn't an expert, but Mr Beyer would want to know if a stash of expensive wine was hidden away. He snapped some pictures to investigate later.

Collecting the flashlight on the way, he closed the door and moved to the other side. He tried the handle, pushing it and giving it a shake. It didn't want to open. He put his shoulder to it and it burst forward, catapulting him into another dingy passageway. Even with the full beam the darkness was stifling in here. If zombies were going to attack it would definitely be on this side. He glanced upwards. This must be the unsafe section. Would it cave in on him? The first section had a wooden framework supporting it, like a mine – or what he imagined a mine would look like; he'd only ever seen them in films.

Further along the earthy ceiling got lower. Zach stooped until he was bent over. And then it stopped. Either the passageway had never been continued or it had caved in at some point. He inhaled a load of stale air, then shifted himself around and ducked back along. He closed the door at the end and nipped back up the stairs. After allowing his eyes to adjust to the light outside, he squinted around at the lie of the land. Assuming that tunnel had once led somewhere, what was the point of it? Where did it go? Or even if it was started and never finished, what was the plan? He racked his brains. *Think like the builders.* Only he wasn't sure who they were or what their purpose was.

The ground above the tunnel was now part of the track from the staff parking area to the guest parking area. Was that why it had caved in? Maybe excavators and heavy vehicles laying concrete had been too much for it to withstand. But where did it go after that? He wandered beyond the track into a wooded area and waded through thick tangled undergrowth for some minutes. Trees swayed above in the wind and his arms were cold. *Should go back and get a hoody.* Was this still part of the hotel grounds? No obvious fence separated it from the wood that curled around the loch side and spread up the hill towards the ruined village he'd visited earlier. He trudged further into the overgrown straggly bushes and bracken, buffing his bare arms, trying to increase the circulation. His feet squelched and dampness oozed into his soles, spreading upwards. His Converse would be fit for the trash after this, but he didn't have any other shoes with him. Trails of bramble vines clawed at him like grasping fingers trying to prevent him going any further.

'Get off. Ow!' He wrestled himself free and heard a ripping sound on the back of his t-shirt. A long scratch ran the length of his forearm. These things were deadly.

If an entrance to a tunnel was hidden anywhere nearby, it was living up to its name, and hidden it would stay. Surely if it existed, someone would have found it before now. Things like that didn't stay secret. Much as he'd love to be the one to stumble upon an old mystery, this wasn't the movie version of his life.

His foot sunk and he reeled forward, straining to pull it free. 'Aw, gross.' He was now ankle deep in mud. Staggering to get out, he lost his balance, wobbled on the spot for an agonising second, then toppled backwards. 'Ow. Jeez. Ow!' He'd landed in a bramble bush. This wasn't really happening, right? He wasn't sitting in a prickly bush with sodden feet and covered in mud. Screwing up his face, he tossed back his head and groaned. Unfortunately, he was.

CHAPTER ELEVEN

Briony

A stream of guests greeted Briony at the reception desk. No surprise there. If ever she left it for even a second, that was the moment everyone chose to call. She checked them in, dealt with their requirements and sorted out the daily requests for extra towels, blankets and coffee supplies – who actually drank that much coffee in a day? She suspected several guests left like smugglers, their suitcases filled to bursting point with coffee sachets.

Her attention strayed to the clock. Zach had been in the cellar for over forty-five minutes. Where was he? Had the ceiling fallen in and crushed him? She needed to go and check, but guests were still milling about, requiring this and that.

'That's you booked in for this evening,' she told a man, smiling, though her gaze strayed to the clock. Zach had said thirty minutes and at this rate it would be nearly an hour.

She smiled at the final person in the queue, a good-looking, but very rough around the edges, man about her age. He gave her a slightly crooked grin, swiped a lock of long hair from his forehead and swaggered forward.

'Hey,' he said, looking around. 'I've been meaning to call in here for a while. Sorry to rock up when you're so busy. My name's Brann. I'm a builder based in Glenbriar. I did some work for the old girl when she was here, bless her. Just wanted to introduce myself in case you're needing anything done.'

Briony tried to ignore the way his gaze seemed to flick automatically between the cracks in the plaster.

'Er, yes, thank you.' No point in denying that she needed work done, but if the deal went through it would be Mr Beyer paying the bills. Would he want to stay local? Or draft in a team of Kentucky builders to complete the renovations? That wouldn't sit well with Briony or the community. 'I'm Briony Dalgleish,' she said. 'There's definitely work needing done. If you leave your number, I'll get in touch when I, um, need a quote.'

'Great. Thanks. Here.' He fished around in the pockets of his work trousers. She couldn't help noticing how muscly he was. Celtic knot tattoos adorned his arms. If Shari caught sight of him, she'd be drooling. She loved men with tattoos and this guy was very easy on the eye if you liked a bit of rough. He handed her a slightly grubby business card.

'Thank you.'

His focus swept around the foyer again. 'I might pop in for the open-mic night this weekend.'

'Can you sing?' She hadn't meant to sound quite so shocked.

He laughed and gave her a wink. 'Sometimes. Depends how much I've had to drink.'

'I see. Well, I'm looking forward to hearing it.'

He tipped two fingers to his forehead and left. Briony couldn't wait another second; she whipped out the Be Back Soon sign and slapped it on the desk. Much as the hotel needed a builder, she could have done without one turning up at the busiest time of day, especially when Zach might be fighting to escape a herd of mad zombies. She nipped into the staff quarters to get flat shoes. These heels weren't made for those stairs.

'Becker, come here. Walkies.' She jangled his lead. He peered at her in sheer disbelief. Clearly after his hike with Zach that morning, he was in no mood for another impromptu walk.

'Come on. This is important. I need you to help me find Zach in the cellar and I don't want to go down myself in the dark.'

Becker eyed her as she explained. People talked to dogs, right? It was a thing. Dogs were famously good listeners. And sure enough, seeming to understand, Becker dragged himself off the sofa and padded over.

'Good boy. Really good boy.' She clapped his bristly chops. 'You've earned lots of treats and unlimited sofa time.' Which he got anyway but at least he was working for it.

With a wag of his tail, he trotted ahead and out of the door, heading across the courtyard towards the woods.

'This way.' Briony patted her thigh. 'Down here. Come on, let's find Zach.'

Becker stood still and cocked his head with a longing look towards the woods before following the command. Briony hovered by the door propped open by the wheelie bin and peered into the darkness. She didn't have another torch.

'Zach,' she called into the opening. 'Zach, are you in there?'

A steady drip answered her call but no voice or sound of movement. Could he have had an accident? Briony's heart raced and her shoulders tensed. She'd have to go for it. If she checked quickly, she could be in and out in seconds. If he was hurt, she'd call for help.

'Right. Let's go.'

Becker snuffled around the top step, then hurtled down nose to the ground. Why couldn't she be this enthusiastic about a new smell? Especially one this cold and musty. With small careful steps, guided by her phone light, she made her way down. Becker was at the bottom, still sniffing merrily. Briony lowered her head with a heavy sigh. Both the doors were cobwebbed and gross.

'I can't touch them. I just can't.' She'd go back and get some thick gloves. 'ZACH!' she bawled. Becker snapped to attention and sat beside her. She patted his head. 'Sorry. I just can't...' *This is pathetic.* She darted back up the stairs. Sitting on the top step beside the wall was the torch. What was it doing there? Becker bounded past her and out of the door.

'Becker!'

He made off towards the woods.

'No. Come back!'

She did a double take. Dragging his way through the undergrowth was a mud-splattered, torn-t-shirt, bleeding-armed Zach. Was he auditioning for a role in his favourite zombie show? Becker darted around, tail slapping off his sides.

'Zach. What the...?' Briony gaped at him as he pulled his way out of the undergrowth and limped towards her. 'Where have you been? What happened to you?'

'Don't ask,' he growled. 'Just don't ask. What do I look like?' He held out his arms and glared downwards.

'An extra from *The Walking Dead*?'

A tiny grin flickered at the corner of his lips. 'My Converse are ruined and I don't have any other shoes with me.'

She pulled a face, trying not to giggle. It wasn't funny but still, it kind of was. 'Why don't you go into my quarters, throw that stuff into the wash and have a shower? You can put the shoes in too.'

'Yeah, ok.' He rubbed the heel of his hand into his forehead. 'I guess I can't go through the hotel like this. I might terrify people.'

'I'm glad you're ok. Well, kind of ok.' She scanned over his slashed arms, restraining the desire to touch them and soothe him. 'Did you fall? What were you doing in the woods?'

'How long have you got?'

She checked her watch. 'Not that long. The community group running the Amber Gold Music Festival are meeting in the bar tonight to check the final arrangements are in place and I should be there.'

'That's what I thought. I'll tell you later. I need to get this stuff off and clean up.' He glanced at his forearms. Red claw marks ran from his wrists to his elbows, front and back.

'I'll get you something to put on that.' She swatted away an image of her helping him out of his clothes, sponging him down and rubbing on some scented lotion. Nice as it was, it had no right being in her head. 'Was it a cat or something?'

'No. A bramble bush.'

'Oh. They can be lethal.'

'Yeah, more dangerous than being pounced on by a cougar.'

Wow. Was that some coded message, warning her to keep her leering eyes away? Did he think she was out to get her claws into him again? He'd been the one to make the move the last time. Was that before he realised what age she was? *Now I'm a cougar, am I?*

'You go in,' she said, opening the door to the cloakroom and utility area of the private quarters. Becker followed, wagging his tail and panting, looking delighted at his muddy visitor. 'The washing machine's right here. Throw everything in and set it to cycle four. That should do the trick.'

'Ok. Thanks.'

'The spare towels are here.' She slid open the ancient wall cupboard and pulled out a white fluffy towel.

'Great.'

'I'll be back with some antiseptic cream you can put on those cuts. I'll leave it here for you, so I don't disturb you.' No way would he get any chance to think she was preying on him.

He nodded, tugging at the hem of his t-shirt like he was about to whip it off.

'I'll leave you to it.' Briony darted out of the door and slammed it. She hadn't told him where the shower was but so what, he could figure it out for himself. She wasn't going back in. Whatever he had under that t-shirt wasn't for her. He'd made that clear. As mud. After saying she could play queen to his dark king or whatever he'd said, now she was a cougar.

Sod's law enforced itself when she returned to the reception area to find another queue of people. How did they time their moments? These guests were not what she'd ordered from the universe – of course they'd help in the long run but if they could just have chosen a better time.

Hitching on her smile, she greeted them. 'How can I help you?'

Her mind strayed to Zach. Where had he been to get in such a mess? Why had he left the cellar?

She sorted out the guests with an extra room key. *Ooh*, she had to get that cream for Zach, but she didn't want to go back and find him parading around in his manly state of undress, no matter how much the idea tickled her fancy. She should fetch him a robe or something to change into as well. A stash of them hung in the airing cupboard, she could lend him one so he could at least get back to his room.

The front door opened and another couple appeared, both laden with bags and cases. How much luggage did people need for a short stay? Briony's internal bemusement didn't filter through her broad smile.

She checked the list of reservations. Only two couples were due in now. So this was either Ms G. Warden and partner or Mr and Mrs McIver.

'Good afternoon,' she said.

'Hi,' said the man. 'I'm Colin McIver. I have a reservation.'

'Of course. I have it here. I've got you in room nine. If you wouldn't mind filling out this card with your information, please.' She passed him the card. He dumped three bags from his shoulder and scribbled on the card.

'Can you walk to the festival from here?' asked Mrs McIver.

'You can,' Briony said. 'There's a footpath along the side of the hedge by the main road that takes you into Glenbriar. It takes about ten minutes to walk, but there's also a shuttle service running on Friday, Saturday and Sunday.'

'Sounds good.'

Briony handed her a leaflet from the desk. 'We also have some acts out here over the weekend, storytelling by the loch and an open-mic night. The full rundown is on this leaflet.' She passed over a glossy sheet.

With everything surrounding the possible hotel sale, she'd neglected the festival. Or in her mind she had anyway. This was a baby she'd been part of developing along with the community group and Felicity. Briony's job was mainly to provide a venue, promote the acts and ply the punters with drinks. The community group were in charge of getting it up and running with sponsorship from the distillery.

Having community group meetings here was a small step to getting the hotel back in favour with locals. Briony didn't charge them for using the small function room off the lounge, but the members usually bought a drink or two. Would Mr Beyer allow her to keep going with ventures like this? In her head she'd imagined him being an absent overlord who provided the cash for her to push the hotel in a new direction, steer it out of its musty overcoat and give it a fresh new life. But since Zach had arrived, she was starting to think otherwise. It seemed he had his own agenda and wouldn't care two straws for her ideas.

She came around and lifted some of the McIvers' bags. 'This is a lovely case. I've always loved Burberry.' Though she couldn't afford it.

'It's that time of year, we never know what to pack,' Mrs McIver said. 'It can be pleasant but it can also be chucking it down. We've been to the Highlands in October before when it snowed.'

'Yes. That does occasionally happen,' Briony said. 'I think the forecast is bright but windy for the next few days. Hopefully the rain will stay away until next week.'

She placed their bags inside the room and left them in peace, nipping back down the stairs. A few committee members were milling around the entrance hall.

'Hi, Nick,' she said, spying a familiar figure dressed in a shabby tweed jacket. Nick worked for a local forestry company and always had a pleasant but forlorn look about him, like he wasn't sure what he was supposed to be doing. Briony knew the feeling but was better at hiding it. 'You look like you've had a busy day.'

'Very,' he replied. 'I'm going to a big conference next week on forestry and conservation, but I've got so much to do before I leave.'

'I know that feeling well. You're ok to go through if you like. The fire's on, warm yourself up. I'll be in to get you some drinks shortly.'

'Thanks,' Nick said.

'Yes, thank you, Briony,' said a low drawling voice. She turned to see an older man, very large around the middle, grinning at her. His teeth were crooked and needed a good brush.

'No problem, Malcolm.' He was the committee chairperson and despite his somewhat off-putting smile – it looked more like a leer – he organised a lot for the community. Almost every event seemed to have his name alongside it anyway, though she never felt wholly at ease around him.

She opened the door for them and watched them heading for the small function room. Ah, no, the robe. *Dammit!* She'd forgotten. Two minutes wouldn't hurt. She made to go up the stairs just as someone whispered from behind the reception desk, 'Briony.'

She jumped and spun around to face the cupboard where Zach had been searching earlier. He peered around the door, gripping the frame. The vision was perplexing and comical like he was merely a disembodied head and hand. Problem was though, he definitely had a body. And it was in that cupboard. Only he didn't have any clothes unless he'd performed the miracle of washing and drying them in half an hour. His furtive glance told her otherwise.

'Are you in there naked?' She tugged at her earring, moving in behind the desk. What was he playing at? If any of the guests caught a naked rambler wandering around it would cement the hotel's place in the gutter.

'No.' His tanned face glowed pinker around the cheeks. 'I have a towel.' He did a quick shuffle into view. She copped an eyeful of a hunky chest, neatly shaped abs and a teasing line of dark hair running down the middle, pointing into the fluffy towel. His fist gripped it at the waist. No sooner had she taken him in than he shot behind the wall again. She'd had a quick fondle of that chest before, but it was in even better shape now. 'I couldn't find the ointment. And I can't get back to my room unless I streak through the hotel like this.'

'I was just going to get the cream and a robe for you to wear, but people kept coming in. Sorry, it's so manic.'

'Can I just run up to my room? Do you think anyone will notice?'

Briony craned her neck towards the stairs and the front door. More committee members were due in but... 'If you're quick.' Crazier things had happened in hotels. But she didn't fancy anyone seeing a half-naked man jumping out of her cupboard. The hotel's reputation was one thing. Hers quite another. That was a road too well travelled. He edged out and she held her breath. Daisy shower gel was her all-time favourite. She was addicted to its fresh, sweet aroma but daisy shower gel on Zacharias Somerton was a lethal drug designed to knock her senseless. Of course he'd used it. It was all she had, but to be parading it up her nose like that was... Well, ridiculously provoking. He gave her a quick smirk, then made to run. Just as she heard the front door's tell-tale click.

'Get back in there.' Her palms slapped against his warm chest, fingertips tingling with the desire to explore, but she shoved him hard and he staggered backwards through the opening.

'What the hell are you doing?'

'Shh!' She put her finger to her lips. 'Guests.'

'Seriously?'

'Yes. So, be quiet. And stay put.' She pushed the door to, but it didn't click completely shut.

'It's freezing in here,' he muttered.

Briony flicked out her hair, confident it would land perfectly. Hayley, her hairdresser, was a magician of a stylist and always gave Briony a tip-top cut. She turned to the desk ready to greet the people she assumed were the final guests for the day: Ms Warden and partner. She froze, her hands still holding the ends of her hair. Ms Warden's partner was no ordinary partner. No way. There stood Darren Dalgleish. Briony's ex-husband. What in the name of god was he doing here?

CHAPTER TWELVE

Zach

Z ach slumped against the wall in the cupboard, hastily
steadying a book before it clattered to the ground and gave
him away. What a crazy day. His brain was fried and his body
broken. He screwed up his nose at the scratches on his arm. Stuck
in a closet, naked, wounded and cold, and still nothing to show
for it. Or if he did, he wasn't sure exactly what. He needed to talk
to Mr Beyer again, but how? His destiny seemed to be to inhabit
this cupboard.

Briony's voice drifted into earshot. He frowned and edged his
head closer to the opening. Her tone wasn't its usual bright and
chirpy self. A sharpness edged it.

'And what are you doing here?' she asked. Zach dodged his
head around the gap, trying to find an angle where he could
peek through. Briony's words sounded abrupt. Usually, she
demonstrated the patience of a saint and that smile never slipped,
but it didn't sound like she was amused right now.

'We're going to the festival,' said a man's voice. 'And I've always been curious about what you left me for, must've been something special... Though not by the looks of things.'

Zach gave the door a tiny nudge so he could see clearer.

'How did you find me?'

'Took me a while, but then your picture turned up in a magazine in front of this place. Anyone would think you were hiding from me, Bri.'

'No. I just have no desire to hang out with the man I divorced because he had one too many affairs.'

What the hell? Zach's jaw dropped and he let the towel slip, grabbing it just in time. That was Briony's ex-husband? And not only that – he was the same asshole who'd extorted money from Zach to ensure Briony kept her job. She'd married him? Or had she already been married to him? Had they been in it together, running some kind of hustle? Zach's brain was now so full of questions he almost missed what was being said. He peered through the gap.

'Don't look at me,' said a woman with heavily bleached hair pulled into a tight ponytail. She was next to the ex and smiling in a way that reminded Zach of his colleagues' wives. The ones who looked at him like he was muck on their shoes. 'I only met Darren at the start of the year. He was already divorced by then.'

Darren. So that was the twat's name.

'Lovely.' Briony's tone was acidic.

'What possessed you to take this on?' Darren said, scrunching up his nose and glancing around. 'The article in Highland Home magazine last month made it look like a palace. I thought you must have inherited a goldmine, otherwise you'd have come crawling back, huh?'

'Hardly.' Briony was ramrod straight and rigid.

'I was imagining The Ritz,' Darren continued. 'Looks more like The Blitz.' Both he and the woman snickered at his crap joke. What a bastard.

'Feel free to leave,' Briony said. 'I can recommend some excellent places I'm sure you'll find more suited to your needs.'

'Na, na,' Darren said. 'This'll do for now.'

Briony slapped a card on the desk in front of him. 'If you wouldn't mind filling out your details, please.'

'Still on cards,' he said. 'How outdated is this place?'

What sadistic kind of man would pull a gag like this? A blackmailing swindling one, that was who. But seriously? He'd travelled from wherever just to get one over on her. Zach barely flattened the urge to leap out and punch him. He deserved it on two counts now. But Briony wouldn't thank him for that, especially in his current state of undress.

'Room twelve.' Briony dropped a key on the desk in front of him.

'Our bags need bringing up,' the woman said. 'Obviously I can't in my... delicate condition.'

Zach gaped. He couldn't see below her chest as the desk was too high, but it looked like she was patting her belly. Was she pregnant? Zach shook his head and silently growled. What a below the belt spectacle.

'I'll leave them there,' the woman said, and she and Darren headed for the stairs, chuckling.

Briony's shoulders rose and fell like she was taking long slow breaths. Once the laughing faded away, Zach peered out of the cupboard.

'Hey,' he whispered.

Briony glared around at him, her cheeks red, her smile gone. 'Did you hear all of that?'

He nodded.

'Great,' she muttered.

'No. It's not great. That man is an asshole. It's fucking outrageous.'

She held her finger to her lips and glanced around. 'Shh.'

'Sorry, but how dare he?' Zach muttered, throwing out his hands, forgetting momentarily about the towel. 'I can't... I just can't get my head around it.'

Whenever he'd been thrown onto the ex-pile, he never wanted to see the thrower ever again. Far from hunting them down and parading a new partner in front of them, he'd do everything he could to avoid them.

Briony's smile returned – a little anyway. It didn't fill her face like usual, but it melted some of the icy wall she'd surrounded herself with for the last few minutes. 'Thanks. I appreciate your indignation on my behalf.'

It wasn't just on her behalf.

'But honestly, Darren is a peasant among men. He hates the fact I left him. No one ever did it to him before, apparently. I'm surprised he hasn't come looking for me before, but I didn't tell him where I was. I never thought he'd see that article.' She let out a sigh. 'I was stupid to marry him at all.'

'And was that before... You and me happened?'

'What? No.' Her eyes flashed with understanding. 'I wasn't with anyone then. He happened after that.'

'Right. And how did that come about?'

'He helped me out of a tough spot. I was grateful.'

'Oh boy.' Zach rubbed his forehead. 'This is such a mess.'

Briony frowned at him. 'You can say that again.'

'I want to punch his nuts and throw him in the loch.'

Briony laughed. 'Ok. That's a bit crazy.'

'No. It's not. He deserves it, I assure you. What a fucking lowlife.'

Some of the resentment was fallout from The Gladstone incident but a lot of it was from the here and now. For Briony. She deserved better. He didn't want her to suffer at the hands of that dick. No more than she had already.

'Don't stress about it. I know what he's like. I better take Gemma's bags up or next thing they'll be leaving horrible reviews all over the place.'

'They probably will anyway.' Zach clutched his towel tight. 'They are definitely the type. In fact, I suspect they'd do worse.'

'You're not wrong.'

'I'll follow you.' He ducked down and nipped out from behind the desk. 'If anyone sees me, I'll say I got locked out of my room.'

'Wearing nothing but a towel?'

'Isn't that what everyone does in hotels?'

'Can't say I've ever had that here. But we know stranger things happened at The Gladstone.' She lifted the cases.

'They sure did,' Zach said. 'Here, let me do that.'

'I don't think so,' Briony said. 'You concentrate on keeping that towel in place. I doubt Mr Beyer would want you moonlighting as a naked bellboy.'

'Good point, ma'am.' Following her up the stairs gave him a neat view of her shapely curves. Her straight, long bob sat neatly below her shoulder, curling under at the ends. Each strand shone a different shade, ranging from toffee to pale gold, blending together in shimmering perfection. 'Don't you miss living in the city?' he asked.

'Sometimes. It's a different lifestyle up here.'

'I've never lived anywhere but a city. I can't imagine what it's like. Don't you get bored?'

'Definitely not. There's never a dull moment around here. I used to think like you. I wasn't sure I could function here, but I decided to give it a go and I love it. I just wish I could have made the hotel a success. You should have heard the ideas I had for it.'

'Tell me now.'

'I wanted to host events like the festival we're having this weekend all year round with different themes and activities. Events that guests could take part in and maybe even come especially for, but also to offer a diverse range for locals. Cocktail making, guided walks, wreath making, quiz nights...'

'How about history talks, writer's workshops, a book festival, painting at the pink hotel?'

Briony stopped walking and chuckled. 'Yes. That's the idea. Will you put all that in your report to Mr Beyer? Do you think he'll let us do it?'

Zach looked over the banister, down into the lobby. 'I'm sorry. I don't think he will. That kind of thing... Well, he just won't care.'

'Yeah. I thought as much.' Briony started walking again with a quickened pace.

'Does your ex know about your book?' Zach whispered.

'Yup. He said it was a waste of time and no one would ever read it. I used to draw and write when he was out.'

'Aw, jeez. What a dick.'

A heaviness pressed in at Zach. He wanted to reach out, tell her it would be ok, but how could he? He was part responsible now for her destiny. Even if he persuaded Mr Beyer the hotel was worth something, what he would turn it into was such a mockery of what it should be, Zach could hardly bear thinking about it. He'd worked five years in the Beyer regime; could he condemn Briony to that? If he tried to stop her, what would that mean for her future? And the tiniest possibility lurked in the thought that if she worked for Mr Beyer too, Zach might be able to see her again.

At the top of the stairs, she turned the other way from his room.

'Hey. I just realised.' He patted the towel. 'I really am locked out of my room. My key is the pocket of my jeans and they're in the washer.'

Briony let out a short laugh and shook her head. 'This day just gets better and better, doesn't it? Ok. Hang fire and let me deliver these bags, then I'll get you a spare key.'

He hovered outside his room. *Please don't let anyone walk past and see me, especially that bastard of a man.* How idiotic did he look? From the end of the corridor, he heard Briony's clipped tones before she marched back along and down the stairs. Darren was a piece of work and no mistake and judging from Briony's reaction she had no idea about the money he'd extorted from Zach. Zach still hadn't discovered if she'd actually lost that job. Or had Darren upheld his promise and stopped her getting the sack? Was that why they got together? Zach simmered, fiddling with the towel edge, a burning nausea in his gut. That dick deserved some kind of public humiliation.

With a jangling, Briony reappeared. 'I'll let you in with the skeleton key and get your other one out when your clothes are ready. That's the beauty of old-fashioned metal keys. You can wash them over and over and they still work, unlike key cards.'

Zach nodded, clutching the edge of his towel. Briony was back to her cheery self – or at least putting on a good face. 'You mean you've got a master key that can get you in here at any time.'

She winked and smirked. 'I most certainly do.'

'So, when that girl burst in on me naked that might not be the last time, huh?'

'Who can tell?' she said with another cheeky smile.

'Can you come in here for five minutes?'

One of her eyebrows almost shot off her face. 'What for?'

'Yeah, nothing like that. Just so I can tell you what I found earlier.'

'Oh, yes. Ok.' She scanned his chest and he struggled to catch a breath. 'But put something on first, will you?'

'Yes, ma'am.' Maybe the view disgusted her more than it distracted her. Who knew what women made of his body? He'd tried a bit of working out recently in the company gym; it was the done thing, and he was trying to fit in, but he was so used to names like weedy, he felt like he belonged to the description no matter what he did. And the new fitness regime hadn't exactly brought hordes of women queueing at his door. The awkwardness he'd felt ever since puberty was still there in some shape or form.

'I'll wait out here, then I can hear if anyone's at reception. Open up when you're ready.'

Yup, best she didn't watch. The jeans from the morning were dry and he pulled them on along with a black button-down that made him feel like a waiter before reopening the door.

Briony stepped inside. 'So, what did you find?'

'Listen up, I'm gonna tell you everything.' And he wanted to. Not just about the stairs and the cellar, the bottles, empty boxes and blocked-up passageway or his ridiculous trek into the scrubland, trying to trace something that may not even exist. More than that. He wanted to open his heart and pour out who he really was, what made him tick, what made him laugh – all the things he suppressed at work and on dates when he was attempting to be part of the crowd. He also wanted to tell her about Darren. But that would have to wait. For now, the facts. He explained, watching her as he spoke, admiring that smile, those lips, and those irises deep as the ocean, sparkling under the wrought-iron chandelier.

'Wow,' she said, as he wound up. 'What an adventure. After I inherited the hotel, or strictly speaking, after my dad inherited it and signed it over to me, we took a quick look. I didn't last long but he said it was a cellar with some worthless old wine bottles and parts of it were unsafe and needed repair before it could be used again.'

'Well, he's right. One side has caved in and the structures should probably be looked at. The wine seems to be the only thing in it apart from empty boxes. I took pictures of the bottles but I left my cell in your apartment. I need to investigate and see if they're valuable.'

'I doubt it. My dad knows quite a bit about wine. If they'd been valuable, he'd have said so or had them valued.'

Zach let out a sigh. 'Yeah. I'm just so curious about that passageway and what it could be.'

'Oh, sorry,' Briony said. 'People are talking out there. I should get downstairs. Look at the time. I need to serve dinner, and the committee people will want their drinks.'

'Ok. You go. I'll catch you later.'

Well, he hoped he would.

He signed onto his laptop and called Mr Beyer. What kind of reaction would his story get? But before he even got to the part about the passageway, Mr Beyer interrupted, 'You know what that could be?'

'No.'

'That could be where they took the stolen whisky.'

'What stolen whisky?'

'Ok, Zach, I'm going to let you in on a secret, but I don't want you blabbing this to anyone else. Your history is against you and I need utter assurance of confidentiality. Make sure you don't screw up this time. Do I have your absolute promise you'll keep this to yourself?'

'Yeah, ok,' Zach said slowly. Must Mr Beyer keep throwing that mistake in his face? And why did he get the feeling he was about to hear something that would have been better knowing before he showed up?

'You know Travis Roswell, the entrepreneur?'

'Not personally, but sure, I know who you mean.'

'We met a while back through business and got talking about stuff. Whisky was something we were both interested in. He told me a story about someone who'd worked with him who was Scottish. This man was quite a character by all accounts and had claimed he'd come over to escape the law because he knew the whereabouts of some very valuable whisky. Whisky he claimed had been gifted to him by a local distillery but he'd been accused of stealing. Now, this man died, but according to Travis he disclosed the location of the place the whisky was hidden. He said it was in a hotel painted pink near Loch Briar and the reason he knew was because he'd hidden it there himself when he'd been accused. The distillery owner who'd supposedly given him the whisky died and his brother wanted it back. The man claimed someone else had stolen it but even his wife believed he was a thief and threw him out. Travis thought it was a silly story and liked the romance of it, but I investigated, I mean, you know what a feature this could be in my collection. These things are hard to trace but a theft was recorded from the Glenbriar Distillery in the fifties and three bottles of a rare whisky were stolen. I can't find anywhere that says those bottles were ever found or sold on. When I also discovered the existence of a pink hotel nearby, it got me thinking. Now, you've provided me with the evidence

I need. Those bottles must be there somewhere. Maybe they're hidden amongst the wine or something. If I buy that hotel, I'll have it excavated. The hotel is worth a pittance next to what those bottles will fetch today.'

'But aren't they stolen property?'

'Not if we can prove the man's claim. Once they're found on my land, I'll get lawyers to investigate. I reckon it'll be finders keepers. Just make sure you don't blab to anyone. And I mean anyone. I don't want the current owner getting wind of this. I'm betting if they knew anything about it, they wouldn't be bothering with selling. I need that whisky, Zach. And I believe it exists. Once I have it, not only will it look great in my collection, but I can make the hotel my Scottish tribute to it. I might even build my own distillery nearby and have my whiskies and bourbons on sale at the bar. Whatever you do, do not let me down.'

When the call ended, Zach slammed the laptop lid shut and threw himself back on the bed. No way. No. No. No. *How can I not tell Briony?* This might save her skin. But if he did, what would happen to him? Mr Beyer would end his career. He'd been lucky once to get out with a reprimand and a demotion when it could have been much worse. How could he risk it again?

Could he pretend he hadn't heard any of that? Find a subtle way of helping Briony find out for herself? But even then, Mr Beyer would suspect his hand. Too obvious.

Was the story even true? Briony had said her grandmother kept secrets and the old Gandalf man knew stories about her. What stories? Was stolen kisses his code for stolen whisky? Things were falling into place in ways Zach didn't really want but the idea still seemed ridiculously far-fetched and unlikely.

He needed his cell, then he could call home or even just play some online games to distract his mind.

Dinners had started and a buzz of guests chattering wafted from the dining room, along with comforting aromas of roast chicken and onion gravy. Zach's stomach rumbled. He'd forgotten to eat since breakfast. Briony would be in the dining room, serving. Was he too late to book for dinner? He peered over the reception desk's high part and saw a clipboard beside the computer. Was that the meal bookings?

He was allowed around the other side now, wasn't he? After he'd spent ages half naked in the cupboard, he could surely claim some territorial rights? With a glance to either side, he nipped around and ferreted about for a pen. The list had several gaps around six forty-five, which was still an hour away, but it was better than nothing – or another plate of cold sandwiches.

'All right there, mate?' a man's voice spoke, and Zach looked up. His eyes locked on the face of that brat who had once called himself Briony's husband. It would have been satisfying to say ugly face, but Darren Dalgleish was blessed with looks that didn't match his mean personality. The urge to rearrange his haughty features rose in Zach again. Completely untrained and unskilled in the art of smiling at guests, he made no attempt to hide his contempt. Would Darren recognise him? Zach clasped his hands and rested his wrists on the high part of the desk, staring at Darren with no hint of a smile.

'Yes,' Zach said.

'Hang on... Are you?'

'Am I what?'

'Are you that American who was caught assaulting Briony at The Gladstone?

'Assaulting? Why you...' He bit back the expletives. Swearing at guests when he was on this side of the desk wasn't smart. 'I did nothing of the kind. Everything we did was consensual. You're the criminal here. You extorted money from me.'

'Oh yeah. That was the story. I forgot. It was so long ago. And for your information that wasn't extortion. Just a fee for a service. I upheld my end of the bargain.'

That was something at least. Zach's jaw tightened.

'What are you doing here anyway?' Darren said with a frown. 'Where's Briony?'

'Why do you need to know?'

'I want room service.'

'Do you? Well, we're not doing room service at this time. If you want something to eat, the dining room's there.' Zach's pulse beat a little too fast. He wasn't sure what he was doing but he was not having Briony running after this dick. If he could bluff his way through his day job, why not this?

'We?' Darren raised an eyebrow. The corners of his lip twitched. 'Are you and her together?'

'So what if we are?'

Darren covered his mouth, barely hiding a laugh. 'You are not serious? Come on, man? Don't tell me you stayed in touch after The Gladstone? Was she two-timing me all those years? Is that why she left me? Bitch.'

'Don't call her that or I'll have you thrown out and barred.'

Darren held up his hands, still laughing. 'You crack on, mate,' he said. 'Don't get your knickers in a twist.'

Zach drew himself up straight and did an internal fist pump. He was taller than Darren.

The door from the dining room belted open and both men turned around. Briony rushed through and stopped dead, staring first at Darren, then Zach, still behind the desk.

'What is—'

'I was just booking this man in for dinner,' Zach said quickly.

'Er,' she said, her brow creasing.

'I'll be down at six thirty.' Darren turned to Briony and shook his head. 'And you blame me for sleeping around? But for three and a half years of marriage you were screwing this one.' He turned on his heel and stormed upstairs.

She glared at Zach. 'What the hell does he mean?'

Zach stepped back from the desk, glancing at his feet. What had gotten into him? Like he wasn't in a big enough mess already.

CHAPTER THIRTEEN

Briony

'Well?' Briony put her hands on her hips. What was Zach's game? There he stood, bold as a neon lightbulb behind the desk, acting like he already owned the place and telling her ex-husband god knew what.

'I'm sorry.' Zach scrunched up his face. 'It's that dick of a man. He mistook me for a member of staff.' He glanced at his black shirt. 'Then, well, he recognised me.'

'How could he have?'

'Because he was the barman on duty when my colleagues bet me I couldn't, you know, in The Gladstone. He heard it all.'

'And he remembered?'

'Of course he did. It was him who came to me the next morning before I left and told me you were gonna be sacked.'

Briony gawped at him. 'He told you that?'

'Yeah. But he said he would help you.'

'Did he?'

'Only if I paid him five hundred dollars.'

'And did you?'

'Yeah.'

'Oh my god. You did not.'

'I didn't want you to get sacked because of me. And I didn't want that money either. It was the winnings from the bet. It felt dirty. I didn't do any of it because of the bet. I did it because I liked you.'

Briony closed her eyes and let out a sigh. 'No way. I thought Darren saved me from getting fired but you know what, I don't think my boss knew at all. It was all Darren. He told me the boss was on the warpath because he'd found out what I did.'

'Which was my fault.'

'But don't you get it? Darren invented the whole thing to get money out of you and to get me to think he was someone special. I started dating him after that. Out of gratitude. And it was all a big fat lie. My boss never knew. I spent years thinking he was watching me and that I was on my last warning when he didn't even know.' She turned away and clutched her face. This was too much to deal with right now. She needed a quiet place to curl up and cry it out. Or some me-time to spend drawing or writing and just not having to care if guests were waiting at the desk for her.

'Briony. I'm sorry,' Zach said.

'Don't be. I'm fine.' She flapped her hand, drying her eyes, and looked back. 'He's such a narcissistic, controlling, fucking bastard. But what made him think I'd been seeing you while I was married?'

'Like I said, he thought I was working here and assumed we were together. He thought we'd stayed in touch.'

'He thought that?'

'Yeah. I didn't contradict him.'

'Why not?' She frowned.

'Because I hate his guts. I hate the way he treated me, then you, and now the way he's flaunting that other woman up your nose. It's shit.'

Briony covered her mouth, barely holding back the dam. 'Thank you. But that's completely crazy.'

'I know, I shouldn't have.'

'I have an idea.' She moved around the desk beside him. 'Instead of pretending to be my lover, how about you pretend to be the receptionist?'

'Um... Are you sure? Me? At front of house?'

'Only if you want to.'

He huffed out a laugh. 'Sure, why not? I'll help.'

'What were you doing round here anyway?'

'Putting myself down for dinner, but now he's gonna be there, I'm second guessing the idea.'

'Yeah, well, not much we can do about that.'

'I could kick his butt if it helped.'

She couldn't help laughing. 'I'd like to see that. But save it until after he's paid up.'

'Ok. So, what exactly do you want me to do?'

'Just look after the desk, that'll save me worrying that I'm missing something. If anyone needs anything and you can't answer the question, come find me, I won't be far.'

'Yes, ma'am.'

She shook her head, just managing to summon a smile. This had been the weirdest day ever. 'Oh, I remembered something about that secret passageway.'

'You did?' Zach shuffled his feet and rubbed the back of his neck, not meeting her eye. Why was he being shifty about it? He was the one who found it after all.

'You know the man you met on your way here, Bruce McArthur, your Gandalf friend?'

'What about him?'

'A while back when I was opening the bar to non-residents.' Before it got too much for one person. 'He used to come in here and make a proper nuisance of himself. He was always talking a load of nonsense, but I remember him telling a bunch of tourists a story one night.'

'Oh yeah?' Zach's cheeks flushed a little. *What is up with him?*

'Yeah. It was about some woman, the one he claimed originally owned this hotel. Apparently, she had an illicit still somewhere nearby and the story went that she distilled moonshine and secretly rolled the barrels to the hotel and bottled them in other whisky bottles so she could fool the excise men if they came knocking. The locals were in on it because they got cheap whisky and better quality, if you believe his story. They made up the legend of the monster of Loch Briar to stop people wandering by the loch at night in case they accidentally stumbled on the illicit still. But one of the men in the village had his eye on the woman and asked her to marry him. Only she turned him down and he shopped her. The inn was raided, she was prosecuted and the illicit still was abandoned. I remembered when you said about the passageway. It sounded like some crazy thing he'd made up for tourists. But what if it's true? Maybe that's why the passageway is there. Maybe she used that to transport the barrels from the still to the hotel.'

Zach rubbed the dark stubble on his chin and frowned. 'Yeah. I wonder.'

'And I'm pretty sure those wine bottles are nothing but cheap wine from about twenty years ago but maybe we should open one and check it's definitely wine in there.'

'You think?'

'Well, it wouldn't do any harm because if it's actually whisky it'll be spoiled now.'

'It doesn't go off, does it?'

'The alcohol content damages the corks and ruins the flavour if the bottles are left on their side. That's why whisky is always stored upright.'

'Ok. Wow. Such a lot to get my head around.'

'Well, you think about it while you look after the desk and I'll get back to the diners.'

She bustled back in, nibbling on the inside of her cheek and flexing her fingers. Her world had spun off in one new direction after another today. And a lot of it was to do with Zach. Then Darren. Who could have guessed Darren's involvement in The Gladstone incident? His behaviour had always been arrogant and self-gratifying. It shouldn't be a shock to her, but it was like a dagger in her side. And he was here. In the same building as her. She had enough concerns with the possible sale without his presence in the mix. And his pregnant girlfriend. Insult to injury. He'd always insisted he didn't want kids. Briony's wishes were of no importance to him. He assumed she'd do whatever he wanted. And silly little her had – until she hadn't. When she grew a pair and started sticking up for herself, he got bored of her and went searching elsewhere for someone to control.

Her face ached by the time dinner was over. She'd smiled so much it almost cracked her jaw but she was damned if she was going to let Darren see her true feelings. If she let them out, she'd slap his face and upend the tattie soup over his head.

Zach must be still watching the desk. Now she knew the bet hadn't been the driving force behind his actions, windows in her heart opened; she wanted to throw them wide and let fresh ideas pour in, but this wasn't the time. Not yet. She made a plate for him, making sure it didn't contain pork and giving him extra helpings of everything. He deserved it after the pathetic offering from the previous evening. Balancing it on her arm, she marched through the dining area towards the foyer door.

'Oh.' She almost crashed into him in the doorway. His lips were screwed up and he was watching Darren and Gemma.

'He boils my blood,' Zach said.

'Don't let him get to you. In a few days, you'll never see him again.' *Or me.*

Zach rolled his knuckle in his palm. 'Men like him,' he growled.

'Here's your dinner.'

'Thanks.' He took it and smiled. When he did that, his whole face benefitted. He was handsome, but the smile transformed him into near perfect, like an Adonis with his thick curls. 'Loving the portion size. This is more my style.'

'Americans,' Briony muttered. 'Everything has to be supersized before you're satisfied.'

Zach's smile widened. 'Ha, too right.' He carried his dinner to the other side of the desk. 'Your grandmother didn't leave any personal papers or diaries or anything, did she? Things that might have clues. About the passageway thing?'

Briony ran her fingers through her hair. 'There's a box of old photos in my quarters but I don't think there's anything important in there. You can take a look if you want.'

'Can I?'

'Tomorrow. I'll be too tired when I'm finished here for anything else.'

'Sure. Tomorrow's great.'

By the time most of the guests started to head up to bed, Briony was dead on her feet. She looked away from the room to cover a yawn. When she turned back, Gemma was strutting out with a face like thunder. Darren was still at the table, his jaw set and a vein pulsing in his neck. A fall out? Shame. Briony let out a laugh as she cleared the plates from a nearby table. She deposited them in the kitchen and when she returned to the dining room, Darren had gone too. Her shoulder muscles relaxed and she briefly closed her eyes. *Phew.*

Once everything was cleared from the dining room, she helped Meg tidy the kitchen then returned to the desk. Zach was still there, glasses on, pouring over something.

'Hey,' she said. 'I thought you'd have gone up.'

'I'm working, remember.'

'Thanks. I should have come out and said you could go.'

'I don't mind. I've been reading through the old records.'

'Anything interesting?'

He took off his glasses and rubbed his eyes. 'Not really.'

'Get some sleep. You've been awake for hours.'

'Yeah. I will.' He got up and came around the desk, passing close to her. That daisy scent tickled her again. It definitely shouldn't be mixed with eau de Zach. It was a hundred times more potent than the Lynx effect.

She switched off the lights and locked up the reception area before heading to the private quarters. Becker would need out for his night-time wee. He staggered out of the door and loped across the courtyard to the bushes. The car park lamps shone, illuminating the path to the loch and a shadowy figure moved along it. Becker looked up, poised and curious. Briony stayed quiet. With any luck the person would walk by and not see her, then make their way back inside via the main door, assuming it was a guest. It was unlikely to be anyone else at this time of night, but a flicker of unease crept up her spine.

The figure got closer. A man. He slowed, his head moving towards where Becker stood next to a bush. Becker barked. The man threw his hands up. His shape and the movement were all too familiar. Darren. So he hadn't gone back to his room to face his girlfriend. No big shock.

'Hey, Bri. Is that you?'

She gritted her teeth. If she didn't answer, would he go away?

'I can see you. Is that your dog? Since when do you like dogs?'

'Becker,' she called. 'Come here.'

He trotted towards her and Darren followed.

'Life's not treating you that well, is it?' he said. 'This hotel is a dive.'

'What's it to you?' How dare he? Even if he was right, it was still her dive, and he had no right to insult it.

'Nothing.' He threw out his arms. 'Fancy a wee drink? Just you and me, for old time's sake.'

'No, Darren. You have a girlfriend—'

'Yeah, but she's hormonal,' he groaned. 'Honestly, her mood swings are off the fucking charts. She's turned into a totally different person and it's driving me mad. Can't wait until she pops the baby out, her family are loaded, they can get us a nanny.'

Briony half closed her eyes and let out a sigh. What the hell had she ever seen in him? And thank god she'd escaped. 'That's your problem,' she said. *Or actually, it's hers, poor woman.* 'Now, excuse me, I'm going to bed.'

'Alone? Where's your Yankee boyfriend?'

'I'm right here.'

Briony spun around at the sound of Zach's voice. Where the hell had he come from? Becker's tail started whipping from side to side and he darted towards Zach.

'Pah,' Darren said. 'Pair of cheats.'

'That's rich coming from you,' Briony said.

Zach slipped his arm over her shoulder. 'You ok?' he whispered.

'Fine.' She didn't move or try to shake him off. Something about his arm there was like holding a talisman to ward off the evil Darren spirit. Protective and comforting. 'What are you doing here?' she whispered through her teeth.

'I—' he began in a low voice, but Darren spoke again.

'How long have you two been together?'

'None of your business,' Zach said before Briony could open her mouth. 'Let's get inside.'

'Briony,' Darren said. 'I can see what you're doing.'

'Which is what?'

'Trying to ease the pain with this kid. Thinking you can buy back your youth. But he's after exactly the same as last time. A quick shag before he fucks off home.'

'Get out of here,' Briony said.

'Only a lowlife would say something like that,' Zach said, increasing the pressure on her shoulder. 'I like Briony so much more than a scumbag like you will ever understand.'

She side-eyed him. What the hell was he doing now? But before she could say anything or even get a sensible thought in, he leaned in and placed a slow, gentle kiss on her cheek. Like a switch had flicked, everything else stopped. Sound, time, brain functionality. The whole universe was solely focused on the sublime sensation of his lips, soft and warm. So beautiful. How much she wanted this – and more. She wanted those lips on hers so she could join in.

Then, just as softly, he pulled away and let his hand fall. 'Let's go inside,' he said, his voice hoarse, almost a whisper.

'Don't say I didn't tell you so,' Darren said. 'I can tell a chancer when I see one.'

'Takes one to know one,' Briony said, though she wasn't sure the words had come out in the right order. What the hell had just happened?

Zach gently steered her around. 'Come on.'

She turned, making sure Darren was gone, then muttered, 'What was all that about?'

'Please. Don't get mad.'

'I'm not. I just want to know why you did that.'

'Because I hate that dick and his attitude and, well, I didn't want you to be alone.'

'What do you mean? I am alone. You're not actually my boyfriend, you know that right?'

'Of course I do. I meant I didn't want you to be alone at that precise moment. Not forever. Well, I don't want you to be alone forever either but that's, well...' He trailed off.

'I think you've lost the plot,' she said. 'You clearly have jet lag and it's impairing your judgement. You should get to bed.'

'Yeah, I'm going.'

'Are you? Then why are you here? Your bed isn't in this courtyard.'

'I came to get my cell. It's still in your apartment. I heard him talking and came out to see if you were ok.'

'I don't need rescuing, you know?' But as soon as the words were out she realised her mistake. That was what she'd spent her life wishing for. Asking the universe to send the right people at the right time. She'd been so desperate to believe in good fortune and *right place, right time*. But was she simply admitting to her own weakness? Maybe she couldn't do anything without a saviour riding in and taking over. Was Mr Beyer just the latest in a long string?

Zach scratched at his wrist. 'Sorry. I overstepped. I'll back off. You're right, I'm exhausted and shouldn't have done any of it.'

His hurt was palpable, flashing from his dark eyes now under a careworn shadow. Briony looked away, her own heart aching like she'd stuck a knitting needle in it. Her mind whirred around panicky thoughts. She'd spent her life trying to be an independent career woman but had she all the while been acting like a weak-willed damsel? Where did that leave her with Zach? Feelings were seeping out and she couldn't stop them, but was that just the damsel talking again? Could she be sensible and resist the undeniable attraction? He'd be gone by the end of the week. She'd vowed never to enter into relationships with guests or colleagues again; he was both, or close enough. And that was before she got onto where he lived and every other objection. She opened the door to her apartment, flicked on the light and saw his phone on the work surface above the washing machine. 'There you go.' She passed it directly to him.

'Thank you,' he said. 'See you in the morning.'

'Sleep well.' Briony shut the door, then put her head in her hands. Becker rubbed his nose on her leg and she scratched behind his ear. Tears escaped, trickling down her cheeks. She tried to sniff them back, rubbing at the corners of her eyes with her fingertips.

What was going on? After months of so little action, no progress in anything and very little excitement, she'd had all this squashed into twenty-four hours and she still had no idea what was going to happen to the hotel.

CHAPTER FOURTEEN

Zach

Why couldn't he just hit the pillow and sleep? After a day like he'd had, Zach's eyes should be ready to close and his brain shutdown for the night, but no. It was as if he'd squeezed a month into a day. And now instead of sleeping his brain wanted to process it. But how?

From stories about stolen whisky and local legends to the incredible coincidence of finding Briony and the revelation that Darren the extortionist was her ex-husband, it was too much. In fact it was causing a mind malfunction, and at this rate could lead to a complete breakdown. To cap it all, nothing could have prepared him for the intensity of the desire burning inside him. An all-consuming raging furnace – all for Briony. And the oddest thing was, it felt like it had been there, simmering away for the last five years. He'd squashed it and ignored it, but now denying it was impossible. Occasionally a pretty face turned his head on the street – he was only human. But no one had ever suckered him like her.

'What's wrong with me?' He groaned. Tomorrow he'd apologise. For whatever. Lying to Darren about his relationship with Briony and kissing her to prove the lie – only that wasn't really why he'd done it. No. He couldn't hold back any longer. The desire was so strong.

Christ. He needed a cold shower or two. And how could he hold himself together until Friday? Tuesday, Wednesday and Thursday to go. Three and a bit days. These thoughts didn't stop him tossing and turning; they picked at his addled brain like clawing zombie fingers, straining to reach his bloodstained arms, desperate to bite him. They carried on into unsettling dreams. Every now and then he'd wake not sure where he was, if he'd been asleep or lost in crazy wanderings. When his eyes opened to a sliver of sunlight poking through the curtains, he rolled over with the intention of getting up in a couple of minutes. The warm pillows engulfed his heavy head and he yawned into them.

Noises woke him. He peeled open his eyelids. People were talking in the corridor outside his room. Stretching his arm out from under the cosy blanket, he fumbled around until he caught his cell on the bedside cabinet. He yanked it from the charger and pulled it towards him. Eleven o'clock? Jeezo. This was like being a teenager again. Waking early, then promptly falling back to sleep for several hours. That had always been a thing of his. How often he'd been woken around lunchtime by neighbours through the wall from his mom's apartment banging the vacuum against it. He'd whiled away long days on his computer games and watching sci-fi until she got out of bed. They'd never been well off and his mom hadn't worked. After his grandma died, his mom had spent even more time in bed, though she was often on the phone. Her gifts to Zach weren't the hugs and solace he needed while mourning his grandma, no, she gave him money and told him to buy all the gadgets he wanted. He had. AI and TV had pretty much brought him up. He didn't know where his mom had found the money, and he'd repaid her by ignoring her, putting on his earphones and shutting out her and everything else. Six years ago, she was diagnosed with chronic fatigue syndrome. Medicines could ease the pain in the short term but made her good for nothing. She was so exhausted. Zach owed her. If he'd helped more when he was younger, she might not have gotten so bad.

He dragged himself up and looked out the window. Grandma would have loved it here. She always talked about visiting other places and seeing the countryside, but she'd never left Kentucky. Zach shivered. The temperature was far too low again. He spent too long in the shower, trying to warm himself up and delaying the exquisite agony of seeing Briony again. The desperation to spend every second he had with her battled against the determination to be sensible. His stomach rumbled as he dried himself. He'd be too late for breakfast. It was almost lunchtime but the hotel only served lunches to those walkers with the foresight to ring ahead. Maybe he should call and pretend to be one of them. As if his role playing hadn't gotten him into enough trouble already.

Letting out a sigh, he opened his laptop and plonked it on the rumpled bed. Maybe Mr Beyer would have further instructions. Mr Beyer, the overlord. He thought himself both president and father of the company, but he wasn't exactly a great role model with his *do as I say not as I do* attitude. Sometimes Zach couldn't figure how he'd made so much money. Obviously he had business sense. Shame his wacky ideas didn't marry with common sense. *Like sending me here without a clue what I'm looking for, then telling me after I found it!*

Was it any surprise Zach was messed up and clueless after having him as a boss for over five years? Nor was his gene pool swimming with sensible fish. His father's identity had always been left hanging – some random man his mom had taken up with for one night, but he didn't exactly sound like a reputable character. Maybe Zach had followed in his footsteps and that was why he hadn't been averse to the one-night stand with Briony – not that it had panned out that way. Perhaps his family weren't in it for the long haul and were the kind of people who were happy with a fling. *Please let that not be true.* He didn't want to be alone forever but so far he'd done a shit job in the searching department.

An email from Daniel Beyer marked URGENT dragged Zach out of his own head; the shouty caps had done their job.

Zach pushed on his glasses, opened the email and read.

Good work yesterday. You cracked things wide open and nice and fast too. I can't say too much in an email as obviously there's sensitive information known only to us. However, I'm concerned about the flow of information and the safety of the assets we discussed.

The what? Zach frowned. He'd discovered a dusty old wine cellar, a blocked passageway and a whole lot of mud, which reminded him, he had no shoes. His Converse were still in Briony's washer with his clothes. He'd never gone back to hang them out to dry. He facepalmed. What an idiot. But back to the email. The assets? Did Mr Beyer mean this stolen whisky? Because he hadn't actually found whisky of any sort.

Please inform the hotel owner I'm putting together a package and an offer. This will take a while as I have a busy week. Therefore I want you to stay on in Scotland for the time being and guard the assets. Make sure any further investigations you carry out are confidential and under no circumstances alert the current owner to their value. This is imperative to the success of the bid. I originally thought it would be possible to keep her in position as manager, though I'm not sure now. I will have to consider the implications carefully. Again, I need not reiterate the need for utter confidence.

As soon as I have the package finalised, I'll let you know what further actions I need you to take.

Once again, I congratulate you on some sterling work.

Zach shook his head. No. Seriously? What was this nonsense? Staying in Scotland? How could he do that? He was on vacation next week and had the *Star Wars* convention to look forward to. Did that mean he would still be here... With Briony? A tussle inside him started. More time with her was something his heart ached for but it hurt his head in a different way. Prolonging his time with her would make their inevitable separation even harder. How could he wrangle his brain into looking at her neutrally and not finding her attractive in any way, shape or form? Maybe he could transpose the image of a tentacle-faced alien onto her every time he saw her. And... oh no. He threw himself back onto the bed and stared at the hangings. How could he break this news to her? And keep 'the assets' quiet? Wrong on every level.

The job never started was the job never done. Nothing for it, he'd have to face her at some point. He pulled open the door and looked about. The door next to his was open and a pile of towels lay outside. The cleaning woman was humming and china clinked and bumped within. Yup, it was a dangerous business leaving his front door and no mistake. Still, like the brave hobbit who first said those words, he had to put one foot in front of the other and walk downstairs.

Briony was at the desk, smile intact even though no one was there to see it. She was beaming at her screen, typing away at the keys. Zach cleared his throat as he approached and she glanced up.

'Ah. Good morning,' she said. 'I thought I must have missed you today.'

'I overslept.' He marched up to the desk and leaned on the high part, trying not to admire anything about her immaculately put together outfit and chirpy expression. 'Look, I should apologise. Last night I—'

She held up her hand. 'It's all forgotten. No need to say anything else.'

Really? Just like that? She was obviously better at forgetting than him. Or maybe it hadn't meant as much to her. But then she was a sensible woman. If she hadn't stopped their kiss five years ago when it got heated, who knew where they might have ended up. Most dramatic scenario: with a baby.

'My shoes,' Zach said, shaking off the mad ideas, 'they're—'

'Dry,' she said, not looking up. 'I put them on the radiator overnight. Your clothes are dry too. I'll fetch them in a minute.'

'Thanks. I forgot about them yesterday. I don't mind fetching them myself.'

'It's not a problem.'

How did she keep up the happy face? Zach rubbed the back of his neck and sighed. Talking business made more sense than trying to unpick his personal life. A personal life that had gone from nought to overdrive in twenty-four hours. 'I need to talk to you about Mr Beyer. He has an offer for you.'

Briony's fingers froze in mid-air above the keyboard and her focus snapped to Zach. 'What? Has he?'

'Yup.'

'Did you tell him that story about the illicit still? Is that what swung it?'

'I, er, I think it must have been.' He shuffled his feet, rubbing his socked toes on the threadbare carpet.

'So, what's he offering?'

'Can we talk about this somewhere private? I don't want to be overheard.' Zach checked around. Nobody was there but his confidence was low after that chambermaid leaping in on him yesterday.

'Sure.' Briony closed the laptop. 'In the lounge. It's empty and not open until later.'

He followed her in and they took seats by the empty fire.

How the hell could he word this without sounding like a complete idiot? Maybe that was Mr Beyer's intention. The idea that this was some kind of test still loitered at the back of his mind.

'So, what's the offer?' Briony's smile slipped and she bit her lip. 'I honestly didn't believe he was interested. But it's real.' She pressed her fingers into her forehead and exhaled. 'I can't get my head around it and what it means.'

'Well, don't get too excited yet.'

'Why not?' She frowned.

'Because he wants to put the offer together and make a package.'

'What does that mean exactly?'

'I'm not sure of the details myself yet.' He rubbed his hand up the back of his neck, not fully able to meet her eyes. What if Mr Beyer decided he'd buy the hotel but send Briony packing? 'In the interim, he wants me to stay here.'

Her mouth opened and closed wordlessly. 'Stay here? For how long?'

'I'm not sure. As long as it takes him to prepare the package I guess.'

'How will that work? I don't have a room for you after Friday. You're meant to be checking out and I'm full with festival goers. Even the attic room is booked.'

'I guess I'll be on the floor with Becker.'

She smirked. 'I'm sure he'll be thrilled. But I don't get why it's necessary.'

Zach's heart nudged him to tell the truth. She didn't deserve lies or to be screwed over by Mr Beyer – as so many had been. A stark reminder of how unbelievably lucky he was to still have this job. But if Briony was sitting on a fortune, she should have the opportunity to use it. Zach let out a sigh. If he told her, Mr Beyer would murder him and his career would be over. Jobs that paid this well were impossible to come by. It wasn't like he could waltz into something else. And weren't his long-term prospects more important? What would his grandma think if she knew he was considering tossing away his career to help a woman he fancied? His heart shrivelled. Right now, nothing felt more important than Briony, and Grandma always told him to be himself. This was Zach Somerton and he wanted to tell her the truth, no matter what Mr Beyer did to him. 'I could get into deep shit for telling you this. I've sworn to Mr Beyer I wouldn't...'

Briony raised one of her neatly plucked eyebrows and her searching look made Zach's gut clench. Electric energy surged through his core and he clamped his jaw shut.

'Tell me what?' she said.

Zach lowered his voice to a whisper. 'He thinks there might be some very valuable stolen whisky in the hotel. He wants me to stay here and make sure you don't find it before he buys you out.'

Briony shook her head. 'You must be joking. That's ridiculous. Why would he think that?'

'He heard a rumour and he's so obsessed with whisky he'll go to any lengths to get it. Even buy a hotel.' And possibly turn it into his Disneyland version of a hotel with its own distillery and who knew what else. Beyer's Scotch Whisky experience with all the pizazz and none of the true heart of the place.

'Why are you telling me this? I mean... Can I trust you? Whose side are you on?'

He let out a huff that verged on a laugh. Had he just crossed to the dark side? Or was he finally finding his way into the light? 'I can't stand lying to you. I did it before and I've always regretted it.'

'Really?'

'I swear.'

They looked at each other for a long time, Zach trying wordlessly to attest to his truthfulness.

'Listen, how about I help you out around here, while the festival is on, instead of getting in your way?' he said.

'Is that your way of keeping an eye on me in case I pull a million-dollar bottle out from under a bed?'

Zach shook his head. 'If the whisky exists and you find it, I guess I'll face the consequences. But it's not very likely, is it?'

'Not at all unfortunately.'

'Yeah. Thought so.'

'And you still want to help?'

'I do. You boss me about. I'm not exactly made for the front of house, the whole smiling thing isn't my strong point, but I'm willing to try.' Couldn't be worse than most of the jobs he was given to do.

'The first time I saw you, you had a great smile. Where's it gone in the last five years?'

'It's been squashed out of me.'

'Aw no. That's sad. It suited you.'

'Thanks.' His lips twitched and he glanced down. 'I'll try and resurrect it if you want me to, but I've never waited tables or served at a bar in my life. But, for you, I'll give it a go.' He held up his arms. This was the least he could do, right?

'Ok. I don't think those jobs are suited to you either. But...' She tugged at her neckline and glanced at the picture books on the table. 'You could look through the photos I left out.'

'Why? Do you think they have clues?'

'Maybe.'

'This kinda feels like we're in a Missy Peck book,' Zach said.

'And who's your character? Inspector Zach?'

'Yeah. I like it. But do you want me to look at those photos without you?'

'I don't really have time just now, but I might later. In the meantime, if I were you and I'd been granted some extra time here, I'd use it to write my books. Why don't you do that? Start your sci-fi novel. Plot it out, see where it goes.'

Their eyes met again and her smile was kind. It tickled him she'd remembered that little fact about him and was encouraging him.

'You remind me of my grandma,' he said. 'I mean, you look nothing like her, but she was like you. She remembered things about people and she smiled a lot.'

'You miss her?'

'Every day. I never got to say goodbye. She went to work and never came back. I kept thinking she'd just walk back in one day and...' Zach rubbed at his eyes. A lump rose in his throat. He'd never talked about this to anyone. 'I'm sorry, I can't...' He got to his feet and Briony followed.

'Hey,' she said, placing her hand on his arm. 'I didn't mean to upset you by asking.'

'It's fine. I just miss her, you know. It was hard growing up without her. I'm not sure I made the right choices.' In his head, he had. His job was well paid. Mom was well cared for. But his heart wasn't in any of it.

'Why don't you take a walk?' Briony said, still holding his arm. 'The fresh air will help and Becker would love to go with you.'

'Thank you, but it's not exactly helping you.'

'It is. Walking the dog is helping me and writing a book is helping yourself. Win-win.'

His facial muscles relaxed and he let go and smiled. 'Thanks.' His heart swelled under her gaze, like it had filled with shiny happy bubbles. An image panned into his brain. He and Briony were sitting by the fire in slippers. He typed away at his sci-fi thriller while she drew illustrations for her latest Missy Peck Adventure. Becker snored on the rug. Domestic bliss. And love. So much love. Love like he'd never known since Grandma. Love of the kind where he could get out of his seat, slouch down beside her and hug her just because. A wrench in his chest made him wish he could do that right now. So badly it hurt. He rubbed at his sternum with his knuckles, trying to ease the knot of pain, and Briony let go of his arm. No one ever hugged him just because... or at all. The last time he'd had a proper hug was when he was thirteen.

What fantasy was this? He must be having an emotional breakdown. Walkers in the barn had more chance of existing than that kind of daydream. Happy endings were the stuff of fiction and not for men like him. That's why he'd always settled for flings and short-term relationships with no strings. Less chance of a broken heart or rejection.

'There's a store of old wellies, you might find a pair that fit you,' Briony said.

He shook his head, returning to their conversation. 'Wellies?'

'You know, boots you wear outside in the rain to splash in muddy puddles.'

'Like rain boots.'

She pointed and smiled. 'Exactly.'

'Great. That sounds sensible.' If he had them, he could trudge about searching for the ruins of an illicit still. Not that it mattered now. Mr Beyer had no interest in the history of place after all – only the sordid kind that might bring him money, or better, the chance to add a unique whisky to his collection. Zach would scoff at how ridiculous it was, were it not for his own collection of *Star Wars* figures. Yeah, he wasn't exactly one to talk. He shared that problem with Mr Beyer but collecting *Star Wars* figures didn't run into the millions of dollars that whisky collecting did.

They reached the door and Briony stopped. Zach walked into her, colliding with her sweet daisy scent. A jolt of awareness zapped through his body. 'Sorry.' The overpowering urge to lean in and kiss her was back.

'Can I ask you something?' She twirled her flower pendant in her fingers.

'Um, ok.'

'If my ex is around, can you... well, keep on pretending to be my boyfriend?'

Zach blinked. *Uh oh.* Shouldn't really be difficult for the master of fakery, only it depended on whether his heart or his brain were playing. 'I guess so.'

'But just, you know, on the surface.'

'Yeah, of course.' Much like his whole existence. 'And no more stolen kisses, huh?'

'Best not.'

'Yeah.'

Zach nodded. He could make it happen. Shutdown the big feelings bubbling from within. Feelings that had been locked away for a long time. And they had to stay locked away. For everyone's sake.

CHAPTER FIFTEEN

Briony

'Where's the American superstud today?' Shari asked, dumping a pile of laundry at the bottom of the stairs.

'Walking. And don't call him that.' Briony glanced around. Zach had evidently taken his dog walking duties very seriously, fallen into another bramble bush, or found the stolen whisky and gone running back to his master. He'd been away for ages. The whole idea was ridiculous. If there was the possibility of valuable stolen whisky in the hotel, why had her dad or Aunt Lottie never mentioned it before? Briony needed to message them and find out if they knew anything.

With Becker catered for, that was one less thing to worry about. Especially after that almost kiss last night had knocked her off balance. Now Zach had put his career on the line by telling her a secret that could save hers, then opened up to her about his grandma. If the kiss had shaken her world, his sincerity wasn't helping to stick it back together again. The knowledge he wasn't the money-grabbing prick she'd taken him for before had changed everything, including the way she viewed that first kiss. He was even more appealing now, like a treat sitting on the top shelf, too high for her to reach and way above her price range. Not to mention one with a short use-by date. Even if he was here for another week, it didn't give her enough time to fully explore the possibilities.

'Have you heard any more about the sale?' Shari asked.

'Nothing's been finalised.' In fact she wasn't sure what to do next. Should she stall the deal and go on a wild goose chase for some stolen whisky? She didn't want to pin any hopes on anything so airy fairy.

'I just want to know if I'll still have a job,' said Shari.

Briony couldn't guarantee Mr Beyer's package would include security for Shari and Meg. Perhaps that would be something she could negotiate now she knew he was interested. But if his interest went no further than a highly implausible story, would he care about staff at all?

'I'll see if I can get clarification on what kind of provision there would be for staff already working here.'

'That would be a relief,' Shari said.

'Remember, I can't say anything for sure, so don't get too excited.'

'Ok. I'll try. Who's the twat in room twelve by the way?'

Briony's heart sank. Darren. This business of pretending Zach was her boyfriend whenever Darren was about was a precautionary measure, though it could easily backfire. Faking something like that to annoy Darren was one thing, but she didn't want Shari catching on.

'Room twelve.' She pretended to look it up. 'Darren Dalgleish.'

'Same name as you. Maybe you're related.'

Briony decided against telling Shari the connection. 'What did he do?'

'He was coming out of the room this morning when I was doing the room next door and he put his head in and said, "Tell the boss this bed's a lot comfier than our last one". No idea what he was on about. Loves himself by look of him. He was topless and making a right show of his six pack.'

'Hmm. If there are any more problems, let me know.' Briony tapped her fingers on the desk. 'He'll be gone in a few days.' She winced like someone had struck her with a stick. Zach might be gone then too.

Shari left to collect her son from school and Briony checked the clock with a frown. She didn't want to go seeking Zach down the rabbit hole again. Give him another hour. First, she wanted to message her dad and Aunt Lottie. Neither were great at quick responses, but she fired off her questions. She also had some phone calls to make regarding the festival gigs at the weekend.

It took a lot longer than she meant. When she finally got off the phone it was late afternoon. Meg had arrived to start dinner and guests were returning.

'Can I have a word?' Meg said, poking her head around from the kitchen corridor. Briony had the feeling she'd been hovering, waiting for her to finish the call.

'Of course. What's up?' She rolled back her chair, got up and joined Meg at the door.

'I had a message from Shari. She said the American boy was going to buy the hotel. She thought our jobs were safe now, but I've been around a bit more than her and... Well, I suppose I'm after some reassurance. Should I be worried? Start looking elsewhere?'

Briony put her hand on Meg's arm. 'Look, Meg, I honestly don't know too much myself. I can't give any assurances right now. I wish I could. We both know this place isn't making money in its current state and I don't have anything to invest in it. If I could keep it going the way it is and offer you job security, I would. Mr Beyer is putting together a package and when I get the details, I'll let you know. I promise I'll do my best to keep you and Shari in a job.'

'Can't you just ask him?'

'It's not up to Zach. He's working on behalf of an employer.'

'I suppose.' Meg dusted her overalls. 'It's just that without a job, we won't be able to keep up mortgage payments and I don't want to move again. We thought this was our forever home.'

'Try not to worry.' Briony squeezed her arm. 'I'll do everything I can.'

She needed to make sure they weren't empty words. Ruining someone's forever home wasn't on her bucket list.

'Hey, Bri.'

She'd barely closed the kitchen corridor door when the voice rang out. Her lips locked shut and she ground her teeth. Only one person ever called her that. The one person she wished would take a running jump out of her life.

'Good afternoon,' she said.

'Is it?' Gemma said.

It was until you two showed up. Briony grinned even wider. 'Can I help you with something?'

'We need a picnic blanket,' Darren said.

Briony blinked and inclined her head. 'And...'

'Can you get us one?'

'No,' Briony said. 'I don't have a random supply of picnic blankets.'

Gemma rolled her eyes and picked on a long talon. 'Useless.'

'Where were you thinking on going? Lots of places nearby have picnic tables.'

'We just wanted to sit by the loch and make out. Gemma can post pics to her Insta feed, she has quite a following.' Darren raised a smug eyebrow and slipped his arm around Gemma's shoulder. Briony tried not to gag at the image. A few years ago, he'd have tried to persuade her to do the same. What had she ever seen in him? Sleaze oozed from him, making her skin crawl.

'The grass is very comfy,' she said.

'Utterly useless,' Gemma said again. 'Come on, Darren.' She tugged his hand and they stalked off up the stairs.

Briony closed the desk. She needed to nip out and have a nosey around for any sign of Zach and Becker. Maybe he'd gone into her private quarters and was in there. Bit cheeky though. She grabbed a coat and stuck her head into the kitchen.

'I'm going out for a bit,' she said to Meg. 'We don't have any new check-ins today, but the first dinners are at five thirty. I should be back but can you keep an ear open for them?'

'Yes,' Meg said, not glancing up from her meal prep. Her shoulders looked saggy and deflated. Briony had to make sure she kept her job – somehow.

She checked her private quarters – empty – then headed for the courtyard, clipping across it in her heels. Where were Zach and Becker? Zach's number was what she needed, then she could call him in future. She tied the belt of her pink coat tight around her waist and nipped on towards the path that led to the loch. Her heels sunk into the soft ground. Should have put on more sensible things, duh. She stopped, shielding her eyes from the low sun, and scanned around. A splash further up the loch under some low trees caught her eye. The water rippled like something was swimming. A fleeting vision of a Nessie-type monster was replaced by a snorted laugh. Was that Becker? He reached the shore, gave himself a shake and dropped something on the pebbles. A man stooped, picked up the object and launched it high into the air. It soared up then crashed into the loch. Becker bounded after it, his legs going seamlessly from running to doggy-paddling. How long had they been playing that game? Zach had a full-time job right there.

Voices on the path behind made her turn around. Darren and Gemma strolled down, hand in hand, chuckling. They both spotted Briony at the same time. She pulled her coat tighter and hugged it against her chest.

'What you doing out here, Bri?'

'Nothing.'

Darren smirked. 'Fancy a bit of a kiss down by the loch yourself? Out of luck then. You missed your chance with me and that American baby of yours has fucked right off too... Again. Maybe his pals bet him he couldn't screw you a second time.'

Briony turned away. *Ignore him.* He was beneath her dignity. 'He's right there if you must know.'

They sidled past her as she spoke.

'Oh yes. With your dog,' Darren said. 'You never answered me yesterday. Since when did you like dogs? Or is that his dog? Maybe he's found a bitch he likes better than you.'

'Grow up,' Briony said. 'You're such a child. You always were.'

'Says the woman who's dating a high school kid who dumped her after he won a bet.'

'You don't know what you're talking about.' Her focus darted back to Zach and Becker. Becker was now bounding towards them and Zach jogging after him. The movement of his body sent tingles through Briony's nervous system. Even in those giant, clunky wellies, he looked exceptionally well-formed and virile.

Becker reached Darren and Gemma on the path first. He stopped, sniffed the air, then shook his hairy coat. A storm of water droplets pelted the duo. Briony stifled a laugh as they jumped to get out of his way.

'Crazy dog,' Darren snapped, wiping his palm down the front of his jeans. 'You should keep it under control.'

'Sorry, sir,' Zach said with a bizarre smile. Briony clutched her mouth before she fell apart at the goofy expression on his face. Was he trying out a 'hospitable' face? His grin was the fakest thing ever. 'This dog is a crazy kid, but he's our baby and we wouldn't change him for the world.'

Briony gaped at him, but he was intently avoiding looking back.

'Are you enjoying your vacation?' he continued.

'We don't call it that here,' Gemma said.

'Beg your pardon, ma'am. How is your holiday?'

'Crap.'

'So sorry to hear that. If there's anything I can do to make your stay any better, just call.'

Gemma looked him up and down. Darren tugged her hand and pulled her away. 'That won't be necessary,' he said.

Zach pulled a face as soon as their backs were to him. 'Dick,' he muttered as he drew level with Briony. He still didn't meet her eyes.

'Where have you been all day?' She ruffled Becker's damp head.

'Playing with Becker.'

'All that time?'

'And walking. It's stunning out here. We saw a herd of deer, like massive ones. This big one was roaring like crazy and running about shaking his huge antlers.'

'It's the rut.'

'Is that when—'

'When the males try to prove they're the biggest, best and most sexually attractive. Yes.'

'Right.' Zach ruffed up his hair. 'Well, that guy was doing a pretty epic job of getting his voice heard.'

'What girl doesn't like a man who can shout at the top of his voice? Irresistible quality.' Briony smirked.

'Ha. Yeah. But it was kinda impressive. Oh for Christ's sake!'

'What?'

He pointed and Briony followed his sightline.

Darren and Gemma had gone about twenty metres to a bare patch of grass between the hotel and the loch. They'd laid out what looked like a bed sheet and had wasted no time in doing exactly what Darren had said they would. Joined at the lips, they looked like teenagers or a horribly showy celebrity couple putting on a display for the press. Gemma had her phone held out to get selfies. Who on earth would want to look at them?

'Are they completely shameless?' Zach shook his head and grimaced.

'It's part of the show.' Briony sighed. 'He wants me to know how happy and fulfilled he is.'

Right on cue, he pulled away from Gemma and glanced towards Briony with a smug grin.

'What a dick,' Zach said. 'I don't think I've ever disliked anyone as much as him.'

Briony's insides surged with hot rage. What was Darren's problem? Or problems – because he was clearly disturbed. What was he trying to prove? If he was happy and had moved on then great, but why rub it in? Why come here? He'd always liked making trouble and he was still at it, jumping in with his big stirring spoon. Only normally he wanted something in return for his tricks. What was his motive other than sheer cruelty? Yup. That was it. Darren always had an unhealthy obsession with revenge and 'getting his own back', often on people who hadn't done anything in the first place. The ignominy of being dumped was obviously eating him and he wouldn't rest until he'd got back at her. His hand slid up Gemma's back though his eyes were still on Briony. He split his pointer and middle fingers, flipping the bird her way, under the pretence of rubbing Gemma's back.

Briony looked at Zach, that gorgeous hair, those brooding eyebrows, luscious eyelashes and kissable lips. She'd wasted long enough squashing memories of their first kiss, trying to convince herself she'd been stupid. Darren's interference had led her to believe Zach was corrupt when he wasn't. The kiss had been as real as Briony had first imagined and it was time she picked up from where they left off. 'Do you know what?' she said.

'No.'

'I really missed you today.' She threw her arms around his neck, pulled him towards her and placed her lips on his, back where she'd wanted them to be for a long time. He'd never been the bad guy, not really. She'd let Darren's influence win, but not this time.

Zach stiffened and let out one of those little huffs of his, like he wasn't sure whether to laugh or go with it, then he coiled his arms around her back, pulled her close and sighed into the kiss. His hands were broad and his wide-spread fingers encased her. His hug was the best thing ever, like he was pouring everything he wanted to say but couldn't into it. It was better than words. The softness of his kiss was like wallowing in deep liquid chocolate. Briony closed her eyes. Who cared if this was for show? If it annoyed Darren, then good. But more than that it satisfied something deep inside her, like bathing a throbbing ache in warm soothing water.

'I missed you too,' Zach whispered as she broke away. He didn't let go. 'Much more than I should. Maybe for a lot longer than I should.'

She smiled and kissed him again, letting go and relaxing into it completely. Zach returned it, still holding her close. Deeper urges to lose clothes, and fast, burned inside her. She'd held it together once before and she had to do it again because they were just acting, right? Putting on a show for Darren. Except every bit of it felt like the real deal.

CHAPTER SIXTEEN

Zach

Warmth beat down on Zach's back. Compared to the heat in Louisville, it was nothing. But blue skies had opened up and everything was bright; the loch sparkled and the golden leaves on the trees fluttered softly.

He held Briony in his arms, not wanting to let her go. Physical urges and obsessions over his next sexual encounter had never got the better of him. He could be disciplined – had to be because he was so bad at dating.

Now, a physical ache burned inside him, not detached and impersonal, but linked intrinsically to the throb in his heart, the one he got every time he locked eyes with Briony. This was where he was meant to be, like all his days had led to this moment. And if he opened his mind to a crazy thought, it was a sensation he'd had since their first encounter. He'd dreamed of getting back to this point. Love at first sight was one of those things that worked in films and was right up there with happy endings. Not something he believed in. *But there is something here and there always was.* Something that was eating him alive. He wanted to rip off his clothes, lie her down and make love to her. Even though it was meant to be fake it was the most genuine thing in his life right now.

'Zach.' Briony held him in the hug he'd been desperately wanting for so long and he didn't want to let go. 'I need to get back to the desk.'

'Oh, sure.' He released her and palmed his forehead, trying to erase a dull throb. Becker nuzzled his nose up Zach's thigh.

'Thanks.' She smiled, rubbing at the lapel of her coat, and blinking several times before meeting his gaze. 'Do you still want to look at those old photos? Search for clues?'

'Sure, why not? I might solve the mystery,' he said, fighting with his insides to revert to normal conversation and make a good show of being interested in something other than diving in for another hug.

'And what then? Who will you give the whisky to?'

'You.' No hesitation.

'But what about your job?'

He shrugged. 'It won't be the first time I've screwed up.'

She tilted her head, a pained expression crossing her brow. 'I don't want you to get into unnecessary trouble for this.'

'It's only gonna happen if the whisky turns out to be real and we both know that's not very likely.'

'True. But will he still want the hotel if you don't find it?'

'I dunno. He's gonna let me know.'

'Well, the box is inside. I haven't really looked at it. My grandmother was a strange woman. She didn't let anyone get close. I found her more intimidating than anything. I loved coming here though my dad didn't. He spent most of the holiday taking my sister and me on picnics, walks and cycle runs. We enjoyed it but he was just doing his duty to his mother while keeping out of her way.'

And in all that time, she'd never heard about the hotel's questionable past. Had her father? Did he know more and want to keep it hushed up? 'Doesn't your dad know any rumours or stories about the whisky?'

'Not that he's ever told me. He and his sister don't like the hotel. They didn't have a happy childhood here. Hilda worked and they were left on their own. I always loved the idea of it, maybe just because it was pink, who knows? The box is in the lounge in my private quarters on the coffee table.' Briony's smile invited him to follow her. 'Feel free to take a look. And please don't judge the decor in there. I hate it, it's so ancient.' She opened the door to her private space from the kitchen corridor. The design was pretty neat, how it opened onto the hotel but also had a back door onto the courtyard. But she was right, it was retro, from the shiny sienna wallpaper to the electric fire with the fake coal moulded into it. The shower he'd used the previous day was probably an original electric shower from the sixties. 'I'll sneak out later and bring you some food, maybe help you look.'

'I'd like that,' he said.

'I'll try.'

After she returned to the desk, Zach dried Becker off, located some doggie treats in a peeling Formica kitchen cabinet and fed one to him. 'You know what? This could be done up. It wouldn't be a bad place to live. Or this could be accommodation and we... Well, Briony could build a house nearby. Here's me about to say *we* like this gig is for real. I'm losing it, Becker. Big time.'

He flopped into the sofa and lifted the box off the coffee table. Becker jumped up beside him and nuzzled in close. 'Hey, boy. You take a rest. You've earned it. That was some walk, huh?'

After trudging around the muddy wooded area armed with a large stick to whack the bramble bushes, Zach had come across the trace of an old stone building, so low and overgrown it was impossible to tell what it was or might have been, but it was within the ballpark area and was possibly the remains of an illicit still. As these stills were never documented, it would be hard to tell one way or another. He didn't really need to know either. Mr Beyer sure as hell didn't care unless the still also happened to be the stolen whisky's resting place. But that was ridiculous, surely?

Zach opened the box and was instantly hit by the smell of old paper and memories. It wasn't unpleasant but neither was it something he particularly liked. He frowned as he lifted the tatty envelope on the top. Inside were some old photographs, none of them named. Some of the people were in late nineteenth century, early twentieth outfits. If these were Briony's ancestors, she must have inherited her smile from the other side of the family. He tucked them back into their envelope with a smirk. Of course, smiling for photographs was a relatively recent thing, but this family looked particularly sombre.

The next envelope had more black and white pictures inside. This time with people in less formal dress. Shorter skirts and flat caps. A car featured in one of them, a long low black model with an open roof. These must be nineteen twenties or thirties. He lifted one, adjusted his glasses and peered closer. A little girl in a frilly white dress stood by an austere-looking mother on a high-backed chair. The girl had strange eyes, slightly creepy, like she was watching him. He slipped the picture back into the envelope and carried on. Each envelope moved forward in time by a decade or so.

When he got to what looked like the fifties, the little girl appeared again, grown up. It was obviously her – same eyes and grim watching expression. She wore a summer dress with a flared skirt and had her arm linked with a young man, who beamed broadly. That smile. So like Briony's. Could this be her grandparents? Was this the formidable grandmother she never really got close to? The same couple appeared in more pictures, including a wedding one. Then some with a baby, a little boy and another baby. Then two young children: the boy and a little girl. As the pictures progressed, the boy's cheeky dimples got more and more like Briony. He had to be her dad. After that, the pictures dwindled. A few of the boy and girl appeared; both were older, standing outside what looked like the hotel. But no more of their parents.

Zach tapped one of the pictures on the envelope. If Mr Beyer's friend's crazy story was true, did that mean Briony's grandad was the thief? Was that why he disappeared from the pictures? Did her dad remember him?

'Aw man. I can't ask her.' He placed the box down and huddled up to Becker. 'I wish I knew what to do. I don't want to be the one who pulls Briony's dreams out from under her feet, then tells her her grandpa was a thief. But if I don't and she finds out anyway? I don't know what to do.'

Zach scrunched up his face at the bright light and took off his askew glasses. He must have fallen asleep. Curse that jet lag. He blinked, trying to focus on the blurred surroundings. The beige velour sofas reformed into coherent shapes.

Briony was in the doorway, her fingers on the light switch. 'Sorry, I didn't think you'd still be here. I couldn't get away any earlier.'

He stifled a yawn and sat up. 'What time is it?'

'Nearly eleven.'

'Seriously? You work far too late.'

She gave a half shrug. 'Has to be done.' Her gaze travelled to the box of photos. 'Did you find anything interesting?'

'Lots of pictures.'

Briony sat beside him and leaned towards the box. 'I never really wanted to look. It's weird, like some kind of mental block.'

'Yeah. I hear you. I have a lot of them around my family too.'

'Because of your grandma?'

'No. She was the best part of my life. When she died, it was only my mom. My dad's never been around. I never knew him. Mom has chronic fatigue syndrome. She's had it for years but wasn't diagnosed until recently. Her medication and care is expensive and she can't work. It's catch-22. She can't work without medication and she can't afford medication without work.'

'So, how does she manage?'

'I pay for it. I want her to be ok. I neglected her...' He stopped talking as a wall of hurt rose in his chest.

Briony put her hand on his knee, a frown etched deep in her brow. 'How?'

'After Grandma died, I didn't know what to do. I just left her... in bed... all day. I stopped even going in to see her. I got more obsessed with computer games and films. I didn't look after her. She got worse and worse. And now... Well, I have to make it up to her. She's the only person left in my family. I don't wanna be completely alone.'

The pressure on his knee increased and he glanced at Briony's fingers, her ring glinting in the hazy lighting. 'Oh, Zach. You were just a child. That wasn't you neglecting her. If anything it was the other way around.'

'Maybe.' He let out a sigh. 'I just feel like I've missed something.'

'Love, by the sound of it.'

He nodded, biting back another lump in his throat. *What's gotten into me today?* 'What about you?' he said, trying to change to a subject that wouldn't make him weep like a baby. 'You seem to have normal parents.'

'I do. But they were always really busy when I was growing up. My sister and I weren't a priority and I often looked after her. They've done really well for themselves, so it paid off.'

'At your expense.'

'Not really. I learned the value of hard work.'

'But you hid your talents, the ones you thought they wouldn't approve of anyway.'

She huffed a laugh. 'Maybe subconsciously but I never thought about it like that.'

'Always be yourself. That's what my grandma said to me.'

'Everything is just so confusing right now. I wish I knew for sure where this deal was going.'

'If you wanna pull out, just let me know.'

'And do what?'

'I'm not sure, but I like your ideas for the hotel, better than the idea of Mr Beyer riding in here with a team of whisky seekers.' He lifted an envelope filled with photographs and pulled one out. 'What happened to your grandfather?'

'How do you mean?'

'I think this is him in the photos with your grandmother. Look.' He ran his hand over the back of hers as he prised the lid open. His fingertips tingled at the warmth of her skin. Batting the sensation out of the park, he skimmed through the pictures until he found the one he'd surmised to be her grandparents' wedding. 'I guess this is your grandparents.'

Briony took it from him and looked. 'I think it is.'

'There are a few of that couple. Then this little boy, who I guess is your dad.'

'That's definitely Dad,' Briony agreed. 'And Aunt Lottie.'

'But your grandparents disappear after a while. I can't find any pictures of them later in life.'

'My grandmother hated getting her picture taken. And I never knew my grandad. My dad and Aunt Lottie never talk about him. He walked out on them when they were kids and from the little they've said, I get the impression my gran was humiliated by it. She ran this hotel but lived like a recluse. She didn't have friends in the village or the community.'

'And didn't your dad or your aunt try to trace their father?'

'Not that I know. I don't think they ever wanted to after what he did. They were pretty young. I suspect he had an affair and went off with someone else. That's the impression I got and the reason my gran was so mortified by it.'

Zach sat back and sighed.

'Is that all you found?' she said. 'Nothing about illicit stills or monsters?'

'Nope. Not a thing.'

'Would you like a hot chocolate? I need something before I go to bed.'

'Sounds nice but shouldn't I get out of your hair?'

'No. Stay for a bit. It's nice having company.'

'Really? Even mine?'

'Especially yours. I misjudged you before. Well, I didn't, then I did, and now I know I shouldn't have. I blame Darren but part of it was me. I should have made up my own mind, not let him make it up for me.'

The warmth of the words spread through his veins and he smiled. 'I always liked you.'

With slightly rosy cheeks, she nipped off and Zach stroked Becker's ear. Becker groaned, rolled further over and lifted his front paw. Zach rubbed his belly, staring at the Anaglypta wallpaper until it blurred.

Two mugs landed next to the photo box and Briony pushed it away. 'So, tell me more about Zacharias Somerton? The man behind the scowl.'

He cocked his head. 'Am I that bad?'

'No. Not really.' She grinned.

'What do you wanna know?'

'Anything.' She lifted her mug and raised it to him. 'I feel like I've known you but not known you for years but also like I've just met you.'

Zach half shook his head. 'That's a bit mind bending but I get what you mean.'

'Strange, isn't it?'

'Yup. I don't believe in coincidence but...' He sipped his warm drink.

'I do but it was a big shock seeing you again.'

'I honestly wouldn't have believed it. I always saw you as a missed chance.'

She glanced away and sucked on her lower lip, before meeting his eyes again. 'So, let's make up for it. I know you like *The Walking Dead* and *Star Wars*.'

'How do you know I like *Star Wars*?'

'The Yoda t-shirt was a clue. Plus I've had a crush on Han Solo since I was seven, so you didn't think I'd miss the line about blasters, do you? It's one of his best cracks.'

Zach smirked before raising the warm mug to his lips again. 'I wondered if you'd got it. No one usually does. Especially not...' Well, women like her.

'Not what?'

'Ah, you know. I'm a nerd. Everyone says it. Yeah, I like *Star Wars*, and *Lord of the Rings*, *Game of Thrones*, *Star Trek*, anything sci-fi or fantasy really. I go to conventions, I have the computer games, the books, the figures and all that. I guess I live in a fantasy world.'

Briony's eyebrows raised in the middle. 'Even if you're a nerd, it doesn't have to be bad. You clearly have a good career as well. You're a trusted part of Mr Beyer's business. If you have hobbies outside of that it's not a crime. Unless you stole the *Star Wars* figures.'

'Ha! No, I didn't. But I've spent a ridiculous amount on them. And I'm not a trusted part of the business. The opposite in fact.' He ruffled up his hair. Her smile invited confidence. The cream from the hot chocolate frothed on his lips and he dabbed at it. 'I made a mistake last year. A big one. It was so stupid. I was duped into believing someone I was working with was an ally. We shared a hotel during a big conference and she asked me to bring her a case of papers she'd left in Mr Beyer's room during a business meeting. I did it, thinking I was being helpful. It turned out they were his confidential papers and she was working for a rival. It was during the time of a big takeover bid and he ended up losing out. I was lucky not to lose my job.' Zach glanced sideways at her. 'He was furious but accepted I hadn't done it on purpose. I was demoted and given all the jobs no one else wanted, which really isn't much different to what I was doing before, only I get paid less.'

'I thought you were a historian?'

'That's my degree but I've never used it at work until now. I was employed as part of the development team where I was totally out of my depth. Now I'm a sort of loose end... and a liability.'

Briony patted his knee and he inhaled at the touch. 'Oh, Zach. I'm sure you're not. But I know what you mean. Some days I feel like I'm drifting and I can't get to shore. I always wanted to be in hospitality, but I lost my confidence after... Well, you and me. I thought I'd thrown away my career and when Darren came along to rescue me, I fell at his feet, thinking the universe had sent me this wonderful man. I didn't for one second think he'd made it all up. I like to see the best in people and situations – even when it isn't there.'

Zach let out a long sigh. 'I'm sorry for my part.'

'Don't be. What's done is done. Darren was a terrible decision. This place might turn out to be another, but I don't regret it. I'd feel worse if I hadn't even tried.'

Zach replaced his mug on the table and shuffled closer. Her tractor beam was working again, pulling him in, and he didn't want to resist. 'I think you're brave.' He put his arm around her shoulder. 'You've made a bold step taking on the hotel, it just hasn't paid off.'

She rubbed his thigh, sending a bolt to his groin. 'You're really sweet.'

'Sweet?' Right now, he was too hot under the collar to be sweet. 'That isn't a word people usually say about me.'

Her smile grew, then faded. 'The woman who worked for the rival company – were you and her...? You know, close in other ways.'

'No. I don't usually throw myself at strangers in hotels, only you.' He loosened the neckline of his shirt.

She pressed her lips into a thin line. 'Are you seeing anyone back home?'

'No... I wouldn't be here, doing this if I was, would I?' He frowned.

'No, I guess not. I'm just used to being around Darren.'

'And women usually think I'm annoying or weird.'

'Stop thinking like that.'

'Yes, ma'am.'

She covered her mouth, holding back a yawny smile and resting her head lightly on his chest. 'I told you, I'm not the queen.'

'Sorry, ma'am.'

She unleashed a giggle and he increased the gentle pressure on her shoulder. It was like holding onto the edge of a cliff with his fingertips. If he kissed her now, it would send him over, landing him exactly where he wanted to be.

'So, what happens now?' he whispered. 'With us.'

'Is there an us?'

'There could be.' He inhaled her fresh daisy scent and her soft hair brushed the tip of his nose.

'We can't,' she murmured. 'It's late. I'm so exhausted and I'm not sure it's sensible to go down this road.'

'What road?' His fingertips slipped on the crumbling rock he was clinging to in his mind.

'To finish the fling we didn't manage five years ago.'

'The fling?'

'Yes. What else can it be? You're not sticking around, are you?' She lifted her head to look at him.

'No... But...'

'Our lives are in different continents, Zach. And if Mr Beyer buys the hotel, we could be colleagues on different continents.'

Zach didn't want to think about it like that. My Beyer had a strict no-dating policy for his employees. To avoid unnecessary conflicts of interest apparently. Zach wanted to see it more as a chance to stay in touch, but how would that work? 'Ok.' He sighed, moved his arm and lifted his mug, downing the remaining hot chocolate and setting the mug on the table. 'I'll go and let you get some sleep.'

'Thanks. And... just thanks.'

'For what?' He shifted his leg from under Becker's head; the dog groaned at being disturbed.

'Your company.'

It was on the tip of his tongue to say anytime except he couldn't. Briony had called it. He was leaving and whatever happened here would be thrown into the memory vault alongside his previous trip.

'You're welcome.' He pulled in a breath, then leaned in and kissed her cheek. 'Sleep well.' Inside his head, he let go of the cliff edge and plunged back into the murky depth of his sad, lonely existence.

CHAPTER SEVENTEEN

Briony

B riony rammed on her shoes, hoping the rest of her clothes were on the right way. Her hair was pretty good at staying in place, but it didn't feel right with just a comb through. No time for the straighteners though. No time for anything. She should have been at the desk two hours ago. Zach. That horribly lovely man keeping her up so late.

Why did he have to be so sweet? He may scoff at that word, but it fitted him. How odd after years of thinking him a prat, then wishing he wasn't, and all the while being glad to have a reason not to like him because it saved her pondering the might-have-beens. Well, they were out in force now.

His position made everything so risky – for both of them. A reason for her to keep a lid on it. She'd risked her job for a kiss before; now she could be risking her livelihood, others' jobs, and Zach's career. But her tummy twinged with an empty pang. Just hunger, and no time for breakfast. It had taken a long time to fall asleep after Zach left the night before and now she was paying for it.

She needed to be at reception and fast. People would be expecting breakfast and to check out and she had to be there. 'Oh god,' she moaned. This was a disaster. It was ten past eight. Any early birds would have been waiting for hours and likely furious. Becker was back in after a two-minute hop into the yard for a wee. Zach might walk him later. Freaking hell, she had to stop relying on him. *Do not let that start.* His time would run out. But then, so would hers. She might have to look for a new home. Mr Beyer might not want her to use the staff quarters any more. He definitely wouldn't want a cheeky dog annoying the guests. What would Briony do with him? How would he take to a new home at his age? She gave him a quick pat. They'd get through this, somehow. And no way was she giving him up.

Dashing into the kitchen corridor, she frowned. What was that smell? Toast? Coffee? Oh no. Had some guests taken the law into their own hands and tried to cook something themselves? Health and safety would have a field day. She pushed open the door leading to the reception area and froze.

Zach stood behind the desk, nodding at a woman. Felicity! Briony had completely forgotten she was coming to set up for the festival.

She cleared her throat. 'Good morning.'

'Ah, morning,' said Zach.

'Hey,' Felicity said, a glint twinkling at the corner of her eye. She nipped over to hug Briony. What had that look meant? Maybe Felicity fancied Zach – they were about the same age. Or maybe she suspected something. *Go away.* Briony shoved the thoughts out and stepped out of the hug.

'Sorry I'm late,' she said, straightening out her top.

'That's ok. I'm a bit early. I've managed to persuade a builder to come and put the stage together in the lounge, which is good because I wouldn't know where to start.'

'It's not someone called Brann, is it?'

'It is. Do you know him?'

'He called in earlier in the week,' Briony said, glancing at Zach. 'Listen, could you give me a second here?' she added to Felicity.

'Sure. I'll wait in the lounge.' Felicity beamed at Zach, flicked her long blonde hair over her shoulder and disappeared through the door.

'What are you doing?' Briony said, the second Felicity was out of earshot.

'Helping you.'

'How?'

'I made breakfast for some guests and I'm looking after the desk so you can get some extra sleep.' He glanced around and lowered his voice. 'It was my fault you were up so late.'

'I shouldn't have slept in.'

'It's ok. Chill.' Zach put his hand on her upper arm. 'I got this.'

She clutched her face and let out a sigh. Her relief was tempered by a niggling worry that Zach didn't have a clue what he was doing. Still, help was help. *Don't knock it.* 'Are you sure?'

'I'm learning all kinds of new skills. Who knew I could cook bacon if I had to?'

'Are you a Muslim or something?'

'No. It's just a nod to the father I never knew.'

'The what?' Briony said.

'Ah, nothing. I'll tell you another time.' Their eyes met in the way Briony knew could open a portal into another world. A world with just them, where everything was possible and no barriers could stop them doing whatever they wanted together.

Zach huffed out a little cough and looked away. 'Shouldn't you go to...'

'Felicity. Hell yes. I should.'

'She works for a distillery, you know?'

'Yes, I do. They're sponsoring the festival and she's here to put up the advertising.'

'Do you think she knows about the stolen whisky?'

'She's never mentioned anything to me but then it isn't the kind of thing we usually talk about.'

'I guess.' Zach rubbed his stubbly cheek and sat behind the reception desk.

Briony made her way to the lounge. Felicity spun around when she came in and her lips widened into a grin. 'I like the new receptionist.'

Briony snorted. 'He's not the receptionist. He's a guest.'

'What? Why is he...?'

'Helping me out.'

'Ooh, why would he do that?' Her face filled with intrigue.

'Because he's the representative of the man who wants to buy the place.' She kept her tone neutral; she wasn't ready for Felicity to poke around too much – not when she didn't want to analyse things too closely herself.

'No! That's him? Oh wow. It looks like he's taken over already.'

'He hasn't but they're working on a package.'

'Seriously? So, the deal might go through soon?'

'Yes. I can hardly believe it.' Briony flopped into a seat. 'I thought it would be a long-drawn-out process. I didn't expect it to happen overnight. It's not given me time to fully process the ins and outs. Now that it's real, I don't know what to do next. It's like being in limbo. Both Shari and Meg want to know what's happening with their jobs. I'll have to consider where to live and what my role will look like.' With a salaried job and fully agreed hours, she'd have more time to herself and to indulge her interests, but something was lacking in being 'just the manager'. Owning the hotel felt so much more her. The summers she'd spent here as child flashed before her. The community she'd written for Missy Peck was what she wanted in real life. This hotel was meant to be a place local people could enjoy too, somewhere they could meet and socialise. The festival was a start, but what would Mr Beyer do? Would he care or prefer to turn it into an upmarket place that only the elite could afford like Donald Trump had done at Turnberry?

'Aww.' Felicity crouched beside the chair and threw her arms about Briony.

'Don't worry about it.' Briony smiled. 'My job's safe. He said I could keep it as part of the deal, so no matter what, I can fight for the hotel.'

'Yay,' Felicity said. 'I'm so glad because this place is such a local landmark and you have the vision.'

'And Daniel Beyer has the cash.'

'Perfect.'

'Let's hope so,' Briony said, slapping her thighs. 'Now, let's get on and sort this festival. Crying over spilt milk never helped anyone.' But even her inner Missy Peck felt deflated.

'I've got the banners in the car. I'll go get them.' She checked her watch. 'I thought Brann might be here by now.'

'Are you and him an item?' Briony asked.

'No,' Felicity said. 'I think he's married.'

'Is he? Oh well. I'm sure Zach would love to help you with the banners and I'll mind the desk and finish the breakfasts. Front of house isn't his forte, but I like the guests.' Most of them, if she excluded Darren.

'Send him out then,' Felicity said, opening the sliding glass door to the outside seating area and letting in a gust of cold air. 'And if Brann turns up, send him too.'

'Sure.' Briony shuddered. 'Close that or the heat will get sucked out and the guests will freeze.'

Felicity snuck out and pulled the door shut with a clunk. She waved through the glass at Briony, pulling a face and doing a huge fake shiver. The gorgeous sunshine reflecting in the loch obviously wasn't making any heat.

Briony waved back before heading into the foyer. Brann the builder had arrived and was leaning on the high part of the desk, his hair falling around his face, laughing.

And so was Zach.

'Fucking always wanted to go to that,' Brann said.

'If you can get a flight, I'll give you my ticket. I'm not going anywhere now.'

'Ah, thanks, dude. I'd love that but I've got too much work on.'

Briony caught Zach's eye before she reached the desk. The corner of his lips quirked up. Those lips she'd enjoyed kissing. And if she'd given in last night, she'd have kissed them again – in private and not for Darren's benefit. Zach's smouldering gaze fanned the fire inside her and she struggled to catch her breath.

'Hi again,' Brann said, and she flicked her attention to him. 'I've been roped into helping.'

'So I hear, thank you,' Briony said, then turned to Zach. 'And can you help Felicity put up the banners, please? You're nice and tall. You can reach the tricky places.'

'Sure. Your wish is my command.'

'I'll follow you,' Brann said.

Zach's focus strayed to the bottom of the stairs. Briony turned, following his sightline. Darren and Gemma stood hand in hand.

'Good morning,' Briony said. Why was she keeping up the false smile? If the hotel was as good as sold maybe she should just tell them exactly what she thought of them, throw them out and ban them, but she needed to stay professional in front of Brann.

'Morning,' huffed Gemma.

'I'll be out getting the banners.' Zach slipped out from behind the reception desk. 'Call me if you need me for anything. And I mean anything.' He slid his arm around Briony's waist, pulled her close and pressed a kiss on her lips. Briony's heart fluttered and her tummy swooped but it was over too fast to properly savour. Zach released her and, with a smug lift of his eyebrows, stalked past Darren and Gemma.

'How unprofessional,' Gemma muttered.

Brann whistled and clapped Zach on the shoulder as they headed into the lounge. 'Way to go, man.'

Briony's pulse hammered. Ok, bang went her image. *Thanks, Zach.* But she couldn't hide a bloom of pleasure. 'Breakfast?' She beamed and clapped her hands.

When breakfasts were finished and Briony was satisfied that all the guests were catered for and ready for their day, she nipped into the lounge. A little stage was now in situ in the corner. Many of the guests had snuck a peek in during breakfast to ogle Brann setting it up. One woman had asked if he was a stripper. Briony could see the appeal, but she only had eyes for Zach. Neither man was about and neither was Felicity.

Briony peered out of the bay window and looked out over the loch. In front of the outdoor seating area, Brann was erecting another stage and Zach seemed to be helping. They were both laughing at something and when Zach lifted the end of a wooden plank that Brann was holding, both men almost tumbled. Briony heard indistinct words and more laughing. Felicity covered her face and shook her head like whatever they'd said was either crazy or rude – possibly both.

Should she go and interfere or leave them to it? They seemed to be getting on fine. Banners now hung around the fence that enclosed the outdoor seating area. Felicity flicked her long blonde hair over her shoulders and turned. She caught Briony's eye and beckoned her.

'How's it going?' Briony asked, exiting through the French door into a bite of wind.

'Great,' Felicity said. 'Mostly. When these two stop acting like a pair of big kids.'

Brann shrugged and Zach smirked as they clicked in the final plank.

'Sorted,' Brann said, dusting off his hands. He clapped Zach on the back. 'Great job, mate.'

'No worries.'

Brann left them to go back to his 'real work' and Felicity and Zach followed Briony inside and back to the foyer, both windswept with ruddy cheeks. Zach rubbed his hands together. 'Breezy out there, but that was a good morning's work, right?'

'Brilliant,' Felicity said. 'You've earned a break.'

'Thanks.'

'Why don't you use it to let Becker out?' Briony said with a quirk of her eyebrow.

'Ok, ma'am, will do.' He flipped her a little wink and disappeared through the door into the kitchen corridor.

Felicity leaned on the desk and smiled after him. 'He's funny. In fact, the two of them, my god.' She shook her head and giggled.

'What?'

'They were talking like a pair of lunatics. They kept going on about zombies.'

Briony chuckled. 'Zach clearly thinks we're overrun out here.'

'And Brann agrees apparently.'

'Is that what they were talking about?'

'That and some other stuff they watch on TV. I was a spare part. They were having their own bromance.'

Briony giggled and her chest swelled. Sounded like Zach had made a friend. Even if it was a friend he might not see again. Just seeing him relaxed and having fun was enough – and better than scowl-faced Zach. 'Well, that's good it's all set up.'

'It's looking great.' Felicity buttoned her coat. 'And with the two of them, it was so much quicker. I should get back to work but I'll see you tomorrow night at the festival.'

'See you there.'

After Felicity had gone, Briony remembered she still hadn't found a place for Zach to stay after tonight. He might joke about sleeping on the floor with Becker, but it wouldn't be a joke at this rate. The private quarters had a spare bedroom, where she'd slept as a child, but it was now jam-packed with stuff she hadn't got round to clearing out. Irony lurked in there. At this rate, she'd be moving out without even knowing what was there. If she even braved opening the door, she usually shut it again straightaway. Her grandmother had loaded it with broken things from the hotel, so the bed and floor were no longer visible. That creeping dread of lifting something and finding a nest of maggots or a spider's lair crawled over her. She couldn't do it.

She put the "Closed" sign on the desk and nipped into the private quarters. Standing in front of the door, she dragged in a deep breath. Before she tried the handle, the main door opened.

'Right, buddy,' said Zach's voice. 'Let's get you some treats. Yes, you were a good boy. A very good boy.'

Briony smirked at his babying tones. 'Hi,' she called.

'Oh jeez, you gave me a heart attack.' Zach peered into the corridor rubbing his chest and Becker bounded towards her.

'I thought I should warn you I was here.' She clapped Becker as his tail worked overtime.

'Thanks.' Zach's dark eyes travelled down her, raising goosebumps. If she dropped the pretence, she wanted him, so badly – both to know him better and to feel his arms around her, deepen that connection they'd started and pour her soul into him. She didn't want this to end but time with Zach came with an expiry date. Was it worth stealing some moments of joy?

'You seemed to be having fun earlier,' she said.

'Yeah.' Zach smirked. 'Brann's cool. We had some stuff in common, you know?'

'Like zombies?'

'Did Felicity tell you that?'

Briony nodded with a grin.

'I reckon she'll have a sleepless night tonight, worrying they're coming for her.'

'Stop your nonsense.'

Zach laughed and his face lit up. His whole body and his movements looked more relaxed, like he was at ease – at home.

'What are you doing?' Zach stepped closer.

'I'm just trying to figure out where to put you tomorrow night.'

'And the night after and the night after and so on.'

'Exactly. You can't really sleep on Becker's bed.'

'I guess not, though he prefers the sofa, so his bed would be free.'

Briony smiled at his goofy look. 'There's a spare room in here but it's seriously overcrowded. I'm not sure I even want to open the door.'

'Can I?'

She pointed to it, her eyes briefly closing as his dreamy scent pitched into her.

He stopped outside the plain chipboard door and glanced at her with the corner of his lips curling up. His fingers took hold of the handle. 'Arrrrghhhhhh,' he yelled, rattling it like he couldn't let go and it was sending violent shockwaves up his arm.

'Oh my god.' Briony leapt out of her skin. 'What are you doing?'

He let go of the handle and took hold of her hands, throwing his head back and laughing. 'You fell for that? The oldest gag in the book.'

'You...' Briony gritted her teeth and pulled out of his grip. 'I did not fall for it. I just got a shock when you yelled. You prat.'

He carried on laughing and she shook her head, determinately looking away until she couldn't help grinning too.

'Sorry.' He peered around trying to catch her eye. 'Do you hate me now?'

She locked her gaze on him and lifted an eyebrow. 'No, but one more trick like that and you can kiss goodbye to sleeping in Becker's bed. You'll be in your car.'

'I'm sorry. I...' He lowered his head, leaning closer to her.

She glanced up and they stared at each other for a few seconds. Then, without words, they pounced at exactly the same time. He threw his arms around her and pulled her close and tight; she slung her arms around his neck and kissed him. This time no one was watching. The deep warmth of his lips was all real and tasted like fresh mint. He smelt so good and his embrace was so strong, yet gentle. With her lips slightly parted, she absorbed just enough of him to tease her nerve ends.

'I think I'm going mad.' His breath tickled her neck, waking her senses. 'Maybe it's being stuck here in a foreign place. I don't have a clue what I'm doing. My job's hanging on a thread and I'm, well, enjoying myself. With strangers and... you.'

'Us?' Briony whispered.

'Yes. You and me. Us faking being a couple to poke your ex in the eye is crazy because that wasn't fake. You can't say it was.'

'No, I can't. But what can we do about it?'

'I don't know. But you can't deny there's something there.'

'I'm not denying it. I never did. Even when I thought you'd done it for a bet, I hated you more for it because it felt so real.' She let out a sigh. 'But, Zach, how can this be more than a fling?'

He tightened his grip and placed a soft kiss below her ear. 'What if we want it to be?' he whispered, then his words seemed to dry up. 'Maybe, there's life without Mr Beyer.'

'What do you mean? We just pack it all in and run away together?'

He looked down on her and tucked a strand of hair behind her ear. 'Is that such a bad idea?'

'Maybe not.'

He gazed at her and an odd helpless expression flickered in his irises. 'I've never thought about doing anything else because I don't know what's out there. I wanna help my mom and be there for her but...' He sighed.

'Don't make any rash decisions. Let's be sensible. Why don't you think about it while you're clearing this room?' She swallowed and pulled away. His look said he'd rather spend that time with her – and she'd prefer that too. Every wall inside her was collapsing, leaving her a wobbly, desperate piece of jelly.

'Ok.' He opened the door, smirking as he turned the handle. 'Wow. This is—'

'A mess?'

'Yeah. But I can probably clear it by tomorrow night. Don't you want to oversee what I do?'

'Not really. It's all broken stuff. If you find that stolen whisky, bring it to me at once, but otherwise throw everything out.'

'Yes, ma'am.'

She tugged at her neckline and let her eyes travel over him. 'Is there anything else you need?'

'No, ma'am.' His returning stare told another story, one her throbbing heart was more interested in. One where neither of them cared if people were queueing at the front desk and where they weren't worried about future complications. They just wanted to have each other there and then.

That outcome was just too far to grasp. Briony wasn't sure how to achieve it. Like everything else in her life and her future, it was uncertain. Would hoping for an answer to present itself work? Maybe this time, she shouldn't leave it to chance. She briefly glanced at Zach before turning and leaving him to the room of lost and broken things. Who knew what he might unearth in there? If that stolen whisky turned out to be real and hidden in that bedroom, it would be like winning the lottery. But right now her heart didn't care about that whisky; all it wanted was to keep Zach close – always.

CHAPTER EIGHTEEN

Zach

Zach collapsed against the wall the second Briony was gone. Whatever was rushing through his veins was burning him. He'd turned into a madman or something had possessed him. Every atom in him wanted to possess Briony and not only that, he'd made friends. Maybe that was an overstatement but builder Brann had chatted to him like an old friend and they'd somehow got onto talking about *Star Wars*, then *The Walking Dead*. Next thing he knew, they were building the stage together and laughing with Felicity – they had definitely been laughing *with* him, not *at* him. What was it all about? An alien planet might have been easier to navigate.

'Aw, man.' Zach rubbed at his forehead. His life didn't make sense at the best of times; now it wasn't just confusing but fun too.

But that kiss. Oh boy. He wanted to carry on that kiss and take it so much further. His body was desperate. Tidying the room was exactly the kind of crappy job he needed to keep his mind off everything else. He lost track of time, throwing broken chairs and cracked ornaments out the window and building a pile of disused artefacts in the courtyard. Any hope of coming across an old cask containing a stolen whisky bottle flew out with the dust. Nothing in the room appeared remotely valuable.

Brann had taken his number and sent him about forty zombie gifs throughout the day interspersed with messages.

You're right in there with Briony

What's stopping you, man?

She's single, you're single... wink emoji, wink emoji, wink emoji

Next time I see you, you better have something to report!!!

Zach let out a snort. *Sees me?* Like that could happen. This wasn't where he belonged. He couldn't even bring himself to imagine his mom's reaction if he suggested moving here. But his grandma's words fluttered into his mind. *Be true to yourself, Zach.* Maybe all the choices he'd made thinking he was doing the right thing weren't really right for him, but he couldn't just walk away... Could he?

Hunger eventually got the better of him. He rubbed his hands together and shook out the dust from his top. The clock showed it was almost five o'clock. Where had the day gone?

He headed for the dining room. It was busy and new guests had arrived for the festival. So much for his last day here and the vacation he'd looked forward to. He sipped a cold beer, watching Briony cross the room, carrying three plates perfectly balanced on her arm. She laid them in front of the guests, then stepped back chatting and gesticulating. Whatever she was saying made them laugh and she smiled along before returning to the kitchen. Zach found himself smiling too. Briony was made for this job. Her writing was important too, but she shouldn't be shackled to one thing or the other. She should be able to have both. What if she really was sitting on a fortune?

Fuck's sake. Zach banged down the bottle. How was he supposed to find something that might not exist and what would happen if he did? Mr Beyer would sack him for sure if he handed over a precious whisky to Briony and not him. Could he live with that?

When Zach had chatted to Felicity earlier, she'd told him that in the distillery where she worked a theft had been recorded in the fifties. The distillers had a space in their collection shelf in case it turned up, but she insisted it was just a talking point on tours, a legend, rather than fact.

What had happened to the whisky? Did it exist? What the hell should he do next? Had the thief sold it to a collector on the black market years ago or was it here, hidden away? Could it be in that passageway? Or somewhere more obvious, hidden in plain sight maybe. He was free to roam the hotel these days; he could go searching. But it wouldn't just be sitting on a shelf somewhere. *How has no one ever found it before?* If that old man knew of some connection to the hotel, surely the police and the people who were investigating in the first place knew too. They must have searched the hotel if there were suspicious circumstances.

Zach pinched the bridge of his nose and massaged it. *What have I gotten myself into?* He thrust back his chair and left the room. His head ached and he needed air. He could take Becker for a quick walk and try to think and breathe.

A cold mist lingered over the loch as he walked along the path on the lower side. He reached a fork in the road with a signpost pointing to a water-sports centre and campsite on one side and a hill path on the other. 'Come on, buddy.' He gently tugged Becker and they headed back towards the hotel. Maybe tomorrow he could walk into the village and have a proper look around. What was the point of coming this far if all he was going to see was a hotel?

The wind rustled the trees above as Zach trudged back. A stag's bellow echoed from the hills above. He checked the horizon but nothing was visible in the fading light. His gaze lingered on the loch surface as mist fell lower. A bird took off, flapping its wings and making him jump. The lights twinkling in the hotel beyond were both eerie and inviting.

Becker gave Zach sad eyes as he returned him to the private quarters. 'Sorry, I can't stay, buddy. I'd like to but... Well, protocol and all that.' He still had his own room and he may as well make use of it one last time. He should give Briony space. Not that he wanted to, he'd much rather be at her side, but if he was still hanging around her quarters when she came back, they might end up talking all night... Or not talking. They might do something they really regretted. Then again, he'd been living in regret for the past five years. What if he didn't take his chance this time either?

'See you later, buddy.' He gave Becker a last pat and headed for his room.

Opening his laptop, he checked for emails or anything he'd missed from Mr Beyer but nothing new had dropped in his inbox. He toyed with his cell for a second. He should call his mom. It had been a while and if he didn't initiate contact she sure as hell wouldn't. He hit call and waited.

'Hi, Mom.'

'Hey, son.'

'How are you feeling today?'

'Ah, you know. Same old, same old. I've had an ok day though. How about you? How's Scotland? You didn't think much of it the last time. Is it any better?'

'Yeah, better this time. It's peaceful and beautiful. I'll send some photos.' He flipped through the ones he'd snapped on his walks and sent them.

'Aw, that's nice, honey. Looks cute. That rainbow, wow. And is that the hotel, the pink place?'

'Sure is.'

'I like it,' she said. 'It's got character.'

'Yeah.'

'And is Dan interested in it?'

Zach half rolled his eyes, hoping his mom never met Mr Beyer. She had an irritating habit of calling him Dan. Zach didn't like to imagine her sidling up to his boss and talking to him like they were old friends. The work world of Zacharias Somerton shouldn't ever be allowed to collide with his private one. They were two separate entities from parallel dimensions.

'Yeah, he's interested, though I'm not sure if his motives are good.'

'Why not?'

'I'm not allowed to talk about it. I just wish I could help the owner.'

'How? You don't have that much money.'

'I know that.' He hadn't missed the panicky note in his mom's voice. 'There might a way, but it depends on so many things.' An old rumour being true to start off with, then proving it was true, finding the whisky, attempting to claim it as finders keepers or treasure trove, having it valued, selling it on and hopefully making enough money to cover the hotel renovations. All of which would be easy for Mr Beyer once he'd bought the hotel. He could draft in a team of archaeologists and investigators to search for the precious whisky. Briony couldn't do any of that. What if she found it and it was handed back to the distillery?

'Son, I hope you're not playing with fire. Do your job and keep Dan happy. It's not up to you to help the owner.'

'Yeah, that's true, but...' He swallowed. 'I like her.'

Silence. He cringed. Why had he said that?

'Like her? In what way?' Mom's voice was loaded, edging on menacing. For someone petite and kindly in looks, she could be a wasp when she wanted and her sting hurt if she used it.

'You know,' he quipped in a non-committal tone.

'I'm not sure I do. You mean in a boy likes girl way or professionally?'

'A bit of both.'

'Oh, son. A love affair in a foreign country? That sounds crazy and not at all like you.'

'I didn't say it was a love affair.' But his heart spiked at the word. He didn't love people after a few days. He didn't usually love people at all. He loved films and books, stories and things he could quantify. Not people. People were changeable and difficult to get to know. But when he talked to Briony and kissed her, he felt easy around her.

'I'm happy for you, son, if it is. You deserve to find someone too. I just wish it was someone a bit closer. These long-distance things never work out and it'd be sad to have you so far away.'

'Stop, Mom. You're cantering away ahead of yourself. I can't stay here.' Saying the words out loud was like bringing down an axe and splitting the last heartstring clinging to a dream. A dream he'd abandoned years ago and never thought he'd find again. Now it had grown like the seed of an idea for one of his books. And Briony was at the core.

By midday the next day, Friday, Zach had cleared enough of the bedroom to see the bed. Screwing up his nose, he lifted the dusty cover and sat on the mattress. Springs jabbed into his backside. He let out a sigh. Not quite as comfy as the Bonnie Prince Charlie suite then. Briony would provide clean linen, but this mattress was beyond saving. Lots of cushions? Rough it as punishment for the unnamed crimes he must have committed somewhere to have been sent here? Well, if that had been Mr Beyer's goal, it had backfired. Mostly. The torture now was not being able to act the way his heart wanted to with Briony. And, yeah, that was Daniel Beyer's fault but not by design.

Now at least he'd cleared space to put the luggage he'd dumped in the corridor. Not that he had much. He'd packed for a few days stay, not an indefinite one. Briony was busy with the festival and he kept out of her way. 'I'm being a good boy,' he told Becker. He wanted to see her, just not get under her feet. This was the job she'd given him and he should put in his best effort.

Becker sniffed around the musty old room, maybe picking up half-forgotten scents belonging to his old owner. Outside, a background hum of music had started, soft and whimsical, in perfect harmony with the environment. It told of vast glassy lochs, tall pines swaying in the breeze, purple mountains towering around and stags strutting through the heather. Zach perched on the bed edge, stroking Becker. The music was about people too. Hardy people who'd worked this land for many years and had big hearts, passion and love for their homeland, their family and their culture. Briony was one of them. She hadn't been close to her grandmother but she had a passion to bring the hotel back to life. How sad that money was the obstacle to her dream. And his; if his mom was able to afford her own healthcare, he could think about moving on, maybe finding a job doing something he cared about, not bumbling along in the first thing that had come up.

'Let's go listen.' He pulled on his jacket and clipped Becker onto the leash. Leaves swirled around the courtyard as he tramped towards the loch. The outdoor seating area where he'd hung the banners was now full of people, drinking in the afternoon sunlight as they watched a male and female duo on a small stage. The man played the guitar and the woman sang a folk ballad with a perfectly clear voice. The mountains reflected in the loch behind, creating a stunning backdrop to the act. Zach watched for a few moments, transfixed.

An invisible force broke his reverie and tugged his vision back to the seating. Briony had appeared with a tray of drinks. She set it in front of a couple. Darren and Gemma. 'Come on.' Zach steered Becker towards the path to the village. If Darren caught Zach skulking about listening to the music while Briony was rushed off her feet, it didn't make him look like a great boyfriend – fake or not. As he walked, he tried to imagine this scenario back home. How would it be if Briony was a girl from Louisville, maybe someone from around the block? Would he have the courage to do anything about it?

He didn't understand long-distance relationships. The communication across time zones would be tricky to start with and how did the physical side of things work? He didn't like the idea of sexy on-screen encounters. He ruffed up his hair. No thanks. Now he was being as bad as his mother for running ahead ten stages.

Strolling along the path beside the road, he looked around, trying to commit everything to memory. Photos and films didn't do it justice. They couldn't capture the place's essence and heart. People passed him in the other direction, chatting and laughing as they headed towards the festival.

A few houses appeared to his left, low bungalows with white walls and the luck of being at the edge of the town where the trees grew behind them. A little purple bus swished by on the road, carrying more festival goers. Buildings continued on the left and a large signpost with Welcome to Glenbriar proclaimed the official start of the town. On the opposite side of the road were some nineteenth-century houses, most of which were advertising as B&Bs. Streets cut off the main road to more shops with apartments above, some of them with mullioned windows. Parked cars lined the main street and the businesses had posters in their windows advertising the festival. Twinkling amber lights glowed from inside a coffee shop and some creepy

Halloween decor hung around the windows like wispy spirits and spider webs. A cute furniture shop called Wood 'n' Chic had a table covered in multicoloured squashes and gourds in weird shapes and all sizes. Next door was a gift store with a display of old crates covered with every whisky imaginable as well as Scottish gins and liqueurs. Zach peered in and his reflection blended with the display. Mr Beyer would appreciate this more than he did.

So this was a Scottish small town.

He continued to where the main road opened into a small square with a fountain. Black old-fashioned streetlights surrounded the area and autumn-coloured bunting was looped between them. He pulled out his cell and took some photos and a couple of selfies with Becker to send his mom. Becker cosied in and nuzzled him as Zach crouched next to him.

'You big crazy thing.' He grinned as he flipped his cell into his back pocket. 'Now let's get the hell back to the hotel and see what we're missing.'

'Excuse me,' said a gruff voice.

Zach turned to see a large man with crooked teeth eyeing him. 'Hey. Can I help you?'

'Is that your dog?' asked the man. 'It looks like Becker.'

'Oh, yeah,' Zach said. 'This is Becker. I'm just walking him to help Briony.'

'You know Briony, aye?'

'Sure. I'm... working with her.'

'Really?' the man said. 'I'm Malcolm, by the way. It's good to know Briony's getting some help. I've been very concerned about what might happen to the hotel. It's been part of our community for a long time. Hilda wasn't an easy person to get on with, but the locals were loyal and used to love nipping along to the hotel. I think she ran up a fair few debts in her old age. Went a bit loopy, if you get my drift.'

Zach kept his mouth shut. This man clearly liked the sound of his own voice.

'I grew up with her kids, Robert, that's Briony's dad, you know? And Lottie. Couldn't wait to get away, the pair of them. Never thought either of them would be back, so it's great to have Briony taking the helm. Too many of these country hotels are being taken over by foreigners who charge so much the locals can't afford a pint. When she started cutting back and stopped opening the bar to non-residents, I was concerned. I'm chairman of the Glenbriar Community Group and we discussed a community buyout but decided it wasn't viable, so we didn't mention it to Briony.'

Zach tried to pull a Briony-style fake smile, though ended up gritting his teeth. Maybe this man didn't recognise a Kentucky accent when he heard one. *Here stands a foreigner and one who may yet take over your world given a spaceship or a laser gun.*

'Aye, tell her I was asking for her anyway.'

'Sure,' Zach said, though he wasn't sure what that meant. 'You don't know anything about stolen whisky, do you?'

'How do you mean?'

'I'm not sure. I just heard a story... On the, er, distillery tour.'

'Pa. Just nonsense the Sinclairs made up to tell the tourists. More money than sense that family. They've exploited workers for years and their whisky's terrible too.'

'Er, right. So nothing happened when you were a child to make you think the story could be real?'

He shook his head. 'Don't believe everything you hear around here. We'll have you believing in the monster next.'

'Yeah. I kinda already do.'

Shari was doing an extra shift, having swapped her cleaning tunic for a black server's outfit. Zach avoided making eye contact. The fact she'd burst in on him naked wasn't forgotten. The dining room was buzzing and a small band warmed up in the corner of the lounge. The old lamps shone brighter and everything was more alive than ever. Would Mr Beyer keep any of this? His plans would be exactly the thing Malcolm and his community group dreaded. Daniel Beyer would gut the hotel, find the whisky if it existed and make the place so modern and exclusive the locals couldn't afford to even look at it. He'd probably ban them from walking in front of the loch directly in front of the hotel and who knew what else. But one thing was sure, it would ruin the place.

Zach returned Becker to the private quarters, then snuck into the dining room to grab some food. Briony was nowhere to be seen. Zach ate his meal, keeping an eye on the gigs in the lounge. It was an open-mic session and who happened to get up on stage but Brann. Zach goggled as he strummed a guitar and sang none too badly. He had a rough edge to his voice, but it worked.

The tables and chairs were pulled back and made a small dance floor. Guests danced enthusiastically, often bumping into each other, and Brann quirked his lopsided grin as he sang.

Zach pushed back his chair to watch properly, then spotted Darren dancing with some random woman and Gemma at a nearby table sucking orange juice through a straw with pouty lips and a sour expression. At the door, Briony came in and pushed back her hair. It looked less kempt than usual and her cheeks were rosy. Zach's heart leapt to her, dragging him up with it. He darted towards her.

'Hey.' He put his arm around her shoulder. With Darren and Gemma close by, he was allowed. Hopefully, they hadn't spied him eating dinner while his 'girlfriend' was rushed off her feet.

'Hi.' She bristled for a second, but the effort seemed to zap her last ounce of energy and she yielded with a sigh, leaning her head on his chest. 'I'm so exhausted.'

A different performer took over the mic and struck up a slow waltz on the accordion.

'Come and dance,' Zach said.

'Dance? I don't have time—'

'Just one. For five minutes tops. Come on. You're allowed some fun too.'

'Am I?

'Sure you are. Come on.'

She glanced up and smiled. 'Ok. Why not.'

He slipped his fingers around her waist and drew her into him. This was where he needed her. Right up against him. She placed her hand on his shoulder and clasped the other in his. Together, they moved slowly on the spot. Zach caught Darren's eyes and he smirked, tugging Briony even closer. She was his. He was the stag with the biggest antlers now and no one was getting close to his girl.

'That's my boy.' A hand slapped Zach on the shoulder. Brann walked passed and winked at him before heading to a table in the corner.

Briony rolled her eyes but Zach smirked. 'I walked to the village this afternoon. It's bigger than I thought,' he said, choosing to ignore Brann.

'People always call it the village,' Briony said. 'But it's more like a town.'

'I met a guy called Malcolm. He thought I'd stolen Becker.'

'Oh him. He's such a busybody. He likes to know everything about everyone and he's got his finger in every pie, but I'm not sure about him. I get a funny vibe from him.'

'He doesn't like foreigners, that's for sure. Though I'm not sure he worked out that I am one.'

Briony giggled. 'He would have known, Zach. But that's Malcolm's way of saying something unpleasant and trying to make it look unoffensive.'

'Ah, ok. I get it. Apart from him, the town was real cute. Everything around here is real cute. Especially you.'

'Zach,' she muttered.

'What?' He rubbed his cheek against hers. 'I missed you all day.'

'You're going to have to get used to missing me.'

'I guess. Unless you fancy getting a job in Louisville.'

'Maybe I should think about doing something out of the box like that. Maybe a clean break is what I need.'

Zach kept her close, wanting to enjoy the moment, but also trying to analyse the implications of what she'd said, all while ignoring Brann's grin, but feeling quite pleased about it nonetheless.

As the song came to an end, he dipped in and placed a kiss on Briony's lips, closing his eyes as he sank into the familiar warmth. She responded gently, opening her mouth to him and they stayed lightly joined at the lips as the outro played. Someone – Zach could guess who – wolf-whistled but he ignored it. If only they could spin around movie style and when they broke apart everyone would be gone, leaving them alone to do as they pleased. The barriers would fall away and they could waltz into the sunset.

CHAPTER NINETEEN

Briony

Briony's eyes were closed. When Zach gently ended the kiss, she didn't want to open them. Her lips burned to make contact with his again but she couldn't legitimately stand still and block out the world any longer.

Slowly she blinked her eyes open and instantly linked gazes with Zach. His smile was warm and his irises glossy, brimming with an expression that toppled directly into her heart. He lowered his head for a second, still holding her tight. 'That was wild.'

She leaned into him, pressing her forehead against his chest. 'Who whistled? One of the guests?'

'Brann.'

'Oh. Your friend.' She glanced into the corner where Brann sat with some friends. He raised a bottle of beer towards them and smirked.

'Yeah.'

Breaking away from Zach was like a cold wind blasting her far from home. Perhaps to Louisville? That could be the answer. Leave everything here for a new adventure. She glanced at her fingers, suddenly warm. Zach had linked them with his and was toying with them, perhaps wondering if he should hold her hand. Briony was about to grasp it when she caught sight of two people close to the kitchen door. Meg and Shari, both still holding empty plates, their eyes wide. *Oh my god, no.* Meg's mouth was open while Shari's bottom lip was clamped beneath her teeth. What must they make of this? *If I was in their shoes or had seen one of them carrying on like that... Shit.* If roles were reversed, she'd have to reprimand them. *Oh hell.* She'd done it again.

'I need to go.' Damage limitation measures were required and fast.

'Sure.' Zach let her go and raked up his hair.

'While your lazy-arsed boyfriend sits in the corner and has another dinner?' said a snidey voice. Bloody Darren.

'Shut up,' she said. 'We're allowed time off.'

'Ooh, listen to you,' he said. 'Not so Miss Professional now, are we?'

'She said shut up.' Zach folded his arms and stared at Darren.

'Ignore him,' Briony said. 'He's not worth it. Would you mind the desk for a bit? Or go and chat to Brann, anything.'

'Sure.'

She almost shoved him away, then beelined for Meg and Shari. Perhaps they thought she was going to give them a rollocking because Meg edged backwards into the kitchen and Shari grabbed an empty plate from a nearby table and followed her in.

'Hey.' Briony marched into the kitchen and closed the door. The heat hit her like a wall. Her palms were clammy. Neither Meg or Shari looked at her. 'I know what just happened must have seemed odd.'

Meg kept her back turned, loading the dishwasher. Shari nodded in a *you could say that* kind of way.

'There's nothing to worry about.' Briony put her hands together, almost praying they believed her. 'That was just fake.'

Shari shook her head, glancing away with a face that said *I wasn't born yesterday.*

'Really. It was.' Briony cringed at her tone of voice. How defensive did she sound? 'I didn't tell you this, but a couple of days ago, my ex-husband checked in. He's the twat in room twelve.'

Shari's incredibly expressive face now said *So what? It wasn't him you were kissing.*

Briony wished she would say the words out loud. The silent treatment was worse. Maybe she deserved it.

'Zach was there when Darren was being... Well, horrible. And he pretended we were together to keep Darren off my back. It's just a front.'

'Ok,' Shari said.

'Good.'

Meg didn't turn around. The atmosphere was heavy with unspoken words. Only the thinnest veil of professionalism was holding it back; it might burst any second. That kiss hadn't looked fake and they all knew it.

Shari grabbed a cloth and a spray bottle.

Briony clenched her teeth. How many times had she told Shari guests were off-limits? 'This is just fake, I assure you...' This didn't sound convincing at all. Briony had broken her own rules and she was playing with fire. Zach wasn't just a hot guy she liked the look of. He was a good guy who she liked for who he was inside. Something had drawn her to him long ago and fate had given her this second chance. His company made her happy and she wanted more, but how could she have it? Unless she did something drastic. And how could she explain that to Meg and Shari when it sounded crazy?

'I should clear the rest of the tables,' Shari said, edging past. 'Then I need to go.'

'Of course. Thanks for doing the extra hours.'

'No problem.' But her gritted teeth said otherwise. Obviously being set to work extra while her boss fooled around on the dance floor with a guest wasn't to her liking. And who could blame her?

With a tightness in her chest, Briony left the kitchen and helped clear up. For someone who usually spent every free second chatting and gossiping, Shari was icily quiet. When the last act finished up and the last guests left, Briony told her and Meg to go home. Not so much a gesture of kindness but a need to free herself from their silent judgement.

Midnight had come and gone by the time everyone had left the bar and Briony turned off the lights. Zach was still at the desk, resting his head in his hands and yawning.

'You didn't have to stay here.'

He blinked and looked up. 'I was chatting to Brann. He'll mix up Darren's face if you want him to.'

'Seriously?'

'Yeah. And I'm gonna help.'

'I'd rather you didn't. Don't lower yourself to his level.'

'I won't really. I let out Becker too. He's all ok for the night. When I came back, I didn't want to leave you on your own, not when that dick was hanging around.'

She let out a slow sigh. 'I'm so tired and... I've upset Meg and Shari.'

'I saw them leaving. They didn't look happy. Is it because of me?'

'Yup. Not you personally but they caught us on the dance floor and they're refusing to believe it's fake.'

'Well, we don't really believe that anymore either, do we?'

'No... We don't.' She linked eyes with him.

He got to his feet and shook his head. 'Let's make it real.'

'How?'

'You like me, right?'

'Yes, Zach.' She couldn't help laughing. He was like a puppy. 'I do like you.'

'Good, because I like you. A lot.'

'That's sweet but it doesn't change the facts.'

'Yeah. I know, life's not fantasy.'

'Exactly and I live here, you live in Kentucky. I'm five years older than you. A cougar, remember?'

'What?' He shook his head. 'No, no, I didn't mean that. Hell no, I just meant the animal. I don't care what age you are. And I lied, you don't look thirty-three, you look younger. Not that it even matters because I like you anyway.'

'Oh, Zach.' She rubbed her cheeks. 'I'm too exhausted to think. I need to go to bed.'

'Can I go with you?'

'What? You cleared your own bed, didn't you?'

'Yeah, but I can't sleep in it. It's got springs coming through the mattress and the sheets are mouldy.'

'Why didn't you tell me earlier?'

'I forgot. And anyway...' He sidled up to her and ran his fingers down her arms. 'I'd rather be with you.'

'But, Zach...'

'I don't wanna waste a second. It's like I'm going to bleed out every time you're out of sight.' He dipped in and kissed her cheek, lingering there and exhaling gently on her neck.

'Oh god, Zach.' She held her breath as his warm lips lingered on her skin. 'I feel the same. I just don't know.'

'Don't know if you want to?'

'Don't know if I should.'

He slipped his hands under her arms and pulled her close. She could feel exactly how much he wanted her. 'No one has ever got to me the way you do,' he whispered. 'I wanted you the first time around, and I'm not asking you to do this so I get out of sleeping in a mouldy spiked bed. I wanna do this because I really, really like you.'

She ground against him with a moan. Why was she resisting? Her body was ready. 'Let's go.'

Giggling between kisses, they backed along the passageway, teasing down zips and unfastening buttons. As she pushed open the door to the private quarters and switched on the light, Zach pulled off his t-shirt.

'You're so fit.' He wasn't a bodybuilder but he was trim and it was nice to be allowed to look properly this time, with a view to handling the goods.

He pulled a Popeye pose. 'I've been known to work out.' He kissed her softly, his hands at her hips, then slowly inched her dress up over her body, breaking the kiss for just a second as he pulled it over her head and dropped it on the floor. He nodded in appreciation before gliding his arms around her again. 'Beautiful, so beautiful.' The skin-on-skin heat burned straight to her core, fuelling her kisses until they were frenzied and desperate.

Who cared if it was almost one in the morning? Just another item to add to the week's catalogue of craziness. Zach slipped his fingers under the strap of her bra and eased it over her shoulder. It had been a while since she'd been with anyone. She groaned and rubbed closer.

'Hey,' Zach said, his voice muffled against her lips. 'I want this. I really do, but I didn't come on this trip thinking I was gonna be, you know, doing this with anyone. I'm not exactly prepared protection-wise.'

'I seem to remember a similar issue before.'

'Yeah, and I haven't learned, have I? I guess I should have thought about it before I suggested it, but this is the kind of fool you're dealing with.'

Briony rested her forehead on his. 'Zach, you really are a case.'

'Yeah. Sorry. I guess I've ruined the moment again.'

'Not this time. Hang tight.' She grabbed a long coat from the rack and shoved it on over her knickers.

'Where the hell are you going? You can't go all the way to the drugstore. Is it even open this late?'

'Don't be silly. You saw the village. It's not exactly a twenty-four-hour kind of place. Get into bed. I'll be back in five. There's a handy machine in the restaurant bathroom.'

He ran his hand over his mouth, covering his grin. 'You're amazing.'

'Five minutes,' she said. Christ. Never would she have thought she'd have to use the machine in her own hotel so she could sleep with a guest – not just a guest but one who could shape her future. Even as she put in the coins with shaky fingers, she wasn't sure she was doing the right thing. Her brain was sending her warnings, but her body was too far gone to listen. She needed to be back with Zach, his lips on hers and his hands...

'Touch me now,' she murmured as she hopped into bed beside him. 'Please.'

'Yes, ma'am.' He rolled her over, gliding his palms across her sensitive skin, waking the nerve ends and teasing them. Finding her hips, he slipped his fingers under the waistband of her knickers. Slowly, he slid them off, shuffling down the bed so he could remove them. His gaze found hers in the dark and he hesitated for a second before leaning in and taking her nipple into his mouth.

'Ohhhh, Zach.' She could hardly breathe. He half laughed against her sensitive skin, sending vibrations zinging to her core and she groaned. His hand moved slowly up between her thighs and he shifted up the bed so his mouth found hers again. His woody scent intoxicated her and she let out a moan.

He pulled back, so they were eye to eye, lying next to each other. 'I've wanted to do this for five years,' he said.

'Me too.' She ran her fingertip over his stubbly cheek. 'I can't believe we're finally here.'

Zach slid his fingers to her most sensitive spot, kissing her again as he did. The build-up of the last few days piled into the moment and it took him only a little time to coax her to the edge. Then the climax ripped through her so suddenly she hurtled into oblivion and cried out. 'Oh god, Zach!'

Her heartrate and breathing slowly returned to normal and he took his hands from her. The loss of heat was like a cooling breeze.

'Let's see if I can do this without any major hiccups,' he muttered.

Briony grinned as she heard the tear of foil. 'Oh, Zach, you're cute. I have every faith in you. But I can help if you like.'

'No need. We're all good.'

She reached for his hand and pulled him close. 'You're a superstar.'

'It's all for you.' He tucked her hair behind her ears as he knelt between her legs.

Briony melted at his touch. Vague wonderings of how things might be between them in the morning vanished as he moved on top of her. His palms cupped her bottom, pulling her close and she wrapped her legs around his waist until his hard body was against hers. 'Sorry if I'm a little nervous. It goes with the territory for me.' He kissed her neck softly.

'It's ok, Zach. You don't seem nervous to me. Just pretty damn hot.'

He grinned, kissing her deeply. She stroked his face and pulled him tighter against her.

'Are you sure?' he said. 'I know it's late and—'

'I want this, Zach.'

He didn't need any further encouragement and pushed gently inside her. She coiled her arms round him, clasping him to her.

He moved slowly, gazing into her eyes. The tenderness took her breath away. She'd never experienced anything quite like it. Darren had liked to get the job done quickly, sometimes roughly, and to his satisfaction – rarely hers. Zach dipped his head and kissed her, his hunger for her unmasked. 'Oh, Briony, you're gorgeous,' he groaned, devouring her sighs and gasps with his mouth. She closed her eyes as he moved deeper inside. He smiled against her lips, increasing in speed as he took her over the edge once more and she lost herself within his arms.

CHAPTER TWENTY

Zach

Z ach usually regretted morning afters. Not that he'd experienced too many. They were generally pretty cringeworthy and he couldn't be sure he'd done the right thing. When he woke this time, a smirk still played on his lips and his chest swelled with contentment. Briony had enjoyed herself as much as him. He hadn't been too nervy or nerdy, grumpy or reticent. This was the first time he'd been with someone and felt real, uninhibited... and happy. The first time he'd met Briony, he'd felt a seismic shift to the status quo and the sensation was back. He was finally starring in his own life, and he liked it.

'You don't have to get up,' Briony said, slamming her straighteners into a drawer.

Unfortunately, with her crazy early rises, it was like they'd just got to sleep when she had to get up again. Why hadn't he listened to reason last night and waited? But for what? And until when? Briony didn't have time off – ever, it seemed. And he couldn't wait another five years on the off chance they'd meet again and circumstances would be different.

'I can walk Becker and do anything you need me to.'

'If you're sure.'

He jumped out of bed and took hold of her before she left the room. 'I am sure. And I'm sure about you and how I feel about you.'

'Oh, jeez, Zach. We don't have time to unpick that tangled mess.'

'My feelings aren't a mess, just the situation surrounding them. I don't want to act like last night never happened. I enjoyed it too much.'

'Me too but...' She put her arms around his neck and he dropped into her embrace, welcoming it as a hug he'd needed for a long time. 'We can talk later, ok?'

'Yeah. Let's do that.' He kissed her cheek, lingering as long as he could. 'I don't wanna say goodbye. We've only scratched the surface of what we could have.'

'I agree. We need some kind of plan.'

After she left, he fixed himself some strong coffee and slumped onto the sofa. 'I could get addicted to this stuff,' he told Becker. 'I've gone from not liking it to needing it in the space of a week. Bit like I've grown to like you, buddy. And Briony. I really like her.' Becker shuffled up closer, lifting his front paw so Zach could scratch his tummy. 'I've gone soft. Maybe I've always been a bit soft. I just didn't meet the right person to be soft on before.' Love wasn't something he'd had much exposure to.

Now he had to find a way of doing this while still keeping his job and looking after his mom. Apart from the half idea that Briony might come to Louisville, nothing new slapped him in the face. The opposite. His head was heavy and full of fluff. He wasn't sure he'd checked his emails at all the day before. Wouldn't it be just the thing to miss something urgent?

After coffee, he was up to facing his laptop but nothing new from Mr Beyer had dropped into his inbox. The shouty caps email about his need for confidentiality was still at the top. He slammed the laptop lid shut. *Too late, Mr B, I've screwed that one up already.* 'Come on, Becker. Let's go walkies.'

Rain had fallen overnight and droplets clung to the almost bare branches. A few colourful leaves held on for dear life but one or two more sharp gusts and they'd fall too. The glory of the season was passing. A tug at Zach's heartstrings made him yearn to know this place all year round. He stopped on the damp path and picked his way through the bracken to the lochside. Becker bounded through and straight into the water. Zach breathed the clean calm air. What would this view be like when the hills were capped with snow? And when birdsong started again and the trees blossomed? What glories would be reflected come summer when the sky was bright and the hills lush and green? 'I wish I could stay and see for myself.' But how would that work?

He ambled around the pebbly shore, lifting stray branches and launching them into the water. Becker bounded after them. As well as the fantasy fear of meeting a herd of walkers crashing through the undergrowth, he now had to battle visions of a monstrous head bursting out of the loch and swallowing Becker. Parking himself on a boulder, Zach opened his cell and dictated some thoughts. He could write a whole series called *Legends of the Loch*. Fantastical creatures came to life and he visualised kelpies charging through the water ready to take on the monster and selkies shimmying out, slipping off their sealskins and luring the hero in to follow them.

The most beautiful one looked like Briony, all rosy-fleshed, rising like the Venus de Milo, running her fingertips over her perfectly rounded breasts, water droplets shimmering on her like glitter. A sound like a moan and gasp jolted him upright. He cleared his throat. Was that sound in his imagination too? A rustling of branches nearby caught his attention and he stood. Was someone in there?

'Come on, Becker.' He stooped and grabbed a branch, then heaved it into the water ahead.

He walked on a few metres, keeping Becker way ahead with sticks, then nipped behind a tree and glanced back. Darren swaggered onto the pebbly shore where Zach had just been. *Dick*. Maybe he was having a snoop to find out why Zach was always skiving off. It must appear like that. Instead of messing around with Becker and fluffing his brain with Selkie-Briony, he should get back and help her. His gaze returned to the pebbles and he gaped at the woman who had followed Darren out.

That wasn't Gemma. It didn't even look like the woman he'd been dancing with the night before. What kind of a man-whore was this guy? *Scumbag*. Where did he get off behaving like that when his girlfriend was pregnant? At all in fact. Shaking his head, Zach made his way back to the path. As soon as Becker joined him, he clipped him onto the leash. 'It's for your own good. Don't look at me like that. I'll give you some treats when we get back.'

From the path it was too steep to see onto the shore where Darren had chosen to take his friend. Probably just as well. Zach didn't want to see or know what was going on. *What I don't know can't come back to bite when shit hits the fan.*

Once Becker was safely back on the sofa with a treat, Zach headed for reception. Apart from Briony at the desk, it was empty.

'Hey.' Zach inched behind her and put his hands on her shoulders as she sat at the computer.

'Hi.' She tilted her head so the side of her face rubbed his arms and he gently massaged her.

'I missed you.'

'I'm right here,' she said.

'I know.' He took a deep breath.

'Zach, I need to work.'

'You work too hard.'

'I found some documents on the computer,' she said. 'Created by you I guess.'

'Oh that.' Heat burned Zach's cheeks. He'd spent the previous evening at the reception typing up the local histories he'd learned. 'I thought it might be something you'd like in the rooms for the guests to read. You know, real history, not Bonnie Prince Charlie woz here after some battle long ago.'

Briony chuckled. 'You're quite right.'

'This place is crying out to have its myths and legends brought to life. The hotel has romance, fantasy and history all in one.'

'Thank you.' She got to her feet. 'Come here.' Grabbing his hand, she pulled him into the cupboard behind the desk.

'We're not going to...' He raised his eyebrows. 'In here?' His visions from the loch restarted. Briony's grey sheath dress was a little too seal-like. If she stepped out of it... Hell, he wouldn't be able to control himself. It was already a struggle.

'Well, it's risky. But—' She stared at him for a split second. He couldn't say who moved first, but her lips met his. Without taking his mouth off her, he cupped her bottom, raising her dress and lifting her. She wrapped her legs around his waist and he drove her up against the shelf of boxes; they rattled and clinked like they were full of old china or glassware.

Her sweet daisy scent and the taste of strawberry lip balm were driving him crazy. If this was risky, he didn't care.

A bell jingled beyond the door and Briony pushed him away, flapping at him to put her down. He lowered her to the floor and she whipped down her dress, flattening it out with a look of shock, like he'd lured her here. He tilted his head. *You started it!* She narrowed her eyes but smirked as she left the cupboard.

'How can I help you?'

Zach sagged against the wall. How could she be so calm? She really was the front of house mistress.

Best way to cool off was to douse himself in cold water, second-best way to check his emails. He pulled out his cell and scrolled, sighing at the name Daniel Beyer. Great. What now? Package info? At the weekend?

A quick update. I've been chatting to some people in the know and the price of those whiskies could be off the charts. I'm also having my lawyers look into Scottish legislation to make sure any bottles found on my property are legally mine. I'm not going to all this trouble to find out that distillery can demand them back. They seem to think if over fifty years have passed then I should be covered. And there's something about an indemnity clause that we might need.

Also, I'm going to have to let Mrs Dalgleish go. She's too much of a liability on the premises. From the advice I got, it would be better if the bottles aren't discovered until after I take over. I DO NOT want you to look any more in case she gets suspicious. Just hang tight and keep her sweet but don't let on a single thing about the bigger picture! I hope I've made that clear.

More than. Zach grimaced and moved the email into a work folder. He wanted to delete it. Horrible images of Briony finding his phone and reading that message plagued his brain. What the hell did he do now? Briony's best bet would be to walk away from this deal but that wouldn't solve her cash flow problems.

From the reception he was aware of an odd sound. He'd thought it was someone chatting, but it was too loud and agitated. Kind of like crying. The crack between the door and the frame was too narrow to see anything through and he didn't want to push it. No one needed to know Briony hadn't been alone in the cupboard. This situation was heavy with déjà vu.

The sound slowly died away and Zach peeked out. Briony was gone. The lounge door clicked open and Zach leapt back into the cupboard.

'Zach.' Briony's voice snapped in sharp whisper.

He peeked around again. 'What?'

'Can you mind the desk, please? You won't believe the irony of this. I've got Gemma Warden in there crying because she thinks Darren's run off with someone else.'

Zach half closed his eyes. 'I can see the irony, but she's not wrong.'

'What?'

'I saw him just now. Down at the shore with someone.'

Briony tossed her head back and stared at the ceiling. 'I so don't need this.'

Zach sat at the desk and tapped it. Never a dull moment around here.

CHAPTER TWENTY-ONE

Briony

G emma huddled in one of the comfy seats by the empty fire, sniffing and wiping her eyes. Briony approached, keeping her footfalls soft in case the proverbial eggshells smashed – which seemed likely. The makeshift stage in the corner stood empty, waiting for the evening's entertainment, reminding Briony of her dance with Zach, and subsequent events. She yawned involuntarily and quickly pushed her hand over her mouth. Lack of sleep wouldn't be a worthy excuse if Gemma caught her.

What to say? No point in asking if she was ok. Obviously she wasn't. Even sympathising felt like slapping her when she was down. If anyone was aware of Darren's inability to keep it in his pants, it was Briony. She'd suffered that for long enough. There were others long before the one that finished them, she knew that now, and she'd suspected at the time, but she'd lived in denial about so many things. The tweed green cushions on the seat opposite Gemma were saggy and threadbare – much like everything else. Briony picked one up and tried to box it into shape, then sat. Should she tell Gemma she was better off without a twat like Darren in her life? Nope. That wouldn't work. The poor woman was pregnant. She'd presumably dreamed of bringing up the baby in a family. Now she was heading for life as a single parent unless she was very forgiving or had the same level of blindness as Briony had had.

And who am I to advise? She was happier without Darren, but financially, definitely not. She hated the idea of needing a man to be financially secure, but two incomes were always going to be better than one – unless she won the lottery, and she'd asked the universe for that too many times without any success.

'I, er, I'm not sure what to say.' Honesty seemed the best policy.

'I want to know where he is.' Gemma made claws with her hands, displaying bright-pink acrylic nails with very sharp points. 'Ugh. He said he was going for a walk but I don't know why I couldn't go too. I'm pregnant, not crippled. I can walk. But he thinks it's too much for me. It's getting really suss, especially after that dancing incident last night. And he was flirting with someone at dinner earlier in the week.' She glared at Briony. 'He has no idea how it feels to be pregnant, and he just doesn't seem to care half the time. It's not like it's my fault. It takes two, you know.'

'Hmm, yes.' But try telling that to an egocentric bastard like Darren. He could never see past the end of his nose and if he was ever pleasant or charming, it was because he wanted something for himself. Oh, the delights of hindsight.

'Plus I get the feeling he only wanted to come up here to see you. He's been obsessed since he saw some article in a magazine at work. Before he got sacked, the idiot.'

'Pardon? He got sacked?'

'Last month. He wanted to leave anyway.'

'Wow, what happened?'

Gemma narrowed her eyes. 'I'm not telling you. My family have enough to support us, so it's not like we'll starve.'

'Lucky you.' But Briony wouldn't have been surprised if he'd been caught with his hand in the till once too often or taking liberties with guests. 'Well, I don't know why he wanted to come here. But, rest assured, it wouldn't be for any kind of romantic reason. It would be so he could crow over me or because he wanted something.' Though if it was the last one, then he was out of luck, because she'd been reduced to almost nothing and if Gemma's family were well off... said it all really.

'He was pissed that you dumped him and said this would show you what you'd lost after you cheated on him.'

Briony choked on a non-existent crumb. She held her fist to her mouth unable to form a reply. What? 'Look, I wasn't going to say any of this, but I am now because I absolutely never saw anyone else when we were married. He knows I...' She stopped herself. He knew she'd been unprofessional with Zach at The Gladstone, but she definitely wasn't seeing Darren then; she'd barely noticed him before that. 'Well, he obviously knows about mistakes I made in the past but none of them involved me cheating on him. But he did it to me. I'd say your suspicions are spot on. Zach was down by the loch walking Becker and saw Darren with someone else.'

'I bloody knew it.' Gemma's face turned scarlet. 'I will kill him.' She jumped to her feet.

'I can sympathise but, honestly, he's not worth the effort.'

'No? Thing is, if I leave him, I'll still have to see him because of the baby. I can't keep him out of our lives forever. He has rights. But I never want to see him again. I can't believe this. But he's done for. Everything he owns my money bought. He's going to wish he'd never been born.' She stalked from the room, smashing open the door on her way out and thumping up the stairs.

Briony let out a long slow whistle and threw her head back on the rest. Thank goodness she'd never persuaded Darren to have children. She didn't envy Gemma's position one bit. Having him hanging round like a bad smell all the time would be torturous. And the idea of having to hand over a precious baby to him made her want to throw up. *I couldn't.* She put a fist to her chest and focused on her breathing before returning to reception. Thank goodness she wouldn't ever have to worry about that.

'Everything ok?' Zach asked slowly. 'Gemma looked furious.'

'She's raging and I don't blame her. It wouldn't surprise me if she cut up his shirts or something.'

'He's a dick. I said so the first time I saw him.'

'Yup. He loves himself. He's blessed with good looks but that's it.'

'Handsome is as handsome does,' said Zach.

'You're handsome too.' Briony leaned over the reception desk. 'Very.' A sigh escaped her. 'But you're also a good man with it. I know I can trust you to tell me the truth, but Darren. Ugh. So glad I'm shot of him.'

'Briony.' He reached out and took her hand. 'I—' The front door opened and he let go quickly. Briony spun around and smiled at the new arrivals. Why couldn't she have more than five minutes' peace? Some time to spend with Zach and actually talk to him about where they were going with this. All too quickly these days might be whipped away from them and life would go on... Alone. Unless she acted.

As she sorted out the new arrivals, Shari appeared at the bottom of the stairs. She hovered until Briony was free. Zach was back in the cupboard, raking through boxes, but Shari either didn't realise or care.

'I've been thinking about what happened last night,' Shari said. 'With you and that American.'

'Look, I'm sorry about that.'

'Yeah, but if I'd done that, would you have accepted that explanation?'

Briony glanced away. 'I don't know.'

'You wouldn't have,' Shari said. 'You'd tell me to be sensible. So, for what it's worth, I'm going to tell you the same thing.

I know he's hot, but how can you trust him? Even if he's pretending because of your ex or whatever, how do you know he doesn't have other motives? He might not be who he says he is or he might have a hidden agenda.'

'I hear what you're saying, Shari. And I appreciate it.' Briony swallowed. Shari was right on so many levels and it made Briony's insides burn. 'Thank you.'

Briony checked Shari had left for the day before confronting Zach in the cupboard. 'Did you hear what Shari said?'

'Loud and clear.' Zach dumped a box on the floor and its contents clattered.

'What's in that?' she asked.

'A hoard of stationery. Check out how many staplers your grandmother had.'

'Shame she didn't spend her money on something more useful.'

Zach tossed them back into the box and pushed it back into place.

'What are you gonna do?' he asked. 'Do you wanna... I dunno, keep out of my way or whatever Shari is suggesting?'

'She's just looking out for me. I should appreciate it.' Though it felt like she'd let her down. 'My future is up in the air but it I think it's an opportunity. I just need to know what's happening with Mr Beyer first.'

Zach let out a slow breath. 'Don't pin your hopes on him. I'd love it if, well... I wanna keep seeing you.'

'Me too,' Briony said. 'But can you find out something more concrete about this buyout?'

'Yeah, about that.' Zach looked away, scratching the back of his neck.

'I need to know what's happening so I can think about my options. I can't keep on like this, floating around in limbo.'

'Yeah, I get that.'

When Zach was here, helping out and present in her life, even crazy things felt possible. She liked to look on the bright side, and trying to imagine her life when he left was painful.

'Listen, the thing is—'

Voices from the foyer stopped Zach mid-sentence.

'No rest for wicked hotel owners,' Briony whispered with a wink. 'We'll chat later. Though it's the festival finale so it'll be a late finish.'

'Ok,' Zach mouthed and kissed his fingers, then turned them towards her.

Later that evening, Briony was rushed off her feet with the number of people who'd turned up. How good was this? If she could guarantee this many guests all year round, she'd be dancing.

She nipped out to the outdoor seating area, bedecked with twinkling fairy lights starting to glow as the sun set, and set a tray of food at one of the picnic-style tables where two rugged young men sat, wrapped in scarves, sipping beer. Both looked more like hillwalkers than festival goers. Maybe they'd stumbled in by accident.

The younger-looking one grinned up at her. 'Are you the owner here?' he asked.

'I am.' She lifted the first plate from the tray and set it in front of him. 'Why?'

'I'm Logan Ramsay, you won't know me, but I'm looking into buying the campsite and outdoor centre at the other end of the loch.'

'Oh, Heather Glen?' Briony said, handing the other man his plate.

'Yeah, the very one. I lived in Glenbriar as a boy and worked at Heather Glen in my teens. It's been a dream of mine to own it ever since.'

Briony recognised the twinkle in his eye. She remembered feeling like that when she first thought about taking on the hotel. How it seemed so exciting – a shiny new project to get stuck into. She needed to channel that enthusiasm again.

'This is my cousin, Matthew Gilchrist,' Logan added. 'We both like hiking, so we're using this as an excuse to do that too.'

'You don't want to buy a hotel as well, do you?' Briony joked. Both men laughed. Little did they how serious she was.

'Logan's the one buying,' Matthew said. 'I don't have the patience for this kind of thing.'

'Says the man who teaches in a high school in Glasgow.' Logan pulled crazy eyes and chuckled. 'But if I'm successful in getting the campsite, that'll be enough. I just wondered if you'd be interested in setting up some kind of package deal. You know, like discounts for your guests at the water sports and I could send the campers here for lunch with a money-off voucher, that kind of thing.'

'Wow, yeah. I would be totally up for that.' The second the words were out a mournful twang resonated low in her tummy. Plans like that were pointless. Great in principle but who knew what Daniel Beyer would want to do? 'Um, things are a bit complicated at the moment. Maybe we could chat sometime in the future when things are less hectic.'

'Awesome,' Logan said. 'It's pie in the sky just now. I haven't even bid for it yet. I want to suss everything out before I make a move.'

She turned to go back inside. The band had started playing on the little stage, all lit with the moon reflecting in the loch behind. So romantic and beautiful.

Zach met her at the door. 'Walk with me a minute.'

'I can't,' she said. 'I need to get the drinks and if Shari sees...'

'She's still inside. Two minutes, please.'

'Why?'

'Come.' He tugged her hand and led her past the stage, towards the woods where it was darker.

'What are you doing?'

'I just wanna kiss you in the moonlight.'

'Seriously, Zach, why?'

'Because it's magic. I saw the rainbow end in the hotel the other day. It wasn't pointing to a hidden pot of gold. It was pointing to you.'

He took her face in his hands and brushed his lips against hers. Closing her eyes, Briony let the warmth flood through her. The soulful tune made a bittersweet backdrop, and she swallowed back a lump in her throat. Tears welled, making her blink them away. *I love you.*

CHAPTER TWENTY-TWO

Zach

Briony's lips were soft and warm against his. Everything was sublime when they were together. Moonlight and music added to a growing sense of surrealness. These moments couldn't last without a plan. Was this Zach's big moment? Could he do something as huge as quitting his job and abandoning his mother? What would it mean for his future? Their future?

'I have to go.' Briony pulled away. 'I'm sorry. That was... beautiful.'

'Briony, wait, please.' Zach ran his thumb down her cheek. 'You're special to me. I'm glad we met – the first time, yeah, but more especially this time.'

'Me too.' She squeezed his hand gently. 'We'll talk tomorrow, properly, when there's no chance of Shari overhearing. There's still so much to do but it'll be quieter when the festival's over.'

'Let me help.'

'You're not exactly a waiter.'

'I guess not. How about I clear tables? I'll leave the serving to you.'

'Ok. Let's do it.'

He'd never had the urge to work in a bar before and this kind of thing made him uneasy – like somehow, he'd mess up or get in people's way – but for Briony he'd do it. And the guests seemed friendly. Screwing up his face, he squinted around. The outdoor seating area was packed and well-lit. Where were Darren and Gemma? After their altercation earlier, he hadn't seen either of them. Was it too much to ask that they'd left?

Tray after tray of empty glasses were lifted and ported to the kitchen. Zach even got a half smile out of Meg, the formidable cook. Both she and Shari had done little but give him the evils all night, so it was a welcome change. He was used to that kind of treatment from women but usually after he'd made some real geeky joke about *Star Trek*. On what was possibly his three-hundredth trip, Meg handed him a plate of food.

'You're a right skinny thing,' she said. 'This'll get some meat on your bones.'

He scanned it with a raised eyebrow.

'It's ok, there's no pig,' she said.

'Thanks.'

'Are you Jewish?'

'Partly. My father is, or according to my mother he is. I never knew him and she doesn't even remember his name. I guess not eating pork is preserving a missing part of my heritage, though

it's just lip service.' Judaism was matrilineal for that very reason.
A person's father could remain a mystery while their mother
couldn't, but Zach made this pathetic effort anyway.

'Oh dear. That's a shame.'

'Yeah. I guess. But you can't miss what you never had.' What a
lie. He'd missed having a dad loads of times growing up. Hearing
friends complaining about theirs hadn't made it easier; it made
him more resentful. Lucky them to have something to complain
about. He just had a mom who never seemed to know what to do
with him and loads of computer games that pushed him further
and further into a world of fantasy.

'Well, you eat that up.' Meg smiled and went back to her work.

Zach took the food into the dining room and sat. With most
of the guests outside listening to the acts, a hush rested over the
room. The faint music from the band was still audible, a gentle
whisper in the background. The food was delicious and Zach ate
quickly. He became aware of voices in the lobby, one of them
louder and more irate. He laid down his fork and frowned. Was
that Darren? Yes, it was. The asshole was shouting at Briony. No
one got to do that, especially on his watch.

Getting to his feet, he shoved a chair out of the way and
stormed through the door. How did Briony keep that smile in
place?

'You better do something about it,' Darren said.

'What's this all about?' said Zach.

'Oh god.' Darren turned and rolled his eyes. 'Not you again. You keep popping up like a bad penny. I still never heard exactly why you're here. Last time you were sniffing around Briony it was for suspect reasons and I bet you're at it again. What are you really up to?'

'None of your business,' Zach said.

'You need to calm down,' said Briony.

'Calm down!' Darren slammed his palms on the desk. 'Gemma has cleared out my room and stolen my car and you want me to calm down? Get the police.'

'Why can't you get them yourself?' Zach asked.

'Because the bitch has broken my phone and this bitch won't call them.'

'Don't you dare call her that.'

'I didn't say I wouldn't call them, Darren,' Briony said. 'I just think it's a bit over the top. She knows what you were doing with that other woman.'

'What are you talking about?' Darren thrust his hands onto his hips.

'You're cheating on her. The leopard doesn't change its spots.'

'Talking about yourself, are you?' Darren's upper lip curled like he might snarl and he glared between Briony and Zach. 'Did you feed Gemma a bunch of lies?'

'I didn't have to.'

'I saw you,' Zach said. 'You weren't exactly being discreet.'

'Like you can talk.' Darren looked him up and down. 'And like it's anything to do with you anyway.'

'I care about what happens around here.'

'Oh yeah? You two getting married, are you?'

'Darren.' Briony's cheeks coloured. 'It's time for you to leave. Otherwise I'll be the one calling the police and having you removed for verbally abusing me.'

Darren laughed, still eyeing Zach like he hadn't heard a word Briony had said. 'What is he? Good for a quick shag? The next knight in shining armour about to jump in and save you?'

'Enough, Darren.' Briony's face reddened further and her gaze flickered in Zach's direction. 'Go back to your room or I'll have to ask you to leave.'

'I'm not going anywhere until you call the police and report the theft of my car.'

'Fine.' Briony lifted the phone onto the high part of the desk. 'You call them and see what sympathy you get. Gemma told me she'd paid for all that stuff, so it's rightfully hers. But maybe the police will take pity on you and give you a lift home.' She bustled out from behind the desk, beckoning Zach with her eyes. As soon as they reached the corridor beside the kitchen, she slammed the door and let out a long sigh. 'The sooner he's gone the better.'

'I couldn't agree more. Listen. I need to—'

Bang!

'Shit. The fireworks have started. I need to get out there.' Briony legged it outside.

Zach spent the rest of the evening clearing tables. It was past midnight again when they got back to the private quarters.

'I can sleep on the sofa.' Zach covered a yawn.

'No, stay with me. I'd like to cuddle up.'

Briony cosied up to him in the bed. The covers were cool but his body was hot.

'I think I'm already asleep,' he said, though he wanted to be awake for her.

'Me too. I'm exhausted. See you in the morning.' She leaned her head on his chest and he held her close, his eyelids drooping.

Briony was up and out before Zach had fully come to the next morning. How did she keep up this relentless cycle? Surely it would break her. He felt broken after a few days, yet here she was fresh as a daisy off to smile and make small talk. Darren was still hanging about. The police had his statement and were investigating, but he'd have to find a way of getting home under his own steam. Zach would drive him to the station if it expedited the situation.

But he couldn't do anything until he'd taken Becker on his morning walk. They took the same path as the day before and Becker diverted towards the lochside at exactly the same point where they'd seen Darren. Zach glanced around, hoping they were alone this time. With a hopeful leap, Becker dropped a stick at Zach's feet and Zach launched it into the water. Yup, he was a sucker.

The game carried on for a few minutes, Zach enjoying lungfuls of fresh air in between tossing the stick into the loch.

Becker stopped frolicking in the water and stood still, his ears perked up. A crash in the bushes behind made Zach spin around. Not Darren again? Surely? Two black shapes came hurtling out and launched straight into the loch. Becker splashed around, jumping and wagging his tail. Zach held his breath. He was supposed to be keeping Becker on the leash. Probably for occasions like this.

He wasn't a dog expert but this looked like a friendly game – no teeth on display anyway.

'Where are you?' muttered a man's voice. 'Get back here.' The dogs ignored him as he shuffled through the bushes.

'You?' Zach said with a flash of recognition. The old Gandalf man came crashing out dressed in an old, waxed jacket and thick black rain boots.

'Do I know you?' he grumbled, hobbling towards the lochside.

'No. But I met you a few days ago, in a car park, then up the hill. You told me to ask about stolen kisses and to look out for a monster.'

The man's shoulders shook as he chuckled. 'Aye. I take it you've no' been eaten yet?'

'Apparently not.'

'And what about the kisses?'

'What about them? Why don't you tell me?'

'Pah. Come here!' he yelled at the dogs who continued to ignore him.

Zach stepped closer. 'Please, tell me.'

The man put his hands on his hips and squinted around, shaking his head that was covered in a khaki beanie. 'This place isn't what it used to be. None of it. The town's changed, the country's changed.'

Zach frowned. Maybe he was just a mad old man. Malcolm, the man in town, had said the story was nonsense and nothing this man had said seemed plausible, but Zach had a feeling he knew more than he was letting on. 'Do you know about the illicit still?' Briony had said this was the man who'd told the story in the first place, so why not find out some more?

'Aye, it's still there. Up in the woods.'

'Is it an old overgrown building?'

'That's the one. You been for a look?'

'Yeah, but I didn't learn much.'

'Nothing to learn. You know the story about the woman who made the moonshine.'

'Yeah. Briony told me.'

'Aye. I was the one that told her, but I don't think she believed me. The woman was a relation of mine, a great aunt. My grandmother often told the story. But once I'm gone it'll be lost. Like so much.' The man fiddled with a holey glove.

'Don't you have family?'

'Nope. But I've tried to tell enough people so the old legend doesn't get forgotten. I've even told a Yank.' He screwed up his nose.

'I might be the one to remember, you never know. I might turn your story into legend one day. We Yanks sure love our Scottish history.'

The old man chuckled. 'Aye. That you do. And if you sell my story and make a fortune then I'd like a cut.'

'I don't even know your name.' Briony had told him but he couldn't remember.

'Bruce McArthur – that's McArthur not McCarthy, very different names. I don't like it when people mix them up.'

'I'll remember that, Mr McArthur, sir.'

'Yes, well,' Bruce mumbled. 'What else did Briony tell you?'

'About what?'

'Did you ask her about the stolen kisses?'

'Yeah. And I was lucky to escape a slap for that one.'

Bruce laughed again. 'So, she really doesn't know?'

'Know what?'

'About the stolen kisses?'

'I don't know if she does or not because *I* don't know what it means.'

'A long time ago now, funny how time flies, feels like yesterday, but it was a long time ago, her grandfather was involved in a theft.'

'The whisky?' Zach's attention was piqued.

'So she does know?'

'Not exactly. I heard a rumour, but I don't get why the stolen kisses?'

'That was the name of the whisky. Whisky Kisses. A daft name really. But back then, two brothers, the Sinclairs, co-owned the Glenbriar Distillery. One of them was a bit of a romantic and apparently had the whisky made – three of them – for himself, his brother and a good friend. I used to work there. A romantic he might have been, but his brother wasn't. He was particularly unkind to his workers. A local man, Jock McClurg was the friend who was gifted a bottle. I think it was partly because the still was on his land. The rumour was that this whisky was made from proofs saved from the still. Jock had good connections and was a popular man. When the kind Mr Sinclair died unexpectedly, all three bottles disappeared.'

Zach frowned. 'And they were never found.'

'Nope. Never. But one of the workers, Tam Wishart, became a suspect in the theft. He was a disgruntled employee. His house was searched and he had a cast-iron alibi. But he was also close to Jock – Briony's grandfather.' Bruce waggled his finger. 'Word got out that Jock was an accomplice, but the police searched the hotel and never found a thing. Briony's grandmother, Hilda, was a sharp woman and didn't take kindly to the bad publicity. Then one day, Jock upped and walked out. Rumours flew around that he'd gone to the US to work. Hilda didn't say much about it but there was so much talk. Everyone thought he must be guilty. He said many times he wasn't and, even if he did have the whisky, at least one of the bottles was gifted to him. But no one really believed that story. The unpleasant Mr Sinclair said no record existed of these bottles being gifted to anyone and the story had been started by Jock to hide his guilt. Hilda, it seemed, couldn't live with the shame so she threw him out.'

Zach ran his hand over his face and sighed. 'Do you believe it?'

'That he was guilty? Possibly. Jock was a good man; he was funny and kind. People liked him but that was his downfall. Tam could have cajoled him into helping and Jock would have gone along with it.'

'What happened to Tam?'

'Moved away for years. Oh, he came back, mind, sometime after Jock had gone, but he's dead now. You know what I think?'

Zach shook his head.

'I think Tam was ill and he came back to apologise to Hilda. Maybe even try to suss out if she still had the bottles.'

'Do you think they still exist?'

'I wondered after Hilda died if they'd resurface. But if Briony knows nothing about it then I guess they're long gone. Hilda probably poured them down the drain and smashed the bottles.'

'Why would she do that? You know how valuable they'd be if they turned up now?'

'She was ashamed, I'm sure. But I also imagine the distillery would want them back. It's still the same family that own it. The pleasant Mr Sinclair's son is at the helm now.'

'Yeah.' Zach rubbed his chin.

'Are you here to find them?'

'Kind of.'

'Did Jock go to the States? Are you his grandson or something?'

'No, I'm not. My boss heard a rumour from someone who might have been Jock. He didn't know the man's name. But if the stories are true, how can I find it? I don't know where to start.'

'Sorry, I can't help you with that. Hilda was tight lipped and never talked to anyone. Hardly surprising her own family don't know. I tried to tell Briony, but she was having none of it. Thought I was spreading crazy rumours about her family and trying to discredit them. That's why I stopped bothering going in there.'

'Thanks for talking to me, sir.'

'Any time, sonny. Do you like fishing?'

'I, er, don't know. I've never tried.'

'I can show you the best places.' He tapped the side of his nose.

'Ok. I'll hold you to that.'

'Good lad.'

Zach called Becker and Bruce's dogs followed. As Bruce walked on, Zach patted Becker on his wet head and stared after him. 'What a bizarre man, but, you know what, I like him. I never knew my grandad, but Grandma always said he was a crazy guy who loved to fish. I guess Bruce is a bit like him. Maybe he's my guardian angel.'

The loch rippled in the light breeze. 'I have to tell Briony.' And that wasn't all. She needed to pull out of this deal right away. *If Mr Beyer is going to sack anyone, it should be me.* He couldn't in all conscience let Briony sell the hotel in good faith only to have Daniel Beyer kick her out as soon as he took over. She might put on a brave face, but Zach was a hundred per cent sure, she was only agreeing to the deal so she could stay here and keep the family connection to the community going.

Why should he be afraid of Mr Beyer? Briony trusted him to do what was right and this time he was going to and screw the consequences.

'Come on, Becker, let's do this.'

CHAPTER TWENTY-THREE

Briony

'D an Beyer?' Briony couldn't contain her shock. Hearing the man's voice was like being put through to the US president. Did he usually consort with lowly people like her in person? Emails had been the limit so far and everything else had gone through secretaries or Zach.

'Mrs Dalgleish, a pleasure to talk to you at last.' His voice was deep, mellow and refined, like a well-matured single malt.

'It certainly is. How can I help you?'

'There seems to be a breakdown in communication channels with Zach. I can't get hold of him. I've been emailing and messaging him for hours but I'm getting no response. Is he still with you?'

'Yes. He's out walking...' She stopped. Telling him Zach was out walking her dog wouldn't win her any favours. 'Walking to look for the illicit still.' If Zach was supposed to be investigating the whisky, then this news would please Mr Beyer and hopefully divert him. It would sound like Zach had thrown dust in her eyes and told her about the legend of the still instead of the truth about the stolen whisky. Hopefully. She crossed her fingers on the desk.

'The what?'

'It's a place where illegal whisky was distilled in the past.'

'Yes, I'm aware of that but... Am I to understand you know about the whisky?'

Shit. How could she say this without getting Zach into deep trouble. 'I know there are rumours about illegal whisky distilling all around this area. Some of it has become legendary.'

'I see. And what happened to the whisky?'

Briony sucked in her lip. When he said it like that it sounded even more insane. Even if by chance something had survived the raid by the excise people, how could whisky from an illicit still exist? How could they prove what it was one way or another without opening bottles? Surely, the locals would have drunk it over a hundred years ago. 'There was a raid and it was all destroyed. That's what the stories say.'

'Really?'

'I suppose there's the off chance that some of it got decanted and smuggled away.'

'Decanted?'

'Yes, it means—'

'I'm aware of what it means. I need to talk to Zach. He needs to return immediately.'

'Return. As in, to you?'

'Yes. I'm going to work on a new package for you, Mrs Dalgleish, but I don't want Zach involved. I'm not sure what he's told you but—'

'He hasn't told me anything.'

'Hmm. That's something. Because after his last business...' Mr Beyer let out a long audible sigh. 'Well, let's just say, he has a history. I'm sorry to say but the new deal I have for you doesn't include you in a managerial role. I'll up my bid so you have a lump sum to invest elsewhere, but I can't keep you on.'

'What?' She gaped at her reflection in the ornate mirror across the hallway.

'I'm glad this is a shock to you, not because I want to upset you, but because at least it assures me Zach didn't let it out. That's a positive we can take away from his visit.'

'Zach knew?' He knew Mr Beyer was planning on sacking her and he hadn't said.

'That's something I can't discuss right now. But be assured I'll make you an offer you can't refuse.'

'But...'

'Please have Zach call me the second he gets back. We have a lot to discuss.'

Briony goggled at the phone long after he'd ended the call. She had to leave for an offer she couldn't refuse? Why? Surely he didn't expect the dregs of some ancient whisky to be kicking around. And why the hell hadn't Zach told her?

That was what putting faith in someone you'd only known for a short time did for you. If she'd practised what she preached and kept socially well away from guests, then maybe things would have been different. Closing her eyes, she sank into her office chair. How could she get out of this?

'Hey, Briony.'

She jumped at the enthusiastic voice behind her. Zach. How could she both be eager to see him but also desperate not to? The tug in her chest she'd known the last time they parted was back. Unease and uncertainty broke back into to her soul, cutting through the happiness of the last few days with serrated blades.

'You'll never guess who I just saw,' he said.

Briony shook her head. She didn't care if he'd seen Darren sneaking away with every female guest plus Meg and Shari. None of it mattered. 'I just had Mr Beyer on the phone,' she said. 'He wants you back in the States.'

Zach froze, his lips forming the word 'what?' but no sound came out.

'Yes.' Briony rubbed her hands together. 'He wants you to phone him.'

'Why? What's happened?'

Briony cocked her head. Was this him still faking? He'd shown her how good he was at that. 'You know all about it apparently.'

His brow furrowed. 'About what?'

'He was never going to keep me on whether you found the whisky or not. He wants me out. Were you going to let him buy the hotel without telling me?'

'No, no. Of course I wasn't.' Zach scraped his hands through his hair. 'He only said yesterday that it might be a possibility. I was gonna tell you, but people and stuff kept getting in the way. I wanted to tell you to pull out of the deal. Part of me wanted to have some good news for you too or a magic solution to the problem, so you could pull out but still save the hotel.'

'Good god, Zach.' Briony threw her head heavenwards. 'You and he are both off your rockers if you think that bloody whisky is still around. The whisky from the illicit still must have been destroyed years ago. Do you honestly believe something as insane as that?'

'But it's not the whisky from the illicit still he's interested in.' Zach frowned at her. 'It's the stuff that was stolen from the Glenbriar Distillery in the fifties.'

Briony's heartbeat flickered and she frowned. 'What stuff?'

'I told you.' He stepped closer.

'No, you didn't. When you said stolen whisky, I thought you meant from the illicit still. I don't know anything about whisky stolen in the fifties.'

'Aw, jeez.' Zach closed his eyes and drew in a breath. 'This is gonna hit like a bus. You better sit down.'

'Now, you're scaring me.' She flopped into the seat.

'Some whisky was stolen from the Glenbriar Distillery in the fifties. This is the whisky Mr Beyer thought was hidden here and it could be worth a mint.'

'Oh my god.' She shook her head. 'Ok. It's slightly more plausible that exists but not much. It sounds like something that the locals have made up over the years.'

'I thought so too, until I met Gandalf in the woods this morning.'

'What?'

'You know, Bruce McArthur. The old man who told me the crazy story about the monster.'

'Oh him.'

'Briony.' Zach fixed her in his gaze. 'I think the story's true.'

'You think the stolen whisky is somewhere in the hotel?'

'I don't know if it's here now, but I believe it once was. And that's not all.'

'What else can there be?'

'I'm really sorry to have to say this but I think your grandfather was involved in the theft.'

'What?' Briony mentally shook herself. Her grandfather? Was that why he'd run away from the family? Could that be the reason Hilda was so closed? She'd lived her life married to a thief. Briony was descended from criminals. And who knew why he'd done it? Was he a helpless fool like her? Willing to go to any length to make money? But it hadn't worked, had it? Surely if it had, he would have been living the high life with his family. He wouldn't have left them struggling to maintain the hotel while he disappeared into obscurity. Or did he sell it and run off to live the high life himself, leaving her dad and Aunt Lottie fatherless?

'I guess he's the man Mr Beyer met. He said he was dead now but he'd worked for a bourbon manufacturer. Bruce suggested your grandmother kicked him out because she was ashamed of his part in it.' Zach recounted the story he'd heard from Bruce and Briony shook her head as she listened.

'I don't know how my dad and Aunt Lottie don't know about this.'

'I guess they were young when it happened, and if Hilda didn't talk...'

'But if this whisky was stolen, would it not still be the property of the distillery?'

'That's what Mr Beyer was investigating and whether or not the Glenbriar Distillers could still claim it as their property.'

'And?'

'I don't know what the outcome was.'

'Zach.' Briony sucked her lip. 'You realise this is it. The end for you and me. He wants you back. I'm not sure he trusts that you didn't tell me. I think he's going to sack you. What will you do then? What about your mum?'

Zach took her hands and she got to her feet. He leaned his head on her shoulder, pulling her close. 'I don't know. I wish I could pull a rabbit out of a hat. This is what I was scared of from the start and I still can't see a way out. I hoped I could find a way for you to save the hotel and write your books, but I haven't.'

'That's not your job, Zach. I don't need rescuing, no matter what my ex might tell you.'

'I know you don't. I just wish there was evidence the Whisky Kisses still existed.'

Briony slowly pulled back and met his eyes. 'Whisky Kisses? Is that the name of the stolen whisky?'

'Yes... Why?'

'Oh my god.' Briony clutched her face; an icy tremor dripped down her back.

CHAPTER TWENTY-FOUR

Zach

'What's wrong?' Zach stared at Briony. Her face had drained of colour and her brows raised to a point. 'You look like you've seen a ghost.'

'Not a ghost. But Whisky Kisses? Oh god. Come with me.'

She grabbed his hand, tugging him along the corridor next to the kitchen and in the side door to her private quarters. As soon as they were inside, she let go and dashed into the kitchen. Zach followed, rubbing his forehead. What was going on?

An upper cabinet door clunked and Briony turned around, holding a clear bottle with barely a glassful of whisky at the bottom. Slowly she revolved it, so the label was facing him. White with a thistle emblem and a swirly tartan sash, the picture and logo had a vintage air to them. Printed in an equally vintage font were the words Sinclair Brothers, Glenbriar Whisky Co. presents Whisky Kisses. The last two words were contained within a purple banner.

'Oh god.' Zach covered his mouth. 'It exists.'

Briony nodded.

'But it's open,' Zach said.

'And nearly finished.'

'Did you drink it?'

'No. But you did.'

'What?'

'That was the whisky I put in the decanter on your first night here.'

'Oh Christ.'

'But it was already open. My grandmother must have opened it and drank it. She probably finished the other two.' Briony passed him the bottle and he took it, staring at the label.

'It was here all the time,' he murmured. 'Taunting us.'

Briony covered her face and a let slip a whimper.

'Hey.'

'I'm sorry.' She sniffed and glanced at him with shining eyes. 'Just to see it like that. Why couldn't it still be sealed? It's like I've had a winning lottery ticket snatched from under my nose.'

'Yeah.'

'I mean with Bruce's story, we could have tried to prove the bottles were a gift and not stolen at all – one of them at least.'

Zach nodded, his heart missing a few beats at the word *we*. Had she meant that or was it a figure of speech? The idea of *we* and a future with Briony called to him more than anything else in the world right now, but he had to pack and prepare to face the music. Not for the first time in his life.

He put his arms around Briony, welcoming her to him, stroking her hair as she seemed to hold her breath. Was she trying to keep it together for him? She needn't bother. 'Let it all out if you want. I get it. I've kinda felt like this all my life. Like something big is just there, waiting for me to grab it but whenever I try it moves out of reach.'

She squeezed him tight and he loved how petite she felt in his arms. The pressure of her fingertips on his shoulder blades was perfect.

'I wish I knew what to do.'

Words failed. He dipped in and claimed her lips. Hands low on her hips, he pulled close, delighting in the delicious friction between them.

'Has your dad never spoken about the whisky?'

'Never. I messaged him and Aunt Lottie but neither have replied yet. They're really rubbish at it,' she murmured, sliding her fingers under his shirt.

He kissed her again, deepening it. His fingers slid upward, finding the pull for her zipper and tugging it slowly down her back. It caught momentarily on her bra then eased down to her bottom. She stepped back and shuffled out of it; the pale grey fabric pooled at her feet.

Zach's hungry eyes skimmed over her lacy pink bra, to her toned waist, full hips and black knickers.

'I didn't manage the matching underwear,' she said, slipping her arms around his neck.

His smiled reply came out like a needy growl rather than words. 'Doesn't matter. You're gorgeous in anything... and nothing.'

She pulled at the edges of his t-shirt and he obliged, easing it over his head. Her cool fingertips brushed the exposed skin, making him tingle.

'I don't think I told you how hot you are the other night... For a *Star Wars* geek.' She smirked.

He snorted. 'Nice. Thanks, but I think you might have mentioned it among some other wild ramblings.'

'Wild ramblings.'

'Uh-huh,' he whispered. 'When you were delirious with pleasure.'

'I'd like to feel like that again and forget about all the other stuff.'

'Me too.'

She kissed him again. Desire slammed into his stomach as he tasted her on his lips. Jeez, she tasted so good, her daisy fragrance overpowering and intoxicating. He cupped the back of her head and she slid her palms down his arms. He pulled her against him, his hands on her waist; the touch of her body was incredible. Her tongue slipped inside his mouth, sending his remaining common sense flying out of the window.

Kissing semi-naked in a kitchen was pretty adventurous considering his fairly pathetic love life to date. When they were naked, he expected them to proceed to the bedroom, but Briony held up a finger, nipped out and returned with a little square packet. She winked.

'How many did you get out of that machine?' he asked, vaguely aware he was doing this in broad daylight in a retro kitchen with a cold lino floor.

She waggled her eyebrows. A shot of need bolted through him and he rolled her backwards onto the veneer table. She let out a little giggle against his lips before she resumed kissing him. He ran his hand over her body and she moaned, tipping her head back to get air. She felt divine: soft, smooth and perfect. Zach ran his hand over her pert breast and a gasp escaped her.

'Are you ok?' he asked, pulling back slightly.

'Oh, yes. Just... happy.'

'You're so beautiful.'

The desire in her eyes was clear. She wanted this as much as he did. He kissed her again and she snaked her arms around him, kissing him urgently. Yes. He felt the same. He ran his hand up her inner thigh, shifting his mouth to her neck.

'Mmmm.... Zach,' she moaned as he coaxed out her pleasure with his fingers, smiling as he watched her tumble over the edge into oblivion. This was his power and it bolstered him, making him feel like the master of the universe. Her ragged breathing tickled his chest and he held her against him, soothing his hands over her hair and her warm skin as she regained control.

When she looked up and smiled, he lifted her. The look of surprise on her face made him grin even more. All those hours working out had finally paid off.

'You're so strong,' she said.

He buried his forehead in her shoulder and breathed, entering her with a low moan. Everything about her was just right. Not heavy enough to be a struggle but full enough to touch the right places and sate his ever-growing desperation. The risk and the unlikely location heightened his senses as he thrust home. The now worthless whisky bottle on the worktop watched his every move and he groaned. Sweat beaded on his forehead. Briony's eyes rolled and she called out, 'Oh my god, Zach.'

A burst of ecstasy fired him into overdrive and his starship spun into another dimension – one he didn't want to leave. Still holding Briony, he leaned one hand on the worktop, panting, eyeing the bottle with a smug smile. It may be almost empty and completely worthless, but he was filled to the brim.

Briony shuffled and slid gently to the ground, shivering as he held her.

'That was incredible,' she said, swallowing in a gulp, then exhaling slowly. 'But, oh god, I so should not be here. What's that noise?'

A buzzing sound was coming from the floor near Zach's discarded jeans. 'I think it's my cell.' Stooping over, he pulled it out. 'Mr Beyer.' He glanced at Briony. 'Ah screw it, he can wait.'

'No. Take it.' Briony lifted her clothes. 'You should. It's your job.'

'Briony, I—'

'Answer it,' she said. 'I'm going for a quick wash, then back to the desk.'

Zach watched her leaving, aware the vibrating had stopped. His foot moved automatically to follow Briony but he should at least check what Mr Beyer wanted. He woke his cell, staring at the string of urgent and angry-looking messages. The sound of the tap in the bathroom gushing on and off filtered into his ears. None of the words of the messages sunk in. The bathroom door clicked, followed by the side door back into the hotel.

Now he was alone and ridiculously naked in the kitchen. Not to mention cold. He made his own quick sprint to the bathroom, hauled on his clothes and called Mr Beyer.

'Where the hell have you been?' Mr Beyer said.

'Sorry. I was—'

'Walking. Yes, I heard.'

Zach smirked at the Whisky Kisses. Walking would do. The truth would be like the guillotine falling.

'Walking around the wilderness looking for something pointless. The woman knows about the whisky, Zach.'

'Yes, she does.'

'It seems to be common knowledge and also everyone knows there's none left. Why didn't you tell me this before?'

'I didn't realise. The stories have got so muddled over the years.'

'So what happened to the goddamn whisky?'

Zach swallowed, his gaze still on the bottle. 'The family drank it years ago. That's the most common line of thought.'

'Unbelievable. One bottle of that stuff was worth more than the damn hotel.'

Maybe to Mr Beyer. He wanted to get a deal on the cheap, buy a property that on its own was worthless to him and would cost a pittance compared to what he'd make back, but to Briony this was a special place full of memories. And it should have the promise of a future too. A future with her in it. Zach had felt the life roaring into the building's fabric during the festival and was there any reason it couldn't happen again? The hotel could succeed. Money shouldn't be a barrier.

'I don't know what to say,' Zach said.

'Nothing to be said. Just get back here. I'll buy her out anyway and then if that whisky exists, I'll have it and if not, I can begin on my Scotch Whisky Resort plans instead. That's not something I need you in situ for. I have other people for that job. I've got another assignment waiting for you.'

'But technically I'm on vacation if this job is done.'

'Your vacation's cancelled, Zach. I need you back here so I can brief you, then you're flying to Venezuela.'

'What?'

Zach's heart bumped down a flight of steps and slapped onto cold concrete. No way. This trip had introduced him to new possibilities and now he was getting dragged away and sent to Venezuela? Scotland might be like an alien planet, but it wasn't unfriendly. What he was going back to would be familiar but hostile. He still had his mom's healthcare needs to consider, and he would, but something new was wakening, a desire to strike back. Did he have to be a puppet and play the game? No. Time to be the hero in his own life again, though it might mean a short break from Briony. But he could and would come back even stronger.

CHAPTER TWENTY-FIVE

Briony

T he string of people Briony expected to find at the desk wasn't there. Thank goodness. Could any amount of cold water on her face take away the flush and heat of what had just happened? Shari was cleaning somewhere about – *please god, let her stay wherever she is*. Briony couldn't face her. Surely something would give her away and what would Shari say then?

Briony ran cold fingertips over her neck. What was happening to her? She'd gone from upset over the whisky bottle to crazy sex in the kitchen. Maybe Zach was more skilful than she thought – not just physically, but he'd made her completely forget about being depressed. Why cry over spilt whisky?

The lounge doors opened and Briony flexed her fingers. *Shit. Not Shari, please not Shari.*

'Oh, hi, you're back.' Felicity emerged from the room, smiling. 'Your sign wasn't up so I thought you might be in the lounge. I came to collect the banners.'

'What? Oh... No, I had to nip into the back. I forgot to put up the sign.'

Felicity leaned her elbows on the high part of the desk. 'The festival went great, didn't it?'

'Yes. Really good.' Keeping her head down, Briony sank into her seat with a sigh. She hadn't meant to let it out but after what she'd just done, the need to curl up and cuddle was strong. Being cocooned by the chair wouldn't do the trick but it was better than standing.

'You look exhausted,' Felicity said. 'You work way too hard.'

'I guess it's all catching up on me.'

Felicity glanced around. 'Where's zombie Zach today? Has there been any word on the takeover?'

Briony hoped the heat in her cheeks wouldn't give her away, regarding just how close they'd got. 'The deal's off.'

'What?' Felicity straightened up. 'Why?'

'It's a long story, but I'm pulling out. I need to contact Mr Beyer soon. I just need to calm down before I compose an email.'

'So, has Zach gone?'

'Not yet.' Briony's heart wavered.

'At least you get to keep the hotel.'

'For now,' Briony said. 'But nothing's changed. I still can't afford to keep it going.'

'Maybe you could talk to Mr Sinclair about sponsorship. He was happy to sponsor this festival and he likes to keep the distillery as part of the community.'

'Yes. I'll do that as soon as I've emailed Mr Beyer.'

'But why are you pulling out? You have to tell me. I can't stand the suspense.'

Briony lounged back and rubbed her temple. 'Mr Beyer thought some bottles of stolen whisky were hidden in the hotel and he planned to find them and claim them.'

'The Glenbriar ones?'

'You know about this?'

'Only what we tell people on tours, but I'm not sure how much of it is true. There's an empty space in the collection in case the bottles ever turn up. But if they're here, my boss will have something to say about it. I'm sure he'd want to fill that space. But this hotel was searched before. It's in my tour notes.'

'And does it say why?'

'Not really. Just that some locals were implicated and some properties were searched, including this hotel, but nothing was ever found.'

'So it doesn't say that one of those locals happened to be my grandfather.'

'What? No. It doesn't name anyone. But he wasn't found guilty. No one was.'

'I know, but it's looking like he did it or at least that he was involved. There are secret passageways around the still in the woods and all sorts of places they could have been hidden.'

'So you believe the bottles could be here?'

Briony drew in a calming breath. 'One of them definitely is. It's in the kitchen.'

'What?'

'Don't get excited. It's open and nearly finished. I suspect my grandmother slowly drank the evidence over the years.'

'Oh my god. Why would she do that?'

'Shame? Guilt? I don't know. No one was close to her, so I guess we'll never know for sure.'

'My boss would probably want that empty bottle, if he doesn't die of shock first. One mouthful of that stuff is worth more than my yearly salary.'

'Ha. Don't I know it,' Briony said, 'The thing is, there's hearsay to suggest one of the Glenbriar Distillery owners in the fifties gifted a bottle to my grandfather and that he didn't steal it at all. Someone else stole them and he helped hide the evidence. He shouldn't have done that, but I guess he felt that one of them was rightfully his. When the older Sinclair brother died, the younger refused to honour the gift.'

Felicity rubbed her chin. 'Kind of makes sense. My boss is the older Mr Sinclair's son and he doesn't think much of his uncle. I wonder if I can find out anything more.'

'It doesn't matter now. The whisky has all but gone. Unless your boss fancies drinking what's left.'

'I'm sorry.' Felicity leaned over to take Briony's hand. 'This is bad for you, isn't it?'

'It's worse than you think.'

'Why?'

'Zach.'

'What about him?'

'We... You know, like each other.'

'No way. Like as in like like?'

Briony nodded. 'Exactly like that. Worse even than that.'

'How?'

'We met before, years ago. We liked each other then too, but... Well, shit happened and he had to leave. Now shit's happening again and he has to leave.'

'Hang on.' Felicity let go of her hand and snuck around behind the desk. 'You met before?'

'In a hotel in Edinburgh. We had a moment when our eyes met and we couldn't stop looking at each other. The looks became smiles and the smiles became flirting. Then he asked me back to his room.'

'And you went?'

'Yup. Crazy. Then it all went to pot.' She explained about the bet and Darren's fact twisting.

'Bloody hell,' Felicity said. 'But didn't you google him after he left?'

'We didn't know each other's names. Deliberately. It was a fling. We both knew that... Kind of. Though it weirdly felt bigger.' She swallowed. 'But that's stupid.'

'Hmm,' Felicity said. 'My gran has The Gift or so everyone says. She believes in all sorts of coincidences and she would think this is fate, for sure.'

'I'd like to believe that too. I've always believed in everything but so far it hasn't worked.'

'Hmm. Then let's make sure.'

'How?'

'We could run background checks and stuff.'

'What?' Briony chuckled. 'This isn't *CSI*.'

'I meant google him. You know his name now.'

'I don't need to. I trust him.'

'Do it anyway. Just in case.'

'Now?'

'Go on, see what comes up. If there's nothing, then good.'

Briony's fingers hovered over the keys. Did she want to? What if something came up? She'd already wrestled with the possibility she was descended from criminals this week. She didn't need anything else.

'Here, let me.' Felicity leaned over and Briony got out of her seat to let her take over. She put her elbow on the desk as Felicity scrolled.

'Well? Is he actually a convicted murderer? Or does he not exist at all?' Briony toyed with the neckline of her dress, not sure she wanted to know.

'There's loads of reports on here about some theft of documents.'

'He told me about that. It was a mistake.'

Felicity frowned. 'It looks pretty serious. Even if it was a mistake, it's odd he's still got his job. I can't see my boss keeping someone on after a breach like that. They would have found a way to pay him off quietly. Maybe he has an understanding boss.'

That didn't tally with what Briony knew of Mr Beyer and the cold way he'd acted throughout.

'Have you seen Daniel Beyer?' Felicity asked.

'No. We've just emailed and chatted once.'

'Look at this.'

Briony leaned in over Felicity's shoulder and followed the line of her nail, pointing at the screen. At first, she wasn't sure what Felicity was showing her, then her brow furrowed. He looked like—

A cough behind made them both jump and turn round.

Zach stood close to the door into the kitchen corridor, looking over the low part of the reception desk, directly at the screen, his eyebrows closed in a thick line. He folded his arms and cocked his head questioningly. Briony sucked in her lip. Caught.

CHAPTER TWENTY-SIX

Zach

The two faces staring at Zach looked guilty of something. Briony was sucking on her lower lip, uncomfortably reminding him of their close encounter, but what was Felicity up to? She shifted to block his view of the screen but he'd already seen the picture of himself and Mr Beyer suited up on a corporate evening out with a couple of other colleagues.

'What are you doing?' he asked.

'Nothing much,' Briony said.

'Really? Why have you got a picture of me on there?'

'We were googling you,' Felicity said. Briony's smile was intact but her eyes almost rolled.

'Why? Are you trying to find out if I'm not who I say I am?' Finally, he'd been caught. They could pull off the mask and see him for the phoney he was... Only he wasn't. He was just a regular guy faking it to survive in his career. The real Zach had been the one Briony met this week. 'Do you think I'm an imposter?'

'Are you?' Felicity said.

'Felicity,' Briony said, glaring at her.

'Of course I'm not.'

'And this job is real? Not a bet or a dare, for example?' Felicity continued.

'What?' He frowned at Briony. She'd told Felicity about that? 'Absolutely not.'

'Felicity,' Briony said again, this time through gritted teeth.

'What's your real name?' Felicity raised her eyebrows and folded her arms.

Zach shook his head. 'My *real* name? My name is Zacharias Patrick Somerton.'

'Not Zacharias Patrick Beyer?'

'What?' He gaped at her. What the hell? He could have predicted a hundred crazy things she might have said but that one side-swiped him out of nowhere. 'No. Why would you think that?' He glanced at Briony. She was watching him closely but didn't flinch or laugh.

'He's your father, isn't he?' Felicity said.

Holy frigging Christ. Had he landed in his own *Star Wars* adaptation? 'No. Of course he isn't. Are you on something?'

'You look very like him,' Felicity said. '*Very* like him.'

'That's crazy.' Though he began to understand where she was coming from. He'd been teased for 'looking Jewish' before. 'I get it. You think I look Jewish and because he's Jewish, you automatically think he's my father, because all Jewish guys must look alike or something.'

'No. I wouldn't think anything of the sort... I didn't even know you were Jewish,' Felicity said. 'Did you?' She glanced at Briony.

'No.' Her voice was quiet. 'You never said.'

'Because I'm not. Not exactly.' He swallowed. Now it appeared like he'd deliberately not told her something about himself. 'My father was Jewish – apparently – but my mother isn't so I haven't been raised Jewish. I stopped eating pork when I started working for Mr Beyer. He never ordered it for company meals and I got out of the habit of eating it.' Maybe Mr Beyer had suggested he gave it up, possibly decreed it. Zach couldn't remember exactly. 'I kind of thought it would be a way to connect to my heritage. Nothing too big or life-changing but so I didn't forget that somewhere out there I actually have a father. Or did have.' He must have done otherwise he wouldn't be there.

'What happened to your father?' Briony asked.

'I never knew him. My mom doesn't talk about him. Some guy she had a fling with. I don't think she even knew his name.' Heat burned his neck. Five years ago, he and Briony had been on the verge of doing exactly what his parents had done. He'd come into existence from a quick fling. His stomach churned as a wheel of thoughts rolled around.

Briony's gaze wandered to the monitor. 'And you don't think—'

'No. I don't.' Zach threw his hands up. 'No way. Just no way. It's a coincidence if I look anything like him, which I don't. And why are you trying to find something on me anyway? Don't you trust me?'

'I just...'

'Just what? Want to make this easier? Well, if it helps, you go with it. Because I have to go back. I don't want to, but I have no choice. If you want to believe Mr Beyer is my father and he's put me up to this or whatever, then you believe it.'

'That's not what I think,' Briony said.

'But why did he let you keep your job after that incident last year?' Felicity asked.

'What?' This was getting worse. Then again, it was something he'd always wondered deep down. Why indeed? He'd committed what was easily a sackable offence but Mr Beyer had kept him on. 'Why don't you ask him? I have no idea why.' His father though? That was so ludicrous, even his crazy fantasy-loving mind couldn't have come up with it.

Fantasy. His life was nothing but. And now everything he'd had felt like it too. That connection with Briony, everything they'd shared. His walks by the loch and Becker. Was any of it real? Was coincidence just another opportunity to have his face slapped? Happy endings were for movies and stories, and this would end the same way everything else in his real life did. Tits up or face down. Unless he did what he should have done years ago.

'I need to go.'

Becker's nose greeted him as he marched into the private quarters. If anything could open the flood gates to his heart it was this. 'Oh god.' Zach sucked his lips between his teeth as he patted Becker's soft fur. Why was he letting emotion get to him? He opened the door to the courtyard and let Becker out. A few steps took him to the side of the hotel and he scanned over the entrance to the cellar, the path to the woods and the loch. Things he wanted to see again. Things he could see again if he was brave enough. The sooner he got out of here, the better. He was going back to the States, but he wasn't going to stay there. He'd face the music all right and make some of his own.

He called to Becker.

'Here, buddy, last treats from me.'

Becker's round glassy eyes had a sad look about them as he took the treat and padded into the living area. 'Goodbye, buddy. Wish me luck. If it works out, I'll see you again soon.'

CHAPTER TWENTY-SEVEN

Briony

'Was that really mean of me?' Felicity said. She hadn't stopped Briony going after Zach, but Briony had already been away from the desk too long, so she stayed put. She needed a few moments to think before she faced him. 'I didn't mean to upset him, but you have to admit he is the double of Mr Beyer.'

'I know. I can see it. But maybe it's just that photo,' Briony said.

'It's not. Look at these other ones. Don't you think I'm onto something?'

'But why would he lie? He looked horrified. Maybe it's true but he genuinely doesn't know.'

Felicity sighed. 'Maybe. But, Briony, do you really think it's a good idea to trust him after such a short time?'

'I just know what my heart's telling me. Maybe I shouldn't have let him go the first time. I let Darren talk me into believing he was bad. Have I done the same again and let you talk me into believing he's up to something? What if he's not?'

'Oh, Briony.' Felicity put her hand on Briony's shoulder, her eyebrows pulled together and her expression stricken. 'He's still packing. Jeez, if it's that bad, go after him. Go now. I didn't grasp how important this was. I'm not trying to stop you. I just don't want you to get burned.'

The string of people Briony had expected earlier had arrived. 'I need to see these guests first, then I'll go.'

'Ok. I'll take the banners down and keep watch. If I see him making a run for it, I'll tackle him,' she whispered with a wink. 'He's not going anywhere. We'll see to that.'

Briony couldn't help smiling. Felicity hadn't deliberately meant to cause harm but her timing could have been better – and she would have done well to keep her assumptions to herself. Could Zach be Mr Beyer's son? How far-fetched was that? And his reaction had been so shocked. No way was that faked.

At the back of the string of guests stood Darren, hands in his pockets, red in the face. Presumably no luck getting public transport then. Not a single ounce of sympathy shifted on Briony's emotion scale. He'd brought this on himself. Just as he'd brought about their divorce. She cringed, remembering how she'd fallen so quickly into his arms after Zach left the first time and look what had happened there.

She served the first guests, smiling through Darren's foot tapping and clenched jaw. Her eyes ever shifting to the side door in case Zach came out. Darren drew closer, getting harder to ignore. The couple at the desk turned, giving him a filthy look before glancing at each other. Briony wished she'd thrown him out the other night. By the time the couple moved off he was practically breathing down their necks.

'How can I help you?' One day this smile might slip but it wasn't this day and Briony was damned if it would be him who dislodged it.

'Why don't you drop that?' Darren's surly upper lip twitched.

Screw him. Never again would she do what he wanted. 'Is there anything I can get you to make your stay more pleasant?'

'Just quit that. When can I get out of here?'

'There's the door, sir.' She pointed, still smiling.

'Not funny, Bri, not funny. Why is it so expensive to get a taxi out of this dive? Especially when the next time slot they have is in three hours. And that doesn't connect with a train. It's bollocks.'

'Patience is a virtue.'

'Will you quit that stupid voice?'

'It's just my normal voice, sir,' she continued in the gently placating tone she knew would irritate the hell out of him. 'There's also a bus service.'

'Yeah, like one every three hours. So convenient.'

The door from the kitchen corridor opened behind her and Zach shuffled out, wearing his coat and carrying his cases. He glanced towards her and the corners of his mouth twitched downwards. A rush of pain stabbed her and she wanted to abandon Darren and run and hug Zach. He looked so low. She tried to catch his eye, indicating he should wait.

'Dear, dear,' Darren said in a fake sorrowful tone. 'Your boyfriend leaving you? Well, that's what he's famous for. What is it this time? Another bet gone wrong? Your mates should give you more of a challenge. This one's too easy.'

Zach dropped his case like he was about to take a swing for Darren, but Briony reached over the desk and slapped his smug face hard across the cheeks.

'Fuck's sake,' Darren said, clutching his cheek and staggering back.

Zach huffed out a half laugh and stepped in behind the desk.

Briony frowned, rubbing her smarting palm. What was Zach doing?

'See you,' he said, leaning in and kissing her cheek. 'I'll miss you. But I'll be back soon.' He blinked, his eyes darting towards Darren, who was still nursing his cheek. 'And I love you.' Without meeting her eye, he edged out, picked up his bag and walked out the front door. Briony stared after him, only coming to her senses when she heard Darren's sniggers.

'What is your problem?' she said.

He threw his hands out. 'Apart from you assaulting me? But I'm glad you've dropped the phoney voice at least.'

'Oh, shut up.' Her focus darted to the door again. She had to go after Zach. He couldn't leave. When was he coming back? Did he mean what he said? Or was it to carry on the act in front of Darren? His last chivalrous act before riding off into the sunset. No. A veil lifted from her eyes. Accepting his love didn't mean she couldn't survive without him, it just meant she'd have someone to share her life with – someone who really cared about her and that she loved in return. She might have made some questionable decisions in the past but this wasn't one of them.

She jumped out from behind the desk, but Darren blocked her. 'So, he lurves you, does he? Or is that part of the bet?'

'Shut up and get out of my way.' She tried to dodge him.

'Did he not have a pony white enough or armour shiny enough?' Darren adopted an irritating sickly voice of his own.

'Piss off. I mean it, move.'

'Did he not have enough cash to save this dive?'

'Shut up and get out.' She shoved him hard. 'I'm banning you from here. You don't ever come back. You're not welcome.'

'Oooh. The cat has claws.'

'Out, Darren. Now!'

With another snigger, he shook his head and let her pass. 'Yeah. Whatever. But will you get me a fucking taxi first?'

She ran to the door. The red brake lights of Zach's rental car were at the exit. She jumped down the steps as he pulled out and whizzed off along the road. Raising a hand in a wave, she tried to catch his attention but he drove around the bend and out of sight. She swallowed back a lump in her throat and looked skyward. Nooooo!

CHAPTER TWENTY-EIGHT

Zach

Rain. Rain and more rain. After days of pleasant sunshine, Zach's departure had signalled a return of the bad weather. It looked exactly like the day he'd arrived. And it matched his mood.

What really was going on in his life? He lived more for *Star Wars* conventions and the latest series of *Supernatural* than anything in the real world. *That's what a sad bastard I am.* Briony had been the first person to drag him out of his fantasy world and give him the opportunity to star in his own life. A life so far removed from what he was used to he barely knew where to start. What would his mom do without him? What she'd always done, he supposed. Put herself to bed and hope someone would look after her. *Fuck me, how uncharitable can I get?* Mom couldn't help her illness, but when did the day come when Zach could think about looking after his own life and not hers?

And what about his work? He'd landed his job straight out of college. It had been easy. Daniel Beyer had approached him, said he'd read his CV on the portal and had just the role for him in his company. Who would turn down an offer like that? His mom had been so proud. Probably the one and only time he could remember her being delighted by something he'd done. Only Zach had proven he wasn't the right person for the job, and was still proving it, because he'd made a total tits-up of this job too. Who came hundreds of miles to do what should be a quick deal and ended up falling in love? Yes, love. This was love. What else could elicit such a powerful ache in his chest and make him think such desperate thoughts? Had he taken an opportunity so far from home to play out a fantasy he knew couldn't come true? This was why he had to take the chance while he could. He'd go home, tell Mr Beyer where to shove his job, then come back to Briony. Maybe he should text her and tell her... He didn't want her to think he'd jumped ship for good, especially when she was back there dealing with that shit of an ex. Crap. Maybe he should go back this minute. He shouldn't leave her with that dick.

The wipers swished across the windshield and he spotted the sign to the Dalarvin Wood Forest Trail Car Park where he'd stopped the day he arrived. Hanging on the post was a brightly coloured scarf someone must have dropped. The colours reminded him of the dresses his grandma used to wear. What would she make of all this? *Be yourself, Zach*. But who was he?

He slammed on the brakes and whizzed into the opening, rolling the car into the same spot as before. The parking lot was empty this time.

What did Briony and Felicity mean suggesting that Mr Beyer was his father? That was truly ridiculous. He frowned. It was, right? But what about the headhunting and the second chances? Nope. Coincidence. But did he honestly believe in coincidences?

He looked nothing like Daniel Beyer, did he? How could his mom ever have met... Zach shook his head. He had no idea what his mom was like before he was born. Nobody would exactly have Zach pegged for the kind of guy who had random one-night stands, but he had – or he'd tried to. Ideas roiled around his stomach like dirty laundry. Dan? She always called him that. Oh god. If he asked his mom straight and it wasn't true, would she be angry or upset? And if it was true... Hell. He rubbed his face. How could it be?

'Only one way to find out, I guess.' Talking to himself now. If only he still had Becker. That furry companion had made as big an impact on his life as his owner. Who'd have thought it? He'd never loved the idea of a pet before, but had he really had the opportunity? He pulled out his cell and sighed. *Here goes.*

The ringing went on for seemingly hours. If his mom was in bed, she might not even pick up. It rang off and he tried again on Messenger.

'Hello? Son... What time is it? Why are you calling so early?'

Oh yeah. He hadn't thought about that. 'Hi, Mom. Sorry. I just wanted to... I need to...' Oh hell, how could he say this?

'What's wrong, honey? You sound strange.'

'I'm fine. I just want to know... about my father.'

'Your father?' She sounded repulsed. 'Why?'

'Just tell me. Is Dan Beyer my father?' He snorted. Did that have to sound so much like asking *is Darth Vader my father*? This was getting worse. He could imagine his online *Star Wars* friends having a field day out of the name play. True or not.

'Why are you asking that?'

'Just tell me, Mom, please.'

'Well, I don't know how you found out, but yes, he is.'

The New York Philharmonic Orchestra had started up his brain, blasting out *The Empire Strikes Back* soundtrack until it deafened him, and he barely restrained the urge to scream, 'Nooooooo! That's impossible!' Because just like for damned Luke Skywalker, it *was* impossible. How? Just how? Why had no one told him?

'Son, honey? Are you there? Are you ok?'

His mouth was moving but words weren't coming out. Was this why Mr Beyer had given him phoney opportunities? A backhanded way of acknowledging an illegitimate son? 'No, Mom. I'm not ok. I don't get it at all. Why?'

'Because we couldn't tell you.'

'Why not?'

'Lots of reasons. Dan was married. I was young. He's Jewish and very traditional – I'm not. We were more of an arrangement than a love affair. He said he'd do the right thing and he did. He just didn't want anyone to suspect his hand in it. He paid for you when you were a child and then your college.'

'What?' Zach facepalmed. No way. Not some unknown relative, but his own father. Hidden in plain sight. Unbelievable.

'We got a good home,' his mom went on. 'And when you were grown, he gave you a job. Even when you messed up, he kept you on.'

'Good god.' *When I messed up?* His whole life was messed up. Nothing he'd done had been chosen by him. He'd been steered down path after path and gone along with it. No wonder he'd been a misfit.

'Did Grandma know?'

'No. Well, she knew there was a man, but I never told her who.' Zach rubbed his face and sighed.

'Son. This can't be easy for you, but, please, don't say anything to Dan. He makes sure you earn enough to have a nice apartment and to help pay my medical bills. I can't afford to have that stop. I can't live without his support.'

'I get that, Mom. I really do. God knows, I don't want you to suffer. But I need to live my own life too. I can't be his pet forever. I took the job with him because it was an easy route to good money. I didn't even question it. But I should have. That life isn't for me. I can't do it anymore.'

'You must.'

'Why? Is it my destiny?' He shook his head and mirthless laugh escaped him.

'No. Your duty.'

'I can earn money in other ways. If that's what this is about.'

'Of course it isn't.'

'No? Well, it feels like it. Aw man.' He threw his head back. 'I don't begrudge paying for you, Mom. But it can't be to the point where I give up everything and all my chances of doing what I want and living out my life the way I need to. I need to be myself.'

'Oh, son. Please don't tell me this is because you want to move somewhere bigger, so you have more room for your plastic spaceships?'

He leaned his head on the window. *Is that what people think of me?* Had his life been so superficial up until now? If it had, it was all part of his subconscious attempts to escape a life he hadn't chosen. 'No. Nothing to do with that. It's about...' He took a deep breath. 'Trying out a new life with someone I love.'

'What are you talking about?'

'I told you. I met someone I like. More than like. I have to try.'

'But you can't have known her more than a week. Don't be so rash. You mustn't throw everything away on someone you don't know and in a foreign country. You'll lose your job, everything. I made mistakes when I was younger, I'd hate to see you doing the same thing.'

'I might lose my job but not everything. And what I might find is more important than what I might lose.'

It hadn't been fake. Nothing he had with Briony was fake. It was the most genuine thing in his life.

'Son, you're crazy. I need to call Dan and get him to talk some sense into you.'

'No, Mom. I'm gonna call him and resign. We can talk again later. Bye, Mom.'

He ended the call and took a deep breath. Now or never. He'd been going to fly home, prepare a speech and do it face to face but before the heat in his blood had cooled, the call connected.

'Zach, this had better be something good. I assume you've woken me in the middle of the night to tell me you've found and secured the whisky.'

Zach's jaw tightened and he stared at his reflection in the rear-view mirror. 'No. I haven't.'

'Then why the devil are you disturbing my sleep?'

'I felt like a chat with my father.' The reckless wording sent a rebellious thrill through Zach's veins. He waited. Silence. He was damned if he was going to be the one to break it.

'What exactly do you mean by that?' said Mr Beyer eventually.

'I know you're my father.'

'Your mother told you? She swore not to.'

And presumably lied on his birth certificate. 'No, I worked it out.'

'Well, I don't know how, but this complicates things. Our working relationship—'

'No.' Zach had never dared interrupt Mr Beyer before but he was going to get these words out if it was the last thing he ever did. 'It doesn't complicate anything. In fact, it makes everything simpler.'

'If you think you're going to get more from me you're mistaken.'

'No, I don't think that,' Zach said gravely. 'The opposite. I don't want anything else from you. Nothing at all. I quit.'

'I beg your pardon?'

'You heard me. I quit. I'm done. Now, you'll have to excuse me. I have somewhere I need to be.' He set the phone on the passenger seat. He hadn't heard the end of that by any stretch. In a few minutes, thousands of messages from Mr Beyer would start arriving, possibly more from his mom once they'd had time to talk. All those years Zach had wondered about his father and now this. Unpicking his feelings would have to wait. A rebellious energy surged through him. No one mattered in this moment except Briony and he needed to get back to her.

Rain was still hammering on the windshield as he drove back into the car park. He jumped out and was heading for the steps when Darren came out flanked by two police officers.

Zach raised an eyebrow.

'Hey,' Darren said, his handsome grey eyes looking desperate. 'This guy's an old buddy of mine. Aren't you, Zach?'

'Me?'

'Yeah. You tell these guys it was Gemma that did the dirty on me. I can't find Bri, I'm sure she'd back me up.'

'Er, what?' Zach asked.

'Just tell these guys I wouldn't assault anyone.'

Gemma must have filed a complaint. Zach smirked on the inside but kept his expression impassive. If Darren got banged up, then it was nothing but karma.

'This way,' said one of the police officers, ignoring Zach.

'Tell them,' Darren said.

'Good luck, sir,' Zach said with a flick of his eyebrows. 'I hope you had a great vacation.'

'You...' Darren growled, but one of the officers took hold of his elbow and steered him past. He shoved Darren's head down none too gently as they bundled him into the back of the squad car. Zach grinned and he gave Darren's glowering face a sneaky wave as the car pulled off.

Zach hotfooted it into the reception area. The sign was up, meaning Briony was elsewhere. Where the hell was she? How had she missed the drama of Darren being picked up by the police? Had she gone out and left the hotel unattended? Didn't seem likely.

He opened the door to the lounge and glanced inside. No one. Checking no guests were around, he pushed open the door to the kitchen corridor. He was about to knock on the door to her private quarters when he noticed the end door was ajar, swaying open in the wind. Maybe she was out in the courtyard with Becker. Rain pelted on the trash cans at the back door. One of the larger cans had been moved to the cellar door and was propping it open again, as it had the day he and Briony were investigating. Had she gone down there again? On her own?

At the top of the stairs, he peered into the darkness. Rainwater gushed over the courtyard like a stream and was trickling down the steps.

'Briony!' His voice echoed into the dark, but no one replied. Could she be there? Through the door maybe? Or along the secret passage? He pulled out his cell and lit the flashlight. One step in and something caught his face, a trailing web. He brushed it off but as he did, he missed his footing on the uneven concrete. The world turned upside down, his cell slipped from his hand and smashed down the stairs with echoing thumps. He followed, landing in a twisted mess at the bottom, his head thumping against cold stone.

CHAPTER TWENTY-NINE

Briony

'Right, Becker,' Briony said, swiping at tears of anger and frustration. 'I can do this, but I need protective clothing and you can help me.'

She pulled a woolly hat and gloves from a drawer. After Zach had left, she'd had a phone call from her dad. He knew nothing about the whisky and only vaguely remembered hearing rumours about a theft but it hadn't at any point seemed connected to their lives or crossed his mind there was reason to investigate. He'd called Lottie and she didn't have any information either. Hilda hadn't been very motherly in her ways, and she'd never confided a thing about their father. But he suggested the roof in the passageway might have caved in and crushed the bottles. Where else could they be?

The ache from watching Zach drive off had been temporarily filled with a burning desire to go down there and look for herself.

Like if she did, it would bring him back somehow. She zipped her thickest coat and tipped her head at Becker.

'I know it's crazy. I know he's not coming back. Not for a long time anyway.' She ruffled Becker's head and bit back a well of more tears. When her marriage to Darren fell apart she'd been upset and angry. Not because she missed him but because she'd been played for a fool. These tears weren't the same. The universe had finally answered and sent her exactly what she wanted. Zach. He'd found the key and the way to her heart. She didn't want him back for financial reasons or to 'save' her, just to hug him and spend more time with him. Maybe all the time she had in the world.

Was this second chance more than coincidence? Someone was looking out for her. Tears flowed again as she remembered Granny Hilda and the pain she must have gone through in her life. Was this Hilda's doing? A message from beyond the grave telling Briony to have a better look. Maybe she'd arranged the second chance at love with Zach's grandma. And what had Briony and Zach done? Made a right mess of it.

An almost empty bottle wasn't enough to save the hotel but hope flickered when she thought of the passageway. It held the answers. Was there some clue Zach had missed? The chances were slim, but she had to check. Even if it meant being suited up like a beekeeper or a crime scene investigator so nothing could touch her.

'Come on, let's go.'

Rain crashed down, bouncing off the wheelie bin tops, and Becker stopped at the door, peering out, then back at Briony. If he could talk, he would have said, 'You want me to go out in this? Get lost, you mad human, I'm going back to the sofa.'

She took his collar and gave him a tug. The back door opened and Shari leapt out, pulling up the top of a bin and shoving a full sack into it.

'There you are. Did you know the police just turned up looking for your ex?' she shouted, ducking under the doorframe.

'What?' How had she missed that?

'Yeah, they came up the stairs and I showed them to room twelve. They went off with him.'

'Seriously?'

'Yeah, I was watching from the window. Zach was coming in too. I think your ex was saying something to him too, but I couldn't hear.'

'Zach? But he left.'

'Must have come back then.'

'But where is he?' Briony's heart was thumping.

'Dunno. Where are you going?'

'I was going to look for something in the cellar.' Should she delay that and go looking for Zach? Where had he gone and why was he back?

Shari shuddered. 'Isn't it a bit creepy down there?'

'Very. That's why I'm dressed like this.' A raindrop ran down Briony's forehead and off the end of her nose. 'Listen, about Zach... Well, I know, I shouldn't have.'

'Yeah. I don't exactly blame you. He was a bit of all right. I would have if I'd had half the chance.'

Briony gave her a faint smile, raindrops stinging her cheeks. 'And you don't know where he went when he came back?'

'Sorry, no.'

'Ok. I need to find him.'

'I'll check upstairs,' Shari said, returning inside.

Briony wiped the rain from her face and glanced around. Where had Becker got to? For a dog who hadn't wanted to leave the building a few minutes ago, he'd made a speedy dash for freedom. She peered through the misty gloom, trying to spot him. Had he gone towards the woods? Daft mongrel.

Before she went searching for Zach, she should lock up the cellar door. Still armed with the giant torch, she crossed the courtyard. An echoing bark boomed around. Becker stood at the open door to the cellar steps, letting rip barks and long howls, turning into whines.

'Hey, quiet,' she called. She'd never heard him make noises like that. He rarely barked at all other than a half-hearted grumble of a woof when someone knocked on the door. Another howling moan issued from him and his neck extended like a wolf. 'What on earth has got into you?' She hurried to him and he ran towards her but before she could get hold of him, he bolted back to the door and disappeared down the steps. Ok, what was going on? She'd been happy to think Granny Hilda might have engineered something from beyond the grave, but she didn't want to meet her ghost. Stolen whisky was one thing; a haunted hotel, no thanks.

At the top of the steps, Briony scrabbled with the torch, her fingers heavy inside her soaked woollen gloves. The memory of arguing with Zach about torches and flashlights zipped into her mind, stabbing her through the ribs. The light sprang on and she moved it around, scanning deep into the dark stairwell. Becker was at the bottom, whimpering and licking something... Something... No, someone. Holy shit, a body was down there. Briony's heart froze. A body? Alive or dead? And who... Not... Oh no... Please, god, no. Not Zach.

Before she got anywhere near the bottom, she could see it was him. Those thick curls couldn't belong to anyone else, but what the hell was he doing here? She shone the torch on the steps and went carefully. Her pulse hammered too hard and fast, thumping in her ears, and she could barely get air into her lungs.

'Zach.' Her voice was squeaky. 'Are you alive? Becker, is he alive?'

She reached the bottom and crouched. *Christ.* What now? Heartbeat? Mouth-to-mouth? What were you supposed to do again? CPR? ABC? Everything was a messy jumble.

'Zach?' She pulled off her gloves and put her palm on his forehead. Her hands were freezing and numb but she felt warmth, definitely heat coming from him. She tilted her head so her ear was close to his nose. A breath tickled her and she gripped his arm. 'You're alive. Thank god.' She felt over his chest until her palm rested over a beat, a strong solid thump.

'Hey,' he whispered.

'Oh, god, Zach. Can you hear me?'

'Yup.'

'Thank god, thank god.' She leaned in and pressed a kiss to his cheek. 'Please, stay with me. Stay awake. I'll call an ambulance.' She fumbled around for her phone, hardly seeing.

A hand grasped her wrist. 'I am staying,' Zach murmured.

'Good. Because I need you.'

'No. I need you. And I don't mean I'm staying awake. I'm staying here with you. As long as you want me. *If* you want me. I'm not going back.'

'What? You mean—'

'That's why I came back. I slipped on those damn wet stairs trying to find you and tell you. I should get up now.'

'No, Zach, stay where you are. I'm calling an ambulance.' She woke her phone.

'Briony.'

'Zach.' She soothed his hair off his forehead. 'I love you. I don't want to lose you. I shouldn't have let you go.'

'I want to...'

'Stay awake. I need to make this call. Becker, lick his face or muddy his shirt or something. Just keep him awake. I need him alive.'

Her fingers tapped nine, nine, nine and she waited.

CHAPTER THIRTY

Zach

Z ach's eyes closed and it felt like warm water had engulfed him. He wanted to smile and let himself breathe in the words he was sure he'd heard. Briony's words. Her voice saying she loved him, telling him to stay. He would stay, he was staying. This was his new home.

'Zach.' Something cold slapped against his cheek. 'Stay with me. The ambulance is coming. Please, stay with me.'

'I'm staying,' he said, though his voice felt far away, like it had come from someone else.

'Are you? Why are you here?' Briony's voice also seemed to be hovering in the distance, like it wasn't really her. With a huge effort he raised the arm that wasn't aching and searched for something physical. Warm fingers entwined with his and he inhaled more purposefully. Something cold and wet nuzzled his neck and he felt his lips twitch. Becker.

'Looking for you. Why are *you* here?'

'I just had a weird feeling like I needed to look down here but as soon as I opened the door I realised I couldn't do it without full body armour... Though maybe it was you I was meant to find.'

Zach's lips twitched again. He wanted to laugh but his head hurt. 'Here was me thinking you'd got into trouble and I was leaping down to rescue you.'

'Yup. That sounds more like it.'

He squeezed her hand tighter. 'But you don't need anyone to save you. You can do this yourself. If you trust your ideas, you can make it work. The person who needs saving is me.'

'I'm doing my best at that too.'

'I don't mean from here. I mean from my life.'

'Why?'

'Because you were right. Daniel Beyer is my father. My whole life has been directed by someone and I had no idea. I need to get off his starship and find my own galaxy. Preferably one with you in it.'

'Oh, Zach.' A soft kiss landed on his bruised forehead. 'You can stay here as long as you want. The longer the better. I don't want you to go anywhere.'

She gently stroked his hair and he sighed. 'You're my superhero in full body armour, riding to my rescue. You can save me from my crazy family...' He chuckled but ow! It hurt all over. 'And I need you to protect me from the zombies.'

'You're funny.'

'Am I?'

'Yes, and I like you just the way you are... Well, preferably without the bumped head, but everything else is perfect.'

'Does that mean I can move my *Star Wars* collection in and sleep with a machete under my pillow in case the walkers attack in the night?'

She chuckled again. 'We'll discuss that when you're feeling better.'

He closed his eyes and smiled.

Returning to the pink hotel with his ankle strapped, a sling and an egg on his forehead wasn't the triumphant way Zach had imagined things, but it didn't matter. Briony was on his arm. Or under it, helping him up the front steps. An odd buzz tingled through him as he crossed the threshold, unrelated to the aches and pains his fall had caused. This was like coming home and going on vacation at the same time. The end of something and the beginning.

His cell had smashed in the fall, which had kept Mr Beyer, aka his father – if he could ever get used to that – off his back. For a little while anyway. Briony had found him an old phone and got his SIM card working. Darren had been charged with assaulting Gemma. Neither Zach nor Briony knew if it was true, but the satisfaction of knowing he'd been caught for something was a bonus. Briony couldn't believe she'd missed him being arrested but between Zach and Shari, they'd filled her in.

Recounting his memories with the new knowledge that Dan Beyer was his father put a different spin on everything and made sense of Zach's insecurities growing up. It was cathartic just being able to talk about it. And surprisingly the fallout from the revelation wasn't as painful as the knock to the head. Zach had the distinct impression Mr Beyer was relieved to say goodbye to him – on a business level. Their personal relationship was something for the future and Zach's head was too full of Briony to think of much beyond that. Zach was on his own adventure now, and no one would force him down a path he didn't want to go.

For now, he was going to work at the hotel with Briony, help out in return for board and lodgings. If things were quiet in the winter, they could cuddle up and write their books together. Maybe one day that would bring in the money this place needed.

'Zach,' Briony said. 'I know you want to start a new life now you've found out about your family but working in a hotel doesn't seem your thing. You're all about stories, history, legends, fantasy.'

'Then let's bring some of that magic here. Let's sell this place on its history and legends. Never mind the Bonnie Prince Charlie stuff. Let's name the bar The Illicit Still and the honeymoon suite Whisky Kisses. That festival was a big hit, and like you said before, it doesn't have to be a one-off. I used to do this stuff for

Mr B— My dad. Don't think I'll ever get used to that. I've been out of my depth there for years because he was breathing down my neck, looking for specific results. But here we have a blank page. We can write our own story. Only this time it won't be fantasy. We'll make it real.'

Briony smiled. 'It sounds amazing. Do you think we can do it?'

'Yes. I do. But one thing...'

'What? Name it.'

'It has to have a happy ending.'

She took his hands and held them in hers. 'Absolutely.' Her smile shone bright and her eyes twinkled. He'd never tire of looking at her. The reality of his new life hadn't kicked in. This was his first day out of hospital and his focus for the past twenty-four hours had been on getting his bones back in the right place. Now, he was ready for a new adventure. He slung his good arm over Briony's shoulder and let her help him to the private quarters. The second she pushed open the door, Becker leapt on him.

'Careful,' she said.

'Yeah, I don't want mud on my shirt... again.'

Briony smirked. 'Funny.'

Zach flopped into the sofa, adjusting his achy body. Becker jumped up beside him and landed on his lap, making it a pointless exercise. Briony sat on his other side and leaned on his unbroken arm.

'This is where I wanna be,' he said. 'In a galaxy, far, far away, with my family.'

Grandma would approve. She'd be smiling down on him. He was finally doing it – being himself. He bent in and kissed Briony's forehead. She nuzzled in. Becker knocked his sore arm with his head and sent a huge slobber up Zach's cheek. He laughed until his bruised ribs ached. Perfect!

CHAPTER THIRTY-ONE

Briony

January

'Zach's shoulder and leg are much better,' Briony said into her phone. 'His mom is dealing with it. I don't think she ever expected him to stay.'

'What about her healthcare?' Felicity asked.

'Mr Beyer has agreed to fund it as part of his ongoing "relationship building" with Zach.'

'Eek,' Felicity said. 'Sounds tricky.'

So far it had been ok. Zach was coming to terms with things, and spending the winter months cuddled up together, thinking up big ideas, had definitely helped. They still weren't sure how to fund them, but it didn't feel like such an insurmountable problem now. A problem shared and all that – it was working for Briony anyway. Just having someone there with her made the jobs easier. George, her financial adviser, was still on her case, but she was desperately trying to draw up a plan involving as much community engagement as possible. Catering for locals meant a year-round supply of paying punters.

'Such a shame the whisky never turned up. Mr Sinclair is getting close to retiring,' Felicity said. 'He's celebrating everything at the moment. He's in such a good mood, he'd probably have gifted you the bottle if you'd found it.'

'Well, we didn't.'

'Ah well,' Felicity said. 'At least I won't be losing my BFF just yet.'

Briony laughed. 'Fingers crossed George thinks the business plan is viable.'

'And I heard the campsite and outdoor centre sale went through. You'll need to find out if that man who approached you at the festival was successful.'

'Oh, yes. Logan Ramsay,' Briony said. 'I'll look him up. The more connections I make the better. I can add his reciprocal deals to my plan.'

'Yeah. And you've got Zach. How exciting is that?'

'I still pinch myself every morning.'

From the cupboard behind the reception, Zach pulled out some more boxes. This was his celebration of a fully healed arm and ankle – finally clearing out that old cupboard. Properly this time. Briony still wasn't sure she could face the heaps of old paperwork but with Zach's company it wasn't so dull and most of it was so old it went straight into the fire. Good winter fuel.

'Ah, well,' Felicity said. 'I'll let you get back to him and whatever you're doing.'

'Nothing more exciting than cleaning, I'm afraid to say.'

'I'll come and see you soon,' Felicity promised before they ended the call.

Briony peered into the cupboard and Zach looked back, one eyebrow high on his forehead. 'I think I'm suffering a dust allergy.'

'Oh? Are you coughing and sneezing?' She hadn't heard anything.

'No. I just don't want to see another speck of it. Maybe it's an aversion.'

'I'm here to help now.'

He sidled up and slipped his arms around her waist. 'I'd rather have you. Can't we throw in the duster for the day?'

Pushing onto tiptoes, she kissed him, enjoying the warmth surrounding her and the overwhelming sensation of well-being.

'Let's finish this cupboard first.'

'Yeah. Ok.'

At the back was a large box with a lid. It clanked as Zach lifted it. Briony pulled a pout and sighed. There had been several like this, filled with old lamps, lightbulbs, remote controls from long-gone TVs and appliances.

'We should have ordered a skip,' she said, prising off the box lid.

Zach put on his glasses and pulled out a tube. 'Is this a poster from nineteen seventy with lots of tartan and thistles on it?' He peered inside and pulled out a rolled-up piece of paper. 'Oh, even older. Looks like fifties. Nice quality artwork.' Unfurling it, he held up a stylised poster advertising the hotel in an overly Highland scene, looking a lot more clinical and sunny than it usually did.

'Very romanticised though. I'm not sure the hotel is *that* pink.'

'I think we should frame it. Would be nice to have a wall of pictures through the years.'

'I like the sound of that.' Briony tugged out another tube, too heavy and bulky to be a poster. She picked off the lid and frowned. 'Looks like a bottle.' Slowly she prised it out and her eyes popped. 'Oh my god, Zach.'

'What's that? It's not... Is it? Are you messing with me?'

Goosebumps rose up her arms and over her shoulders as she stared at the label just like the one on the half-finished bottle in the kitchen. She turned it to Zach. 'It's real, isn't it?'

'Be careful with that. Like seriously careful.'

She clung to it and he put his finger to the cork. 'It's not open. Jesus.' He let out a low whistle. 'Hidden in plain sight.'

Briony lowered it back into the tube. 'Let's check the others.'

Zach pulled out an identical tube. 'Too obvious?'

'Let's see.' Briony's heart catapulted against her chest.

Screwing up his face, Zach prised off the lid and slowly raised another bottle. Briony slapped her hand across her mouth.

'No way. We've found them,' she said.

'I can't believe it.' Zach shook his head slowly.

'What the hell do we do?'

'Call Felicity back, get her to tell her boss we have his whisky. Then we can try and persuade him the other one was a gift to your grandfather.'

'And if he agrees, what do we do with it?'

'Well... I know a man who desperately wants one of these bottles. We could see what he's willing to offer.'

Briony grinned. 'I can't believe it.' She could barely wait for him to replace the tube in the box before throwing her arms around him. 'I don't know what's going to happen, but I have a good feeling about it.'

If this was Granny Hilda's legacy, she'd take it.

April

Zach clutched Briony's hand and she beamed at him, her eyes travelling over his dress kilt and black jacket with shiny silver buttons. People milled around them as they made their way towards the little podium in front of the loch, the same place the Amber Gold Music Festival had taken place.

He leaned in and whispered. 'If anyone had told me a few months ago I'd be in Scotland, beside a loch, dressed like this, I'd have had them locked up, or told them I'd more likely be in my Starfleet Academy uniform and jetting off for the semester.'

Briony poked him in the ribs. 'You're the mad one around here.'

'I'm mad about you alright.' He squeezed her fingers. 'Hey,' he said to Becker, as he sniffed his knees. 'Watch where you're putting your nose. I'm not used to this kind of gear.'

'Suits you, but you'll never be as hot as a true Scot,' said Brann the builder, whacking Zach on the back and winking. Brann was in a kilt too but had paired it with a black t-shirt and heavy boots.

'Get lost.' Zach smirked and elbowed him away.

Brann laughed and slung his arm around another friend, or possibly his brother. 'Catch you later, mate.' He saluted Zach.

He and Briony reached the podium and had barely been there two seconds when Felicity appeared in a slick navy suit with a short skirt, purple blouse and killer heels. Briony looked her up and down. 'Check you out.'

'Right back at you,' Felicity said. 'You're looking gorgeous as ever.'

'Isn't she?' Zach beamed at Briony.

'Totally,' Felicity said. 'This is going to be the best start to Mr Sinclair's retirement year. We need all the publicity we can get.

I'm already freaking out about what'll happen when he goes. I've heard a rumour he wants to pass the business onto his son, who's completely clueless about whisky.'

'Oh dear,' Briony said. 'That doesn't sound sensible.'

'Tell me about it. But Mr Sinclair is obsessed with keeping the business in the family.'

Beside the loch was the grey-haired Mr Sinclair in an equally grey suit beside a small, smiley woman in a long pink coat. Briony side-eyed Zach when she saw who they were talking to. He let out a sigh. Dan Beyer in person. And instead of flying over with a wife – Zach had told her he'd had at least four in his life, though he wasn't sure if any of them were current – he'd chosen Ms Somerton, Zach's mother. Pale and thin she may be, but she was still managing to make eyes at Dan Beyer and he seemed quite pleased about it.

'I'm going with the flow,' muttered Zach. 'I'm not sure what else I can do.'

Briony's parents were also present. Her sister, Teagan, was halfway around the world singing on a cruise ships, but she'd met Zach on FaceTime and seemed to like him. The whisky sale brought in more than enough to go around the whole family and Briony's share was going straight back into the hotel and some of it towards her books.

When a good crowd had amassed, Briony called everyone together and took to the stage. A local reporter hopped around, snapping photographs.

'Thanks for coming, everybody. Today is a special day for the Loch View Hotel. It's not just day one of the brand-new Whisky Kisses festival, but it's the day we let everyone know exactly how this came about.' In the crowd, she spotted a wizened old face and recognised Bruce McArthur, chatting to her dad and her aunt Lottie. 'This hotel has a long history and one closely linked to the local whisky trade. Some of the activity over the years was somewhat suspect, including the use of an illicit still in the grounds during the nineteenth century. If you'd like to know more about that, we have a display inside with information collated from local accounts and presented by my partner, Zach Somerton.' She beamed at him.

He tipped her a wink and she went on. 'Zach came here last year on a recce mission to seek out some legendary whisky known as Whisky Kisses. For a long time we didn't believe it existed. Once we established that it did, we had to figure out who it belonged to and then the seemingly impossible task of finding it. You know that phrase, things turn up when you least expect them? Well, that's what happened. We'd long given up the idea of finding it when we accidentally stumbled over the two remaining bottles.'

She glanced at Mr Sinclair, who nodded.

'Please welcome Mr Frank Sinclair, the owner of the Glenbriar Distillery chain.'

Mr Sinclair gave an almost royal wave to the assembled onlookers. The reporter snapped away. 'Thank you ever so much. I'm honoured to be here at this wonderful pink hotel, such an iconic local landmark. Glenbriar Distilleries has a long and colourful history very like this hotel and some of these histories are linked. Most notably because of Whisky Kisses. The distillery was previously owned by my father and my uncle. Unfortunately my father passed away as a fairly young man, but not before he, my uncle and a friend, Briony's grandfather' – he gestured towards her – 'conspired to create a unique and legendary whisky made from a barrel preserved from the original illicit still. This whisky was already valuable but now, seventy years on, it's almost priceless. The story got twisted in many ways throughout the years but it's my belief that my father gifted one bottle to his friend and the allegations of theft were mistakenly placed on him, leading to his departure and exile from this community. We understand he has also now passed and last year we lost Hilda, his wife. Sadly for Hilda, she died not knowing her husband's innocence and coercion into a plan that ultimately removed him from his family. Partly to honour that and because I do believe my father bequeathed this whisky to him, I have decided to keep one bottle for the distillery and gift the other to Briony in honour of her late grandfather.'

Briony shook his hand and smiled. They weren't crazy enough to exchange the actual bottles. Those were safely locked away in the vaults of the bank.

'As Mr Sinclair knows, I have no need for a whisky, no matter how rare. But one man who is desperate to get his hands on it is Mr Daniel Beyer, bourbon manufacturer. It was him who originally sent Zach here to discover the whereabouts of the whisky and he's agreed to a purchase price for it. A generous price. And with the profit from that sale, we'll have enough to carry out full hotel refurbishment and keep it going as the *iconic landmark* you all know and love.'

The crowd clapped and gave a few appreciative whistles. Zach took Briony's hand as she stepped off the podium. She finally had the money to make the hotel work, plus employ a few more workers so she and Zach could sneak in some fun... ahem... writing time. Mr Beyer had his whisky. Mr Sinclair had his missing bottle and could spend his final year before retirement in peace.

Briony's parents patted Zach on either shoulder, her mum leading him away to show him something by the loch.

'You cracked the case,' Briony's dad said. 'And solved a big mystery.'

'You really did,' Aunt Lottie said. 'Mother never mentioned that whisky or why Dad left.'

'It's good to have the truth,' said her dad.

'And the hotel's in good hands,' Lottie added.

'It really is,' her father said. 'I knew you could do it.'

'Thanks, Dad.' Maybe her mum and dad hadn't always been the most hands on and present parents but knowing she had their approval was worth a lot.

Zach returned from his wander with Briony's mum and linked hands with Briony.

'This hotel always had a vibe,' Briony said, clutching Zach tight. 'When I was young I loved the thrill of it. When I was on my own, I was kind of freaked by it, and now it feels exciting again and happy, like someone's watching over us.'

'I think it was always good,' Zach said. 'We just needed nudging in the right direction'

'From Granny Hilda and Grandma?'

'Exactly.'

'You kids are funny,' said her dad. He, Lottie and her mum made their way towards the hotel, but Briony held back. She wrapped her arms around Zach and sighed into his chest. He placed his palms on her back and held her close. A breeze from the loch tickled their cheeks.

'Are you truly happy here?' she asked.

'Couldn't be more so... Well, unless there's enough money to build me a neat little shed for my *Star Wars* figures.'

Briony chuckled and patted his back. 'Yeah, ok. Just watch Luke Skywalker doesn't turn into the other kind of walker. You won't want to find them in the barn.'

'Ha. You awesome gal. This is why I love you. I've never met anyone else who got my jokes.'

'Jokes? I thought you were serious.'

'Yeah. I kind of am.'

'Oh, Zach. I wouldn't change you for the world.' Becker sniffed around her legs and she ruffled his head. 'It doesn't feel like stolen time anymore, just a blank page waiting to be written.'

'Exactly. It's our story. You, me, Becker and one big crazy old happy ending.'

The End

More Books by Margaret Amatt

Scottish Island Escapes

A Winter Haven

A Spring Retreat

A Summer Sanctuary

An Autumn Hideaway

A Christmas Bluff

A Flight of Fancy

A Hidden Gem

A Striking Result

A Perfect Discovery

A Festive Surprise

The Glenbriar Series

New Beginnings in Glenbriar
(A free short story to introduce the series)
Stolen Kisses at the Loch View Hotel
Just Friends at Thistle Lodge
Pitching Up at Heather Glen
Two's Company at the Forest Light Show
Highland Fling on the Whisky Trail

Free Hugs & Old-Fashioned Kisses

A short story only available to Newsletter Subscribers

ACKNOWLEDGMENTS

Thanks goes to my adorable husband for supporting my dreams and putting up with my writing talk 24/7. Also to my son, whose interest in my writing always makes me smile. It's precious to know I've passed the bug to him – he's currently writing his own fantasy novel and instruction books on how to build Lego!

Throughout the writing process, I have gleaned help from many sources and met some fabulous people. I'd like to give a special mention to Stéphanie Ronckier, my beta reader extraordinaire. Stéphanie's continued support with my writing is invaluable and I love the fact that I need someone French to correct my grammar! Stéphanie, you rock. To my lovely friend, Lyn Williamson, thank you for your continued support and encouragement with all my projects. And to my fellow authors, Evie Alexander and Lyndsey Gallagher – you girls are the best! I love it that you always have my back and are there to help when I need you.

Also, a huge thanks to my editor, Aimee Walker, at for her excellent work on my novels and for answering all my mad questions. Thank you so much, Aimee!

ABOUT THE AUTHOR

Margaret Amatt

Margaret has told and written stories for as long as she can remember. During her formative years, she spent time on long walks inventing characters and stories to pass the time.

Writing books is Margaret's passion and when she's not doing that, she's often found eating chocolate, walking and taking photographs in the hills around Highland Perthshire. Those long walks still frequently bring inspiration!

It's Margaret's pleasure to bring you the Scottish Island Escapes series and The Glenbriar Series. These books are linked (even the two series have crossovers!) for those who enjoy inhabiting Margaret's world of stories but each can be read as a standalone if you'd rather dip in and out with individual books.

You can find more information about Margaret on her website or by signing up for her newsletter.

www.margaretamatt.com